I PLAY ONE ON TV

BOOKS BY ALAN ORLOFF

Novels
Diamonds for the Dead
Running from the Past
Pray for the Innocent
I Play One on TV

The Last Laff Mysteries
Killer Routine
Deadly Campaign

The Anderson West PI Thrillers
I Know Where You Sleep

Writing as Zak Allen
Ride-Along
First Time Killer
The Taste

ALAN ORLOFF

I PLAY ONE ON TV

Down & Out Books
3959 Van Dyke Road, Suite 265
Lutz, FL 33558
DownAndOutBooks.com

Cover design by Zach McCain

ISBN: 1-64396-213-2
ISBN-13: 978-1-64396-213-9

To my family: Janet, Mark, and especially Stuart,
my thespian inspiration.

Chapter One

He watched as a teen in a dark hoodie emerged from a storage closet and crept into the high school locker room. In the dim light, the shadowy figure advanced, slowly. methodically. In his left hand, a knife blade glinted.

The man's insides constricted as he observed. He could almost smell the stale sweat left behind by the athletes after football practice, soon to be replaced by the stench of fear and the coppery odor of fresh blood.

The feelings he experienced now—rage, fear, excitement—mirrored those he had felt then, five years ago. When he had been the teen in the hoodie in that locker room. When he had been wielding the knife.

When he had been stalking his unsuspecting victim.

On the TV screen, the teen actor portraying the killer peeked around a corner and laid eyes on his quarry, an asshole named Will Ogden.

Ogden had returned to the locker room to look for his lost wallet, but he wouldn't find it. It had been swiped earlier, from his locker, thus setting the trap.

Ogden fiddled with the lock for a moment, then swung open the door, a metallic clang reverberating throughout the cavernous locker room. He proceeded to root around for his missing wallet, to no avail.

As he searched, the teen with the knife crept closer.

Ogden scoured the locker for his wallet.

The teen killer inched closer still. And raised his weapon.

The actor on the crime reenactment show was milking things for all they were worth. Hamming it up. He looked like a caricature of a madman. Ridiculous. Insulting. Outrageous.

"That's not right," shouted the man staring at the TV. "That's not the way it—"

He hurled his can of beer across the room where it bounced off the wall, spewing sudsy foam everywhere.

"No! No, no, no!" He jumped to his feet. For a moment, he wished he were back in that locker room, gripping the knife again. "I am not going to rot in jail. No way. No fucking way."

A shot of adrenaline cleared his mind, and he grabbed a piece of paper and a pen. When the closing credits rolled, he furiously began taking names.

Chapter Two

The temperature in the room seemed to have dropped ten degrees. I watched in silence as a teen in a dark hoodie emerged from a storage closet and crept into the high school locker room. In the dim light, the shadowy figure advanced slowly, methodically. In his left hand, a knife blade glinted.

With each footstep, my pulse quickened. *I'd* been the one in that locker room months earlier. That knife had been in *my* hand.

I'd been sneaking up on *my* unsuspecting victim.

Of course, I'd just been acting.

I watched myself as I peeked around a corner and spotted a kid named Will Ogden searching for something in his locker. Next to me, on my family-room couch, my best friend Miguel "Patch" Gutierrez gasped. I shushed him with a quick elbow to the gut while concentrating on the scene unfolding before us. On my other side, Trinity Thomas watched in complete silence, her eyes wide with horror.

Watching one of your close friends preparing to murder someone will do that to you, I guessed—even if it was just acting.

According to the news reports I'd read to prepare for the role, the killer, a lowlife kid named Homer Lee Varney, had gotten into a few fights with Ogden during the weeks preceding the incident, each worse than the one before. Varney had threatened Ogden—on more than one occasion—but Ogden, a star line-backer on the state champion high school football team, had laughed in his face. Now Mr. All-State Linebacker would pay.

With his life.

Ogden rummaged through the stuff on the floor of his locker, looking for his wallet. No luck.

Varney inched closer.

Ogden kept searching.

Varney inched even closer. And raised his knife.

The camera zoomed in for a close-up. I watched as a maniacal expression spread across the killer's face as if he were going to enjoy eviscerating his victim with the razor-sharp, eight-inch blade. Eyes bugged out. Wild clown grin. Evil personified.

I nodded to myself. Not bad.

"Dude!" Patch exclaimed. "That's over-the-top insane!"

"Hey, it's what the director wanted." I shrugged, mostly pleased with my performance, but a tiny bit ashamed, too. I mean, I looked as if I were having the time of my life, about to carve up someone.

"Well, you captured crazy, all right."

I hit rewind on the DVR remote and backed up a few seconds, then hit play. I advanced it in slo-mo, so I could get a good look at the killer's rabid face.

My face.

I'd landed the role to portray the young Varney in a true crime reenactment show—the "High School Hitman" episode of the series *Teen Killers*—and I was always looking for ways to improve my acting technique.

I rewound again. Analyzed myself critically on-screen as the action advanced, one frame at a time. Knife held aloft as I approached my victim. Too stiff? Was my grin too comical? Did I face the camera too much? Was my breathing controlled? Did I really, truly, come across as a teen killer?

The screen faded to black, and the sounds of a struggle intensified. Scuffling, shouting, screaming. Then the noise slowly petered out, leaving the viewer with four full seconds of dead air.

Literally.

No picture. No sound. Just a mental picture of a guy getting stabbed to death.

My heart hammered in my chest as my friends applauded. A commercial for a pawn shop burst on the screen, and I hit the pause button on the remote. We could have watched the episode on the rough-cut DVD that the production company had sent over, like I had with my parents—multiple times—but somehow it seemed more official to watch the actual cable network feed, complete with cheesy commercials.

"Great job, dude," Patch said. "I smell an Emmy."

"You were fantastic." Trinnie's brown eyes were huge. "You nailed it."

"Thanks." When I'd shot this four months ago, I'd just turned sixteen. This was my first TV gig, and although I didn't have many lines, I was totally pumped. Every actor had to start somewhere, and I was proud of my effort, even if I was portraying a cold-blooded killer.

"Your face was the best part," Patch said.

"Looked bad ass," Trinnie said.

I'd done my research on the killer, Homer Lee Varney. Every news article I could find. By all accounts, he was an angry, demented, vindictive, abusive, poor-excuse-for-a-human being. I think I pulled it off pretty well, and it was nice to know I was growing as an actor. The experience was cool. The exposure was great. The pay sucked on these crime reenactment shows, but you couldn't have everything.

On the other hand, I wasn't sure it was nice knowing that playing an angry, demented, vindictive, abusive, poor-excuse-for-a-human being came so easily to me.

"Tell me again why they rushed this to air, though?" Trinnie said, wincing a little. "The quality did feel a little...B-movie. No offense."

"First of all, that's how all of these reenactments look. And secondly, the killer, Varney, had just been released from prison on some kind of technicality. Corrupted evidence, or something.

It's been plastered all over the news." Patch scooped up the last piece of pepperoni pizza from the box on the coffee table and took a huge bite.

The murder had happened in the next town over, and Varney's release seemed to be the lead story on every local news network and paper. The producers of *Teen Killers* liked to film their episodes near the place where the crime had occurred so they could shoot in actual locations, and because it generated extra homegrown interest when the show aired. Every additional tenth of a point in the ratings mattered.

"Sorry, must have missed it," Trinnie said.

"Really? There are all kinds of protests going on. People are pissed that they're releasing a murderer. Hard to believe, I know." Patch's words were soaked with sarcasm. He stuffed the rest of the pizza into his mouth and took a big gulp of Coke to wash it down.

Varney had claimed his innocence all along, but the circumstantial evidence had been enough to put him away.

"The whole thing is crazy, right? What if he does it again? If there's one thing I've learned from watching all these reenactment crime shows, it's that once you're a killer, you're always a killer," I said.

"Maybe he's a changed man," Trinnie said. "Maybe he's found religion. That happens."

"Based on my research, I doubt it." I shook my head. "In any event, the cable channel wants to capitalize on all the publicity. They think the show's going to have huge ratings, especially around here."

"Tonight, a star is born." Patch grabbed his hipster black porkpie hat with one hand and performed some kind of elaborate curtsy-bow. Trinnie joined in, and she and Patch took turns creating their own unique bows, each more ridiculous than the last, singing my praises as they contorted their bodies. My parents were upstairs, and if they came down now, they'd think we were all high.

"Okay, okay. Don't worry, I'll remember all you little people when I'm famous. Or more precisely, my assistant will remember you—whatever your names are."

Patch stopped fawning and looked me square in the eyes. "You know, you sure seemed comfortable with that performance. Like you were born to be a killer." He raised his arm and pretended to slash me repeatedly with an imaginary knife while cackling like a madman.

Trinnie followed suit, adding a screechy horror movie soundtrack. "Eek, eek, eek."

One minute they were worshipping me, the next they were trying to kill me. Drama kids.

I let them have their fun for a minute or two. "Had enough yet?"

They stopped. "I guess. For now," Patch said.

Trinnie touched my arm. "Hey, don't you have an audition tomorrow?"

"Yep. For a bank commercial. The part is 'teenage son.' I sit at the breakfast table and say, 'Please pass the syrup.'"

"Another breakout role," Patch said. "How about this? PLEASE pass the syrup."

Patch could sing and dance like a pro, and he was awesome with accents, but his acting was still a definite work in progress.

"No, no. Like this: Please PASS the syrup," Trinnie said.

"Please pass THE syrup. Please pass the sy-RUP. No, wait. How about this?" Patch cleared his throat, once, twice, then blasted, "PLEASE PASS THE SYRUP."

Trinnie and I both clapped our hands over our ears as we recoiled.

I spoke quickly so Patch wouldn't deafen us with another attempt. "No offense guys, but what if I say it like a normal human being and save the over-the-top delivery for when I'm slashing someone to death?"

"You're no fun," Trinnie said.

"Do you think Cam will be at the audition?" Patch asked.

By some cruel twist of perpetual fate, Cam Carter and I always seemed to show up at the same auditions, vying for the same parts. And by that same cruel fate, he managed to beat me out for most of them. I sure hoped he'd caught my performance in "High School Hitman." "Wouldn't surprise me. But I've been eating pancakes for a week to get into character."

Trinnie laughed and touched my arm again. Drama kids on the whole are very demonstrative, and she's more so than most.

"Well, I hate to cut this party short, but not all of us have auditions tomorrow. Some of us have to work in the morning," Patch said.

Three days a week—Monday, Wednesday, and Friday—Patch, Trinnie, and I worked as counselors at the summer acting camp run by our high school drama teacher, Ms. Zhang. "I'll be there after my audition's over. I cleared it with Ms. Z. See if you can keep things from falling apart until I arrive."

"Without your talented leadership, it will be tough, but we'll make it through somehow."

We gathered up the debris from our little viewing party—soda cans, pizza crusts, dirty napkins—and detoured through the kitchen to throw it all away, then headed for the front door.

At the door, we said goodbye. This time, Trinnie touched my shoulder. Was it my imagination, or had she gotten even more demonstrative lately? "Break a leg tomorrow, Dalton."

"Okay, guys. See you later."

My friends shuffled out, and I closed the door behind them, making sure to lock the deadbolt. Watching my performance was cool. Thousands of people, people I didn't even know, had seen me, Dalton Black, on television.

On the other hand, seeing a guy get killed, by me, was a bit unnerving. I couldn't help but think back to all the research. How evil some people could be. As my mother reminded me periodically, the world could be a scary place.

I double-checked the deadbolt.

Chapter Three

The next morning, I sat at the breakfast table, trying to make the immortal words *Please pass the syrup* as engaging as possible. A few Eggo waffles on my plate helped create the mood. My big sister Annie slouched across from me, staring at her phone as she ate her yogurt. Accustomed to what she called my *acting nonsense,* she pointedly ignored me while I repeated the same line over and over.

"Please pass the syrup." I put some cheer into the words.

"Please pass the syrup." I put some urgency into the words.

"Please pass the syrup." I put some hunger into the words.

"Please pass the—"

"Enough!" Annie glared at me. "You've got the delivery down cold, but maybe you should go see what you look like in a mirror. Upstairs. You wouldn't want your face to be all scrunched up on camera. I mean, you wouldn't want to be any uglier than you already are."

"You just want to get rid of me." I forked the last piece of waffle into my mouth.

"You're not as dumb as you look." She flashed me a fake smile and fluttered her eyelids.

"And what do you have on your schedule today?" I rose and picked up my plate. "Oh, that's right. Summer school. Sounds like a lot of fun. I wish I got to sit inside for hours going over tedious math problems."

She went back to ignoring me.

I ran up to my room and flopped on the bed. Three seconds later, my manager, Alfred McMaster, called, and I picked up. "Hello, Alf."

"Hello, my boy. Congratulations on a very fine TV debut. I watched it last night on the edge of my seat. You captured the essence of a murderer. I truly *believed* you were a deranged killer. Fine job, fine job." Alf was a young seventy-years old, and I pictured him with his baby-blue high-top Chucks up on his desk, stroking his immaculately trimmed white beard or playing with a flashy silk scarf around his neck. For some reason, he spoke with a vague British accent, although I was pretty sure he'd grown up in Indiana or Illinois or Iowa—one of those Midwestern states beginning with an "I." Maybe it was left over from a performance of *My Fair Lady*.

"Thanks, Alf. And thanks again for getting me the part."

"Au contraire, my boy. *You* got the part. I simply got you the audition. A little birdie named Meryl Streep once told me that being a good actor is all about being a good auditioner. Or something like that. And speaking of auditions, I have some good news and some bad news. Which would you like to hear first?"

"How about the bad news?" I braced for the worst.

"Very well. Today's audition has been canceled. The mother of your stage family got sick, and because it's all about the look of the family as a unit, they canceled your entire group's auditions. Nature of the beast, I'm afraid."

So much for passing the syrup with gusto.

"But the good news should make up for it. I got you another audition. For a better spot. A national commercial, with more lines. A wireless carrier. And you know what that means. More exposure. And more money, too."

That *was* good news. Sometimes those national spots aired for months, or longer. And that meant residuals. Money to put away to travel to auditions, for acting workshops, or for college. "Great. When is it?"

"Ah, well, there's the rub. Tomorrow. I'll send over the sides and details. I know you can do it. You're a quick study, Dalton, and you've never yet failed to give it your best effort. I'm confident you will acquit yourself superbly. And I've cleared it so you don't need a parent at the audition. Break a leg, my boy. TTFN!"

He hung up immediately after spouting his signature old-timey "ta-ta for now" farewell, without giving me a chance to respond. Alf had approached me about working with him four years ago when he'd seen me play the title role in a community theater production of *Oliver!* My dad had been okay with the idea of my having professional representation, but I practically had to beg my mom to let me go ahead with it. She was afraid it might distract me from my schoolwork and derail me from what I really wanted to do with my life. I'd told her—repeatedly—that what I really wanted to do with my life was act.

Three months of constant nagging on my part had worn her down.

Alf was one of the top managers on the East Coast, and he gave me invaluable guidance about my career. As part of his role, he acted as my agent, doing a good job of getting me auditions, mostly for local commercials and voice-overs. The role in "High School Hitman" was the highest-profile gig I'd ever booked, and I couldn't help but think it was the beginning of an ever-expanding career.

I fired up my laptop, and Alf's email with the sides—the script for the audition—was already sitting in my inbox. I opened the attachment. Three pages of dialogue between two teens talking about their phone service. I skimmed the scene. *Never miss a call or text. Fast download speeds. Best coverage area.* All boring. But it wasn't my job to critique the writing. I was supposed to bring the words to life and get across the message—no matter how dull—to the audience.

I printed out the sides and highlighted the part I was reading for—Teen One—with a yellow marker. Then I settled in for a session of memorization. For whatever reason, remembering lines was something I excelled at. Mom thought I had something close to a photographic memory, and I think it helped me skate through most exams with a minimum of study time. Most of my drama friends also found memorizing lines easy, but I sure sympathized with those who didn't. Guys like Patch. It had to make acting so much more difficult.

Sometimes, I'd call up Patch or have my dad run the lines with me, but this didn't seem too hard, so I dug in and tackled it myself.

Fifteen minutes later, I'd memorized the first page of dialogue.

I was about to dive into page two when my phone buzzed with a text from Patch.

> Patch: My mom saw the show last night and was worried you seemed too comfortable playing a killer. She said she didn't want me hanging out with you, lol. Seriously, she loved your performance.
> Me: Thanks. How's camp?
> Patch: Tommy Harrison puked. Otherwise, fine.
> Me: So, business as usual.

Tommy Harrison was trouble. After the first few days, the counselors caught on and tried to rotate him into different groups, so the same person wouldn't always get stuck with him.

> Patch: Break a leg on the audition.
> Me: Got canceled.
> Patch: So you're coming in?
> Me: Yeah. In about an hour. Later.

First, I'd memorize the sides, then I'd go in to camp. I'm sure Ms. Z would understand; she was as supportive a teacher, director, and boss as you could ask for. Probably why everybody loved her.

I set my alarm, just in case I lost track of time.

Forty minutes later, I had the whole scene down pat. I thought I could even read for the role of Teen Two, if someone asked. I tried to be as prepared as possible, because you never knew what might happen during an audition. An actor who the casting director thought would be perfect for the role might bomb, and you might get an opportunity to audition for a better role. Someone trying out ahead of you might grab a role with a great audition, leaving you without even a *chance* to audition.

It was a tough business, full of rejection and dejection around every corner. Sometimes it was a simple, *no, thank you*, while other times you got the all-purpose, faux-polite, *we're going in a different direction*—casting-speak for getting rejected.

I put the sides down and leaned back, hands clasped behind my head. It had been cool to see myself on TV last night, and it felt great to have Alf and Patch's mom give me thumbs-up reviews. All I could ever remember wanting to do was act.

When I was a kid, I'd put on puppet shows at family gatherings and do monologues for whoever would listen. My parents' attention, on me. Laughing and applauding when I finished. What kid wouldn't eat that up? And when I got older, I kept at it. Took classes after school. Went to drama camp every summer, two sessions. Once I started getting parts in things, I couldn't wait to audition for the next show. Whenever I didn't have another gig lined up, I felt a little anxious, a little empty, afraid my time onstage might be over.

That's why I worked so hard—I hated the idea of never acting again.

My mother claimed I was obsessed with being an actor. I preferred to be called *passionate.*

Of course, acting was a tough, tough field. To be successful, you needed talent, drive, and some good old-fashioned luck.

I closed my eyes and visualized where things might go if I got a few big breaks.

My name, Dalton Black, in lights on a Broadway marquee.

My very own Beverly Hills mansion, complete with a double-decker pool and a hundred live flamingos.

A tricked-out trailer on some movie set in the Australian Outback.

Leonardo DiCaprio opening the envelope and calling my name at the Academy Awards.

I was about to reach the podium to accept the Oscar when my daydream was interrupted by the *zzzzzt* of the alarm. Time to go to camp.

Chapter Four

According to my father, every few years our town, Vienna, Virginia, would get named to some magazine's list of Best Small Towns to Live In. Never mind that Vienna was basically a suburb of Washington, D.C.—one of probably a hundred communities outside the Beltway, providing workers to our Nation's Capital. The restaurants and shops on Main Street didn't care, proudly displaying their "Best Small Town" signs in every place possible.

But it was a decent place to live, where people knew their neighbors yet didn't hate them. The crime rate was low, there were parades on the Fourth of July and at Halloween, and most of the town showed up for the Friday night high school football games.

Maple Avenue—the town's main street—cut through the heart of the commercial area. Shops, restaurants, the library, Town Hall, the police station, the fire department, two grocery stores, the village green, and the funeral home all were located within a square mile or so. All within walking distance of my house.

And right on Maple Avenue, across from the McDonald's, was my school, South Vienna High.

As I opened up the double doors to the school's auditorium—where the summer drama camp was held—a wall of noise rose up and smacked me in the face. Yelling, singing, music, laughing, hammering—the sweet sounds of putting on a show. This year, the camp was performing *The Wizard of Oz*, a perennial favorite.

That familiar feeling of excitement grew in my chest as I soaked in the scene. The kids had been divided into various groups. Some practiced new songs; others learned their lines. Pretty much everyone had seen the movie, so it wasn't like they had to learn something entirely new. Ms. Z felt it was a good way to introduce middle schoolers to theater.

I took a picture of the frenetic activity in the auditorium, careful not to capture anyone's face, and posted it on Instagram, with a plug for the upcoming show. The more publicity, the better.

Patch waved me over. He was teaching a group of kids some dance moves, but it looked more like a crazed mosh pit. A dozen bodies all going in different directions. "Okay? Got it? Now you try. I'll be back in a moment," he said to his crew. Then he walked me off to the side, away from where the flailing arm or leg of a sixth-grader could do damage.

"Too bad your audition got canceled."

"Got a better one tomorrow. For a national spot."

"Cool!" Patch put his arm around my shoulder. "Here's a bit of friendly advice: when you go in for the audition, leave your knife at home."

I shrugged out of his grip. "Thanks."

"Don't mention it. Did you see Ms. Z yet?"

"No."

"She was looking for you. Said she wanted to talk to you as soon as you came in."

"Know why?"

"Nope. But she seemed a little stressed out."

From the stage where she was working on a gigantic neon-bright cardboard rainbow, Trinnie spotted us and waved. She said something to another counselor, then left her station, climbed down from the stage, and made her way across the room to join us. Red and blue streaks of paint decorated her shirt, and a smattering of white paint spots were flecked in her hair. "How'd the audition go?" she asked me.

I told her what had happened and about the upcoming audition.

"That's great!" She squeezed my arm and held on a beat too long.

"Thanks." I turned to Patch. "Did you sign up for the Christmas Cavalcade auditions yet?"

"Nope."

"What are you waiting for? The deadline is soon." Trinnie shifted toward Patch and stared at him with full focus—a habit that made some people uncomfortable, but always got the middle schoolers in line.

Patch shrugged. "I need to get back to work before my kids kill each other. See you after?"

"Sure," Trinnie and I said almost simultaneously.

He returned to his group and started demonstrating how to do a jazz square, as part of a dance he was choreographing.

Trinnie inched closer and lowered her voice. "I'm worried about him. That's like the fourth audition in a row he's blown off. We've got to do something."

Patch had trouble remembering his lines, especially when he was onstage. Last winter, one of the leads in the play got sick, so Ms. Z drafted Patch to stand in. He blew his very first line on opening night and never recovered, a huge hit to his confidence. He always did fine during rehearsals, or in a musical when he could shine with his singing and dancing, but getting him to audition for a significant speaking role had become a challenge for the last three years, since his uneven performance as Captain Hook in *Peter Pan*. The only good thing to come out of that role was his nickname.

"What do you suggest?"

"I'm not sure, and I'm worried. And I know you are, too. We can't stand by and let stage fright ruin his life."

"Ruin his life? I think you're being a little over-dramatic. He'll overcome it. I have faith in Patch."

Trinnie turned her intense stare on me, and I felt like an ant caught under a magnifying glass, about to get incinerated. "Dalton Black. You and I are going to help our friend. Whether you want to or not."

"Well, if you put it like that..."

"Uh-oh. Here comes Ms. Z. I need to get back to painting. Later." Trinnie zipped away, right as Ms. Z walked up.

She was about Trinnie's height with medium-length sandy hair bisected by a purple streak running through it. Last spring the streak had been red, and the semester before that, green. Nothing ever seemed to get her down. In fact, the only time I'd ever seen her without a smile was...right now.

"There you are. How was the audition?"

I repeated what I'd told Patch and Trinnie, and she nodded, telling me I could take off as much time as I needed—for the auditions themselves, as well as to prepare for them. Her words sounded normal, but something about her less-than-cheerful delivery bothered me.

Ms. Z motioned for me to follow her. Instead of finding a quiet corner as I expected, she led me all the way out of the auditorium and down a short hallway to her office. Which would have been fine, except she closed the door. She never closed the door.

"Have a seat." She pointed to a chair with a flying monkey costume on it. "You can set that aside. Carefully."

I picked up the costume and set it on the floor. Took a seat. My heart raced.

She perched in her chair, back perfectly straight, and her gaze drifted to the framed photo of her wife, Whitney, on the corner of her desk. This was completely out of character for laid-back Ms. Z. Had I screwed up somehow? Was she going to kick me out of camp? Was she going to tell me I shouldn't even bother auditioning for the next show? Don't call us, we'll call you.

As Ms. Z. gathered her thoughts, I tried to remember if I'd done anything to deserve her wrath. After a moment, Ms. Z turned toward me and forced a smile, but dropped it quickly.

"Someone stopped by earlier looking for you."

"Who?"

"He said his name was Tom Smith. Do you know anybody named Tom Smith?"

I thought for a second. "I don't think so."

"Ordinarily, I wouldn't think twice about what happened. But..." She pursed her lips. "Something didn't seem right. He seemed a little creepy, if you want to know the truth."

"Did he say what he wanted?"

"He said it was a private matter." She looked at me kinda like how my mother looked at me when she thought I was screwing up. "Is there something you want to tell me?"

"Like what?"

"Look, Dalton. I've known you a couple of years. You're a good kid. A *real* good kid. But even good kids sometimes make bad choices. If there's something I can do to help you out of a jam, please let me know. I understand that sometimes there are things you might not want your parents to know, but I assure you, if your safety is involved, you can tell me and I'll keep things confidential as much as I can."

What the hell was going on? "Exactly how creepy was this guy?"

Ms. Z sighed. "Pretty creepy. Early, mid-twenties. Unkempt. Talked fast. He seemed desperate, too. For the record, I told him I wasn't able to tell him if you worked here or went to school here. I gave him the standard, 'You need to talk to someone in Administration.' He didn't seem to like that answer. In fact, when I picked up the phone to call the main office, he said he was running late for a meeting and had to leave."

"I have no idea who it might be. Honestly."

"I'm not accusing you of anything, you understand, but..." Ms. Z said, and sighed. "You're not involved with drugs, are you?"

"No!"

"I didn't think so, but I had to ask." She exhaled. "One

more thing. He was looking for Dalton Black."

A few years ago, I'd adopted the stage name Dalton Black, instead of using my more-boring given name, David Berglund. Everyone seemed to go along with my wishes and call me Dalton, except for my mother, who still called me David. Of course, all the teachers knew my real name from the student rolls. "Seriously, I have no clue who might want to talk to me."

"I'll report this to Principal Shirazzi. She can decide what to do, if anything. When he left here, I followed him out and watched him drive off, making sure he left the school grounds. He's probably just someone who saw you on TV and wanted to talk to you about how you got the part or something like that. I've been around enough frustrated actors to know the extremes many would go to with hopes of landing a part. But you never really know, so please be careful. How are you getting home today, after camp?"

I was going to walk home with Patch and Trinnie, like I always did. But if I told that to Ms. Z, then she'd insist on something else—and it would probably involve contacting my parents. But no way did I want them—my mother, especially—to hear about some creepy dude stalking me. She'd lock me in my room and forbid me from booking any jobs until I graduated. "My mother is picking me up."

I'd never lied to Ms. Z before, and it felt terrible. Acting might be lying onstage, but it's a lot different doing it to a person in real life.

"Good. Better safe than sorry."

Chapter Five

"Pass the meatloaf, please." I'd practically inhaled the first piece, along with a baked potato, but it had hardly made a dent in my appetite. There's something about corralling kids at camp all afternoon and having a potential stalker that makes you ravenous, I guessed.

"Here you go." My dad handed me a platter. "The most delicious meatloaf ever made." He smiled at my mom, who gave him that look. The sappy one that said how much she adored him. Almost enough to ruin my appetite. "Why are you sitting in Annie's place, anyway?"

"Hey, nothing wrong with a little change now and then, right?" I asked, shrugging like there was nothing really wrong. My usual seat at the dinner table was right in front of the large bay window facing the street. With whoever it was on the prowl, I decided not to make it any easier for them, and with Annie out someplace, I took her spot.

"This from the kid who has to drink from the same blue plastic cup every night at dinner?" Dad asked.

I mumbled something about baby steps.

"So, David." Mom stabbed a piece of meatloaf with her fork and stared at me. "I was thinking about the fall. About your classes. Maybe you should take an academic class for an elective, instead of both chorus and drama."

"I like chorus. I like drama." I said, tired of this routine. "I don't like Intro to Business or Coding or whatever it is you think I should take."

"Don't get me wrong. I think drama is fun." She slowly shook her head, as if I were having trouble understanding her. "But I'm sure you want to get into a good college and study something that will allow you to make a living. Why don't you come into work with me one day? Get an up-close and personal view of what I do. Or better yet, why not come with me the next time I try a case? You can sit right in the courtroom and see how the law works. I know it might not sound exciting, but I think you'd be surprised."

We'd had this discussion before. Many times. Mom was a high-powered attorney who thought money and job security were the barometers of success. Every time we got into it, I would hold off talking about happiness for as long as I could, mainly because that didn't seem to factor into her thinking. At least not when it came to careers. Eventually I'd bust out the "Don't you want me to be happy?" line, and she'd counter with "You sure won't be happy struggling to make ends meet." Voices would get raised. Feelings would be bruised.

Then we'd go to our respective corners to cool down. I didn't want to ruin dinner tonight, so I simply nodded and said, "Sure, I'll think about it."

I glanced at my father. He never hassled me about what I wanted to be. Of course, right now, he seemed mesmerized by his baked potato.

"I've heard that before," Mom said. "It's what you say when you're blowing me off. I've been suggesting you come into work with me for a long time."

My father looked up from his plate, ready to step into his role as family peacemaker. Predictable, but sometimes I wished he'd take my side, outright. "Hon, he said he'd think about it. Why don't we agree to table this conversation until a future date? Maybe after he's had time to consider it. Hmm? What do you both say? Of course, maybe he'd like to come into work with me one day." He winked.

My father was a regional manager for a movie theater chain. When I was younger, I went in to work with him on many occasions, and he'd set me up so I could preview movies. Lots of movies. *He* cared about my happiness. I fist-bumped him.

Mom turned to Dad, scowling. My parents rarely disagreed about things, but when they did, it usually involved me. And more specifically, my drama pursuits. "We've been down this road before. All I'm asking is that we sit down and discuss options. Figure out what classes might be most beneficial to sign up for. Maybe expose him to something else besides acting. What's the harm in that?"

I bit my tongue.

"Exactly. I think we're all saying the same thing," my dad said.

"Well, that's the problem, isn't it?" She turned to me, an eyebrow raised. "David talks a good game, but he doesn't always follow it up with action." Even though she was facing me, it sounded like she was still talking to Dad.

"Dalton," I said. "Please call me Dalton."

"I *know* what your name is," Mom said. "I named you, remember? And for the record, there's nothing wrong with David."

I couldn't hold it in any longer. "Don't you want me to be happy?"

"You sure won't be happy struggling to make ends meet. I can tell you that, young man."

I picked up my plate, second helping of meatloaf untouched. "I'm not hungry anymore. May I be excused?"

Without waiting for an answer, I rose and, careful not to step in front of the bay window, stalked over to the sink to dump my plate in. Then I rushed up to my room, taking the stairs two at a time.

The next morning, I woke up early to review the sides for the audition. After a once-over, I was happy I still had the lines down pat.

I scarfed down a quick breakfast while waiting for Dad to get ready. He'd offered to drop me off on his way to work, and I'd gladly accepted.

My phone buzzed. A Twitter DM from an account I didn't recognize.

> Johnsmith9988: I need to meet with you.
> Me: Who is this?
> Johnsmith9988: It won't take long.
> Me: Who is this? What's this about?
> Johnsmith9988: It's about life or death.

Seriously? I'd gotten an occasional scammy message on Twitter or Facebook—I suppose everyone did from time to time—but I couldn't help but picture Ms. Z's concerned face. It would be an awfully big coincidence if this *wasn't* related to that guy looking for me.

> Me: Tell me more.
> Johnsmith9988: In person. Must be face-to-face.
> I wasn't an idiot. No way was I going to meet some stranger in person.
> Me: Nope. Sorry. If you can't tell me now, then forget it.
> Johnsmith9988: I won't forget it. I won't give up, either.

A chill rippled through me and I couldn't block his account fast enough.

A minute later, my dad came downstairs. "Ready to go?"

"Uh, yeah," I managed to say, still shaky.

"Okay, then. Let's roll."

Unlike many of my auditions held in Baltimore or Richmond,

this one was in Tysons Corner, located only a few miles north—or was it east?—or was it northeast?—along Route 123, otherwise known as Maple Avenue.

Tysons Corner was jam-packed with hi-rise office buildings, and during morning rush hour, it also was jam-packed with cars. I reached into my backpack and pulled out a pair of Ray-Ban knockoffs and a Nationals baseball cap, and put them on.

"New look?" My dad glanced over at me in the nearly-stopped traffic.

"Yeah, maybe..." I thought about the stalker or fan or whoever it was searching for me back at the school. The ominous message on Twitter. My heart raced. "Hey Dad, look, there's something I should maybe—"

The car jerked back and forth, as we stopped yet again in traffic.

"Damn it!" Dad pounded the steering wheel with his fist. "I can't stand this town during rush hour." He turned to me again. "What were you saying?"

We'd only moved a hundred yards in the last five minutes. I consulted my Maps app and realized my destination was only a few blocks away.

"You know, I'm good, Dad." I unbuckled my seat belt as we waited at a light. "We'll talk about it later. I'll walk from here." The fresh air would also help to clear my head, get me in the right frame of mind for my audition. I'd tell Dad what happened later, when the time was better.

Mom probably would have argued about letting me hop out in the middle of traffic, or pressed to keep me in the car until I told her what was on my mind. Dad just said, "Break a leg, Sport!"

I grabbed my backpack and climbed out of the car, slamming the door behind me. Zigzagged across three lanes of traffic to get to the other side, and I made it right as the light turned green. One guy blew his horn at me, but I just smiled and waved.

I'd been to this casting office a few times before, so I knew what I was looking for: a row of non-descript townhouse offices.

A couple of law firms, an insurance company, an import/export business specializing in oriental rugs. Capitol Casting occupied the top floor over a bathroom renovation showroom. A small sign with two fancy-fonted "Cs" surrounding the silhouette of the Washington Monument marked the place.

I walked up the narrow flight of stairs, both shoulders brushing against the paint-peeling walls. Why was it that most of the casting offices I'd been to were shoe-horned into odd places? Before I'd been to my first one, I pictured luxury penthouse suites with thick carpeting and sleek brass-and-glass furniture. What else would be appropriate for a business catering to movie stars, or at least, would-be stars?

It had only taken my first visit to one to knock me crashing back to reality.

On the landing outside the entrance to Capitol Casting, I removed the cap and sunglasses, stuffed them into my backpack, and smoothed my hair. Then I opened the door and slipped inside. A young woman—not too much older than me—looked up from her desk. "Hello. Can I help you?" Crystal-blue eyes sparkled and, for a moment, I forgot what I was doing there.

"Uh..."

Her smile grew. "Yes?"

I snapped out of it. "Oh, sorry. I'm Dalton Black. Here for an audition."

"Of course." She slid a clipboard across the desk. "Please sign in. Someone will be with you shortly. You can have a seat over there while you wait." She pointed to a cramped waiting room with eight chairs, all full. More people stood and a few leaned against the wall, checking their phones.

"Thanks." I filled out my name, leaving contact information for me and for Alf. Then I scanned the waiting area, for anyone...someone... Strange looking? Dangerous? I still wasn't sure what to think about the Twitter message or what had happened at school. Who would be looking for me? Why? Despite my initial fear, the most likely explanation pointed to some overzealous—but harmless—fan. I just needed to calm down.

I found six inches of free space, squeezed in, and leaned against the wall. As I was attempting to get comfortable, my backpack bumped into the guy behind me. I turned around to apologize, and as I did, the guy spun around, too.

I found myself face to face with Cam Carter.

I wasn't surprised. "Hello, Cam."

He tipped his head at me. "Dalton."

"Here for the phone spot?"

"Yep. Teen One. You?"

"Same."

We nodded at each other. By my count, we'd been up for the same roles five out of my last seven auditions. We were both the same age, we both had a certain look—average high school student—and we were both represented by top managers. Unfortunately—for me, anyway—Cam had that something-something casting directors often preferred.

We also both attended South Vienna High, and Cam got juicier roles in the school plays. Trinnie once let slip that she thought it was because Cam was just a tad better-looking and just a tad better actor.

I told her it was because he was a better kiss-ass.

Our staring contest continued. Finally, I broke it off. "Well, break a leg."

He tipped his head again. "Likewise." Then he turned away.

I glanced around the waiting area and took stock of the other actors. All casting offices were alike. A bunch of similar-looking people auditioning for the same part.

Today, there were two distinct groups of teens, obviously auditioning for the same commercial. As described in the Role Description that came with the sides, Teen One was your "typical" teen—dressed in regular clothes, decent haircut, boy-next-door face. In addition to me and Cam, there appeared to be three other Teen Ones.

Another five boys looked as if they were there to play Teen

Two, a jock. Each was tall and muscular, and they had come prepared, wearing sports jerseys and flashy sneakers. One kid even had a basketball tucked under one arm. Nice touch.

Virtually everyone in the room stared at their phones. I could bet what ninety percent were doing—running lines in their heads, reading and re-reading them off their screens. Some of the actors' lips moved and if you listened carefully, you could hear a few audible recitations. At an audition once, a guy had gone out into the adjoining hallway and screamed his lines, trying out different deliveries, putting emphasis on various parts of the sentences. That had caused everyone in the waiting room to crack up. I was pretty sure he hadn't gotten the part.

Ah, the crazy life of an actor.

I pulled out my own phone, called up the sides, and ran the lines in my head.

Ten minutes later, another young woman, clipboard in hand, came over to the waiting area and called half a dozen names, mine and Cam's included. Three of us fit the Teen One mold, and three were clearly jocks. "Follow me, please."

She led us down a short hallway, into another waiting area, not quite as crowded. "Please wait here. Dalton Black and Eric Weiss, please follow me."

She led me and Eric—six-two and ripped—into a small room, where a twenty-something man and an older woman sat in chairs at a folding table. The guy wore a casual plaid shirt and trendy black-rimmed glasses, and the woman wore a black blouse, black jeans, and black flats. I had the feeling she was the casting director, the one in charge. A stack of headshots and resumes sat on the table, the biggest pile of them right in front of her. A video camera perched atop a tripod in the back of the room.

"Welcome, guys," the man said. "I'm Finn. Ready?"

Eric and I both nodded, and Finn got us set up in front of a plain wall, checking from behind the camera to make sure we were framed properly in the shot. After a couple of adjustments, he gave us the thumbs-up.

"All set. Could you please introduce yourselves? The usual is fine. Name, age, height," he said.

Most of the time, the casting directors didn't want a lengthy bio. They just wanted us to "slate"—give our vitals—for the video recording. After all, they'd already seen our headshots and resumes when they selected us to come in for the audition.

After Eric slated, it was my turn. "My name is Dalton Black. I'm sixteen, and I'm five-ten." I paused, then decided to add a little personality, trying to stand out from the pack. "Most recently, I had a role in an episode of *Teen Killers* on True Crime Network. You might have seen it the other night?" I paused to let that sink in, then added, "It's also been, for as long as I can remember, my life's dream to play Teen One in this particular commercial. And I'm not just saying that to get on your—"

Finn held up his hand. "That's fine. Really."

I nodded, conjuring up my brightest audition smile.

They didn't smile back, and an uneasy feeling grew in my gut. "Okay, then. Let's get started," Finn said.

I glanced over at Eric, his mouth a thin line. I felt like I might have just ruined my chances before we even began.

Dammit.

Eric began with his line, delivered smoothly, with feeling. I responded equally well, and we went back and forth. About halfway through, my mind went blank. I opened my mouth, but nothing came out. I licked my lips, mind racing to come up with the line.

"Sorry. I, uh...sorry." I cleared my throat and took the line from the top. And screwed it up again.

Unprofessional.

Eric scowled, and Finn frowned. Weirdly, the woman remained stone-faced as she glanced down at my resume.

Once more, I tried to deliver my line. Before I'd gotten five words into it, the lady held up her hand and spoke for the first time. "Thank you. Thank you very much."

My mouth dropped open. Eric's scowl deepened. Finn didn't look at us as he put our headshots aside and plucked the next two off the pile. "Sorry, I messed up. Can we try again? Please?"

"I think we've seen what we needed to," the casting director said. "Thank you for coming in." She turned to Finn. "Can you get the next pair?"

Finn hustled out of the room; Eric and I gathered our things and plodded out behind him. As we trudged down the hall, Cam and his audition partner passed us coming in. Judging by the smirk on Cam's face, I'm sure he could tell by my super-short audition things hadn't gone very well. They disappeared into the room behind us.

"Hey." I turned to apologize to Eric, pretty sure my attempt at standing out might have ruined his chances, too. "I'm sorry, but I—"

"Save it." He held up his hand, and then turned and stalked past the reception desk and out the door. One of the perils of auditioning in pairs is getting stuck with some loser who made you look bad.

In this case, *I* was that loser.

I stopped for a moment back in the waiting area, taking a seat to collect my thoughts. Usually I was pretty good in my auditions. In fact, I prided myself on my ability to nail them. Had I been overconfident? I didn't think so. I had the sides down cold. Was something else stressing me out?

Regardless, I still felt terrible about blowing the audition. For Eric. For me.

I glanced around. No one seemed to be fixated on me. Maybe—hopefully—my stalker had a short attention span.

The faces of those in the waiting area had changed, but in some sense, they remained the same. Distinct groups of people with similar looks. All rehearsing their lines. All with that slight edge of nervousness or anxiety or fear—or whatever you wanted to call the butterfly rodeo in your stomach right before an audition.

Actors wanted to succeed. Actors wanted to get good parts. Actors wanted to make a living, keep working, become famous. There had to be some reward for being brave enough to turn yourself inside out in front of dozens, hundreds, thousands, and millions of people, didn't there?

I wondered how Cam's audition was going. He'd already been in there longer than me. I decided to wait until he came out before leaving. The minutes dragged. Sure, my audition had been cut short, but that wasn't *so* unusual. Even though most auditions were scheduled after the casting director sorted through dozens of resumes and headshots, sometimes people presented differently in person. And because looks were such a big factor, especially in commercials, there were times when a casting director could tell in mere seconds a candidate wasn't right for the role.

Usually, but not always, the directors allowed the actors to run the lines, more as a courtesy than anything else. It sure sucked when you spent hours memorizing sides, then drove for an hour—or more—then waited around even longer, only to get a "Thank you very much for coming" after a cursory three-minute audition.

Welcome to the world of acting.

Finally, Cam came around the corner, chatting it up with Finn. They seemed to be sharing a joke, big smiles all around. When Cam spotted me sitting there, he threw a quick wink my way.

"Well, Cam. You'll be hearing from us shortly," he said. "Thanks so much for coming by."

"The pleasure was all mine," Cam said, in full suck-up mode, reaching out and shaking Finn's hand. "Truly an honor."

They said goodbye, and Finn and I locked eyes. His smile vanished quickly. I guess my audition really had been that bad.

He called out the next names on his list and escorted them back to their auditions. Cam stepped over to me. "How did it go?"

I shrugged. "Okay."

He beamed. "Yeah. Mine, too. Give you a ride someplace?"

A ride would save me time. But sitting in a car with Cam after he'd all but booked the job? I could walk the three or four miles. "No thanks. I'm good."

"Okay, then," Cam said. "See you around."

I wanted to smack the smarmy smile right off his face, but instead said, "Sure. Around."

He turned to leave and I thought about the stalker, lurking in the shadows. "Hey, wait up, Cam. I think I'll take you up on that ride, after all."

On the ride back, I stared out the window, boiling inside, as I listened to Cam's success stories.

Chapter Six

Later that afternoon, Patch, Trinnie, and I relaxed on Patch's back deck, engaged in one of our favorite hobbies—arguing about actors. As so often happened, we wound up debating the relative merits of Leonardo DiCaprio versus Ryan Gosling.

"I don't know how you can have Leo ranked above Ryan," Patch said. "He's a great actor, sure, but come on, he's been phoning it in lately. And all the roles are the same character."

"Oh please," I said. "You need to consider the entire body of work."

"I've been considering both of their bodies. And I think it's pretty close to a tie," Trinnie said.

Patch and I both glared at her.

"What? They're both hot. And their acting isn't bad either."

"Who's hungry?" Patch asked.

I'd wondered what had taken him so long to ask that question. He usually couldn't go more than thirty minutes without thinking of food.

"I could eat," I said.

"Only water for me," Trinnie said.

"Be right back." Patch scurried off to raid the pantry.

"So, how's it feel to be a big TV star?" Trinnie asked.

"I think I had my fifteen minutes of fame." And it was pretty cool, if short-lived. Most of the kids at school congratulated me, but after the initial buzz, I was just another drama kid walking the halls. "Aside from a few dinner theater performances, I've got nothing on the horizon."

"You're doing great. Lots of auditions. Something will come through."

I shrugged. "Maybe I should kneecap Cam."

"I can do it for you. He won't know what hit him." Trinnie ducked her head and threw a few punches. Then she kissed her biceps. "I'm tougher than I look."

"You look plenty tough."

"Thank you, sir." She paused for a second. "You know, he's really not such a bad guy."

"You mean for an arch-nemesis?"

"Get over yourself. You need to be a super-hero before you get a nemesis, arch or otherwise." Her expression turned serious. "You really should give him a chance."

"Why do you care so much?"

"Maybe I don't like seeing you make an ass of yourself." One of Trinnie's eyebrows arched.

"Next topic," I said. The less time spent talking about Cam, the better.

"A little touchy, are we?" She sighed. "What time is your dinner theater thing tonight?"

"Dinner begins at six, and the performance begins shortly thereafter." I'd agreed to be in a mystery dinner theater production, something one of my father's co-workers was putting on. Tonight was the third performance out of four. Trinnie and Patch were coming to provide moral support.

"Okay. How long does the show last?"

"Hour and a half. You know, you guys don't have to come. My part is really small, and the food is really bad." According to my dad, the dinner theater idea was experimental—an attempt for a new restaurant to get some publicity and generate business on a weekday night. They were paying me twenty dollars per show and free food. And I loved free food, no matter how lousy it tasted. Besides, the more paying gigs on my resume the better, at least during this stage of my career.

"Wow, how can I possibly turn that down?"

"Just be sure to lower your expectations. Like I said, my part is very small. No lines, even."

"So you've said. It'll be good research for when I have a very small, no-lines part. Then I'll know how to behave."

"Suit yourself."

Trinnie's expression softened, and she cocked her head at me. "You okay? You seem a little...off. Something going on?"

Trinnie had always been the perceptive one. I hadn't mentioned my stalker to her or anybody else. Part of me—the bigger part—hoped it would all blow over, no harm done. But part of me also didn't want to risk having limits put on my acting. If my parents found out, I'd be done. I knew I could trust Trinnie, though. "Well..."

"I knew it." She sat forward on her chair. "Talk to me, Dalton. Whatever it is, I can help."

I blew out my breath. "Okay." I paused, looked directly into her big brown eyes. "I think someone's after me."

"After you?"

"Yeah. Like a stalker."

She ran a hand through her hair. "Whoa. A stalker?" She bit her lip and I could tell her brain had gone into overdrive. "I need some details."

I told her about the creepy guy who came to school looking for me, Ms. Z's reaction, the strange Twitter message, and the fact I've been seeing stalkers hiding in every shadow, a by-product of my wild imagination.

"You know, you could have told me sooner. That's what friends are for." Her eyes flashed.

"So you think I should be worried?"

"Worried about what?" Patch said, returning with two armfuls of snacks. He dumped them on the glass-topped table.

"Go ahead, tell him," Trinnie said.

No sense sugarcoating it. "I think I have a stalker."

Patch did a double-take. "What? Seriously?"

"Yeah." I repeated what I'd told Trinnie.

"Come on. It could be a lot of things. Maybe he saw you on TV and wants to be your manager. Trying to get in on the ground floor, before you hit it big." He plucked a bag of chips from the table and popped it open. "Maybe he's a casting director and wants you to be in his project. Maybe he wants you to endorse some product of his. Could be anything." He reached into the bag and grabbed some chips. Stuffed them in his mouth.

I'd been thinking of logical explanations myself, but I kept coming back to "stalker."

"I think we have to assume the worst here," Trinnie said. "We need to be careful."

I noted her use of the word *we*. "What do you suggest?"

Trinnie chewed her lip some more. "Maybe we should call the police."

"And tell them what? Some guy was looking for me? Patch is right, this guy could be looking for me for some perfectly innocent reason. Besides, if the cops get involved, my parents will find out, and then my career is finished." I shook my head. "Look, I don't think I'm in any real danger. I mean, who would want to hurt me? It's just creepy, you know? Regardless, we are absolutely not calling the police. Or telling my parents."

We sat in silence, digesting the situation.

A minute later, my phone rang. I glanced at the screen. *Agent Alf.*

"Guys, quiet. It's my manager."

"Oooh, his manager," Patch teased.

I answered the call. "Hello, Alf."

"Hello, my boy," Alf said.

Patch mouthed the word, *speaker*.

I hesitated while Patch mouthed it again. What the hell. If you couldn't show off for your besties, who could you show off for? "Is it okay if I put you on speaker?"

"Sure, why not?"

"Thanks." I hit the speaker button, placed the phone on the table, and put my finger up to my lips. Just because I was letting Patch and Trinnie listen didn't mean I wanted them involved in the conversation.

"Are you sitting down?" Alf said. "I've got stupendous news."

"I got the phone company role after all?"

"Uh, no. They said they were going in another direction. But don't be disappointed."

"I'm not. After I bombed, I figured—"

Alf talked right over me. "A certain actor you may have heard of, one Mister Bradley Charles Cooper, says that every *no* you get at an audition puts you one audition closer to getting a *yes* and booking the gig."

I glanced at Patch and Trinnie, who were staring at my phone, mouths agape.

"Bradley Cooper is your client?" Patch blurted out.

"What? Who said that?" Alf asked.

I faked a cough. "Sorry, got something stuck in my throat." I mouthed *shut up* at Patch. "I didn't realize you worked with Bradley Cooper."

A beat of silence. "Yes, well, I don't actually work *with* him. Coop is a friend of a friend...of a friend. Smart guy, a true professional, too. We all could take career pointers from master thespian Cooper."

"Uh-huh. So, your terrific news?"

"Ah, yes. Yes, of course. Still sitting?"

I wasn't sure why it was so important to be seated, but I knocked loudly on the metal frame of the deck chair, twice, so he could hear me. "Yep."

"True Crime Network wants to film a sequel to 'High School Hitman.' And they want you to reprise your role as the dastardly young Homer Lee Varney."

Trinnie clapped a hand over her mouth, and Patch did a little dance in his chair.

I waited a second for the hammering in my chest to slow

before answering. "Wow. That sounds—"

"They can't do it without you. You're one of the leads, and you delivered a magnificent tour de force with your breakout performance. This time, you'll have many, many more lines. You're in the proverbial driver's seat. I told them my client is very busy and would love to do it, but scheduling may be a sticky wicket. They offered to work around your availability, *and* they doubled the pay. Of course, I know you're not doing it for the money. It's about the three E's: experience, exposure, and excitement!"

I took another deep breath. Exhaled. Tried to keep my voice from wavering. "Thanks, Alf. That sounds awesome. When's the shoot?"

"They want to rush it into production in order to capitalize on the first show's ratings bonanza and the press surrounding the recent release of Varney. They want to commence this weekend."

"I think—"

"You're available?" Technically, a question, but not the way Alf said it.

"Sure." I glanced at Patch. His eyes were big and his lips were slightly parted, and he looked like the proverbial kid in a candy store. An idea came to me.

"Very well, then. I'll send you all the details: locations, call times, and—"

My turn to interrupt. "Alf?"

"Yes, my boy?"

"You said I was in the driver's seat, right?"

"Figure of speech, but without you, they'd have to come up with a totally different angle for the show. Why do you ask?"

"I was thinking it would be great if they could find a way to use a couple of my friends in the shoot." I picked up my phone and took the call off speaker. If Alf said something harsh, I didn't want Patch and Trinnie to hear. Putting the phone to my ear, I smiled at them.

Trinnie smiled back, a huge grin, and Patch smiled, too, but it didn't seem completely genuine, as if there were a layer of anxiety preventing him from being entirely happy. I nodded reassuringly at both of them.

"Well, Dalton, let me make a call. Knowing how these reenactment shows are always looking for warm bodies—as extras and for small speaking roles—I think your request may be doable. Are these friends actors?"

"Yes, they are."

"All the better." He paused. "Do they have representation?"

"Not at the moment, no." I smiled again at my friends.

"Excellent," Alf said, more pep in his voice. "Excellent."

We said our goodbyes, and when I put the phone down, Trinnie hopped out of her chair and practically jumped into my lap, hugging me harder than she ever had before.

"You're...crushing...me..."

She gave me a final squeeze, topped it off with a pinch, then let go, still beaming. "We're going to be on TV!" She tried to grab Patch's hands and haul him up out of the chair—presumably to hug the life out of him, too—but he wanted no part of it.

"It's not definite," I said. "But hopefully, all three of us will be on TV."

Patch appeared a little shell-shocked.

"What's the matter?"

"Nothing. Like she said, we're going to be on TV. Exciting." Patch said *exciting*, but the way he said it was anything but.

"It'll be fine. If it comes through, you'll be an extra or something. You can stand around looking like a hipster. I know you can do that. You've been preparing for that role all your life."

Patch's uneasy expression didn't change.

Trinnie tried again to haul him out of his chair, and with a little more effort, she succeeded. She draped an arm around his shoulder. "You've got this," she said, and then went on, poorly impersonating Alf and his already-terrible, probably-fake British accent. "A fantabulous friend of mine, one Mister Ryan Gosling, thespian extraordinaire, says he thinks you'll be *fawn-taws-teek*."

"Okay," he said, starting to smile a little. "No one even notices the extras, right?"

"That's the spirit," I said. "And really, what actor wouldn't want complete and utter anonymity?"

Chapter Seven

Trinnie and Patch met me at Villa Roma at six o'clock sharp. I ushered them to a small table toward the back of the restaurant with a slightly obstructed view of the performance area. It wasn't a raised stage, merely a space cleared out at the front of the dining room.

"So, the show goes on while people are eating?" Patch glanced around the restaurant. Most of the seats were full, and most of the patrons were my parents' age or older. I'd made a sweep of the room earlier, when I'd first arrived, looking for anyone suspicious.

"Yes, the show goes on while people eat. It's a little distracting for the actors, although most of the meal is finished before we start. We get going right as people are digging into their desserts."

The other cast members—five besides me—were putting on their makeup and getting into costumes backstage. In this place, backstage consisted of one cramped corner of a walk-in storage closet full of shelves holding twenty-pound cans of string beans and tomato sauce.

Because of my role, I only needed three minutes to get ready. That gave me time to eat with Trinnie and Patch. When the director found out I had invited a couple of guests, she'd somehow arranged for the restaurant to comp their meals, along with mine. I loved directors who took care of their actors.

The server brought our dinners, and even though they were

free, the chef didn't skimp. Baked chicken in a tomato sauce, pasta, and broccoli. Bread and butter. Nothing super fancy, but it looked edible. And plentiful.

Patch made a face. "Don't we get to order our own dinner?"

I shrugged. "This is the deal the director made. Chef's choice. What do you care? You'll eat anything."

Patch shrugged. "I guess that's true. Never mind."

I finished my chicken and pasta, then dabbed my mouth with my napkin and rose. "Well, time to earn my pay."

"We're rooting for you." Trinnie flashed her effervescent smile, and my heart skipped a beat. "Break a leg."

"Yes, break whatever you have to," Patch said. "By the way, what role do you have?"

"I'm the corpse."

The lights flashed twice, then went dark. A voice from the wings welcomed everyone to Villa Roma's Mystery Night and the production of *Murder in the Mansion*. The narrator set the scene, and the lights went up.

I was stretched out on the floor, completely still, a sheet covering my body except for my head. My eyes were shut, but I cracked one open a millimeter so I could see what was going on.

The actor playing the detective walked over to where I lay. Gestured at my body. "He's dead. Poisoned, by the looks of things. Ate some bad..." He paused and faced the diners. "Ate some bad chicken and pasta."

The audience laughed, exactly as they'd laughed the past two performances.

He turned back toward me. "Poor kid. Showed such promise. Captain of his high school football team. Valedictorian. On his way to Harvard."

A female came up to the detective, sobbing. "But who would want to kill my baby? He never harmed a soul." The actress delivered the line like a southern belle during the Civil War. She was only thirty years old or so, way younger than my real mom, but the director had some trouble getting enough actors for this gig and had to make do with what she had.

"Maybe he wasn't the intended target," the detective said.

Out of my eye slit, I noticed a waiter standing next to a table right in the front. Even from my weird angle, he seemed out of place. Too young. The rest of the waitstaff were older than forty, at least, and he was in his twenties. Plus he seemed a little too focused on the show, rather than the patrons. The waiter shifted slightly out of my line of vision. I opened my eyes a little wider, straining to get a glimpse of him. Was this my stalker?

"Oh my! Then who was?" my stage mother asked, clutching a hanky to her chest. "My poor, poor baby!"

I tried to move my head, ever so slightly, to get a better view of the suspicious server, but all I could see were his black pants and the bottom of his white shirt. My heart pounded.

The detective stroked his chin, then spun around, pointing at my distraught mother. "We must investigate this terrible crime."

I tuned out from the play as my imagination ran amok. I knew I was supposed to be dead, but my self-preservation had priority. I tilted my neck to get a better angle. Now I could see halfway up his torso.

"Have you made any enemies lately?" the detective asked.

I stretched my neck as far as I could, but it wasn't enough. I didn't have the right angle. From my vantage on the floor, I saw a lot of pants and shoes and feet under the tables—no faces. The waiter shifted again, even farther out of sight. Very slowly, I wormed my entire body to the left, one inch at a time, and rotated my head. Surely no one would be looking at the corpse on the ground, not when the detective was about to grill my mother.

"I...I can't think of anyone who would want to harm me, or my son," my stage mom said.

Now I could see the bottom of the server's chin. If I rolled onto my side and scooted to the left another few inches...

"Look," a lady said from the audience. "The dead body is moving!"

Someone else called out, "Is that part of the show?"

At first, only a couple of people realized I'd moved. Then the actors seemed to notice, and the audience began to snicker. Titters at first, but the laughter mushroomed until everyone was cracking up, big time.

The detective recovered quickly. "Uh, maybe we should call Nine-One-One. Your son may still be alive."

"Oh, that's wonderful." My faux mom rushed over and knelt beside me, mouthed, *Play Dead* to me.

Hoping the actors could somehow save the scene I'd ruined, I froze.

My stage mom put her ear to my chest. "No! No! His heart isn't beating. Now he's really dead. Oh, dear Reginald!"

Dear Reginald, indeed.

I waited in the restaurant's kitchen for the play to end. According to my parents, I had always tried extra-hard to be the center of attention, even as a toddler. At family gatherings, at the grocery store, or at the playground, I was the one "hamming it up" as my dad loved to say. So they weren't surprised when I'd somehow managed to land the lead role in the second-grade, end-of-year production. In fifth grade, I begged to go to an audition for a community theater musical—*Seussical*. Much to my parent's surprise, I got a role. Which was great for me, but I wasn't sure how much they liked driving me back and forth to rehearsals. Anyway, to say I caught the acting bug would be an understatement. That bug plowed me over like a runaway freight train.

I mean, what could be a better pursuit for a kid who craved the spotlight than one where he got to receive applause—and admiration—for doing what he loved?

In my playbill, nothing.

However, being the center of attention because I'd screwed

up wasn't my idea of fun.

When the scene ended and I got up off the floor, I managed to get a good look at the server in question. He had a bushy moustache and looked nothing like how Ms. Z had described him. I found a quiet corner and sipped a large glass of ice water to calm down while the troupe finished the show.

After the performance, the director nabbed me before I could escape. My insides clenched as I prepared to get reamed out for my unprofessionalism.

"Dalton, sometimes things just happen. Don't worry about it." Her lips twisted into a nervous smile.

My muscles relaxed. "Sorry."

She handed me twenty bucks. "Here. This is for tonight. And, uh, we've decided to go in another direction for tomorrow night's performance. It was nice working with you. Good luck." She scooted away before I could react.

Tomorrow was closing night, so I was done. Let go from a job I'd taken only as a favor to my dad. One more example of an actor's roller-coaster life. As I moped, Trinnie and Patch appeared.

"There you are." Trinnie hugged me. "Quite a performance."

"I'm pretty sure dead people don't move around," Patch said.

"It was an accident," Trinnie said, glaring at Patch as she tried to comfort me. "It could have happened to anyone."

Maybe, but it had happened to me.

Chapter Eight

Thursday was a camp off-day, so I was able to meet with the director/producer of "High School Hitman"—and the upcoming sequel—at a Starbucks in a strip mall in the City of Fairfax. His name was Ranjay Kapoor, and he was probably around thirty years old. He wore an old Pearl Jam T-shirt, ripped jeans, and a pair of mirror sunglasses wrapped around backward, as if he had eyes in the back of his head.

I could only hope to be half as cool when I turned thirty.

We'd developed a good working relationship filming the first episode. He gave me his vision and guided me through the scenes, but was very open to any suggestions I had, trying to incorporate my ideas into his direction. All the other actors loved him, too. I had no doubt he'd be directing big-budget films in another ten years. A guy could do worse than hitch his wagon to Ranjay's rising star.

"I'm so glad you were able to clear your schedule to shoot the sequel. Your agent is quite a character. And quite the negotiator." He winked at me, making me feel as if I were in on the joke.

I smiled back, as if I was. "I'm glad you're filming a sequel."

"With ratings like we got, and all the media hype surrounding the case, we'd be stupid not to. And one thing TCN isn't is stupid. Not when it comes to ratings, anyway." He took a sip of his coffee, then dug a script out of his sleek messenger bag and handed it to me. "Here. Saved you the trouble of printing it out yourself. You know the drill. Memorize your lines. You need to be totally off book before our first rehearsal." He held up two fingers. "Two days is fast turnaround. Can I count on you?"

I riffed the pages of the script. "You got it."

"I gave your friends a couple of lines, too. That's the great thing about some of these cable productions—you don't need to be in the union to get a part." Ranjay smiled. "Nice thing you did, asking that your friends be involved."

"Not too forward?"

He waved his hand. "On the contrary. This is a very tough business. You do what you can for your peeps, and Mr. Karma will pay you a visit down the road sometime. I need to follow your example and stick my neck out for friends more often."

Ranjay leaned back, took another sip. His expression turned serious. "I should warn you. I have a feeling this shoot is going to be a little different from the last one."

"Oh?"

"Way different, actually. More scrutiny. More media attention. TCN has given me a bigger budget, so we'll be able to use an extra location or two. We've got to step up our game. I've talked to the other actors, and they're all in on this."

"Count me in, too."

"Good. As for the tone of the show, you'll see when you read the script, but this one focuses more on what Varney was like *before* he killed Ogden. Sort of a 'How He Became a Monster' examination. Which means you've got a much bigger role. I've got confidence in you."

"I'll do my best."

"I know you will. I wouldn't have given you so much responsibility if I didn't think you could handle it." He set his cup down and looked me in the eye, a direct, no-blinking challenge. "You're going places, Dalton. Keep working hard and taking advantage of your opportunities, and good things will happen."

I thought about the dinner theater disaster, and attempted to shake it out of my head. "Uh, thanks. I'll try."

"Seriously, Dalton. We can't do this show without you. I wanted you to know that." He laughed. "No pressure, of course."

I laughed too, although mine came out a little shaky. I felt a *ton* of pressure. If I screwed up, I'd be taking a bunch of people down with me. Other actors. Crew. Production team. And my friends, too, now that I'd dragged Patch and Trinnie into this.

"I don't know if you saw the press release. As soon as all the principals signed on, we sent it out."

"Press release?" I asked.

"More of TCN's marketing. Sometimes all it takes is one big show to boost a network to the next level, especially a fairly obscure cable channel. TCN is really putting their muscle behind this one."

A scary thought occurred to me.

"Did the press release say where the shoot will be?" I asked, swallowing, worried that would make it easier for my stalker to find me.

Ranjay gave me a sly smile. "Nope. Because I've declared that information need-to-know only. Cast and crew. And I'm only going to tell you guys the night before shooting begins. I don't want any looky-loos, or worse. A lot of people aren't happy Varney was set free, and I've heard rumblings they're going to try to disrupt things." He cocked his head at me, and he must have seen something in my expression because he furrowed his brow and asked, pointedly, "Why do you want to know?"

Should I tell Ranjay about my stalker? I tried to run through his possible reactions in my head. Would Ranjay cancel the shoot? Would he hire extra security? Would he replace me? Would he call my parents about it? None of those outcomes were good. If the shooting location remained secret, I was probably okay.

"No reason," I lied. "Just curious where it might be."

"You'll know soon enough." He picked up his phone and glanced at it. "Well, got to get going. Just wanted to give you the script and make sure we're on the same page. The pep talk was an added bonus." He raised an eyebrow. "Did it work?"

"You bet," I said, forcing a smile. I was plenty excited about the shoot. I just hoped my stalker wouldn't get excited about it, too.

After my meeting with Ranjay, I dropped by Patch's house. His mom sent me down to their basement, which had been turned into an exercise room. A stack of weights took up one corner, a yoga mat was unfurled on the floor in another, and an assortment of miscellaneous workout equipment was strewn about—exercise balls, a bunch of colored elastic bands, and a contraption made of metal with lots of thick springs that looked like a medieval torture device.

Patch was on a balancing board balancing when I entered.

"Hey, man," he said, still rock solid on the board, hands at his sides.

"What's up?"

"Just doing a light workout. Gotta keep my dancin' legs in shape, right?" He calmly maintained his balance. I wasn't sure how he did it. Whenever I got on the balance board, there was a lot of arm flailing and knee bending and body contorting during the four seconds I could actually stay balanced.

"Well, you'd better warm up your acting muscles."

Patch frowned and the board dipped to the right. He stepped off. "What do you mean?"

"'High School Hitman II.' You got a part. A *speaking* part." I thumped the script in my hand.

Patch tensed and a look of panic spread across his face.

"Dude. Relax. It's only three lines, and one is 'Those guys are bad dudes, for sure.' I think you can handle that."

"I only agreed to be an extra."

"They give anybody with a speaking part thirty bucks, minimum."

"How about if I give you thirty bucks to give my lines to someone else?"

I rolled an exercise ball over and sat on it, bouncing gently. Looked him in the eyes.

"Repeat after me. 'Those guys are bad dudes.'"

Patch stared at me.

"Come on." I said. "Humor me."

"Those guys are bad dudes,'" he said in a singsong voice.

"For sure."

"For sure what?" He began pacing in front of me as he spoke.

"Repeat after me. 'For sure.'"

"For sure."

"Good. Now, 'Those guys are bad dudes,' and 'For sure.'"

"That is sure bad news for this dude."

"Do me a favor. Sit down, will you?" I slid off the exercise ball and sat on the floor.

Patch sighed and sat on the floor facing me. "What?"

"We're bros, right?"

"Yeah."

"So I want to know what the deal is. Why you've blown off the past five auditions you could have had. Why you don't seem interested in pursuing any speaking roles."

Patch stared at me, unblinking. His Adam's apple bobbed when he swallowed. "I don't really know what you're talking about."

"Come on, man. It's just us here. What's the problem?"

"No problem."

"Right. So why didn't you go to those auditions? Why haven't you signed up for the Christmas Cavalcade auditions?" I raised an eyebrow. "I just want to help. Trinnie and I are worried about you."

Patch's nostrils flared. "You brought Trinnie into this? Why would you do that?"

"I didn't do anything. She knows something's bugging you, too. You're lucky it's me talking to you now. Trinnie wouldn't be so...easy on you."

"Yeah, lucky."

"She's not going to let it go, my friend. You've got a choice here. You can tell me what the problem is. Or you can tell her. It's your life."

He looked down at the floor, picked at some nonexistent lint on the carpet. "Look, I'm a dancer. I like dancing. I like doing voices, impressions. Goofing around. I'm not good at memorizing lines and playing it straight."

"You could be if you wanted to."

He looked at me. "Yeah, well, maybe I don't want to. It's no big thing, at least not to me. I'll let you know if I need any help with anything, okay?"

Upstairs, the doorbell rang. Then footsteps and the front door opened. Patch's Mom talking to someone. Tough to make out, but judging by the trill in Mrs. Guitteriez's voice, it was Trinnie. She had that effect on people. Besides, I'd asked her to meet us here.

"This conversation isn't over," I said.

"Yeah, it is," Patch replied.

Footfalls on the stairs, then Trinnie appeared. She stopped on the bottom step, stared at us staring at her.

"Why do I get the feeling I'm interrupting something?" she said.

"You're most definitely not," Patch said, a little too loudly. "What are you doing here?"

"Dalton told me to come over. Said he had some big news." She put her hands on her hips. "Well?"

I retrieved the script from where I'd set it down and raised it over my head, as if I was holding a trophy. "You got a part in the sequel."

Trinnie squealed, rushed over, and grabbed the script from my hands. "What page? What page?"

"Around page forty, I think."

"Do I have any lines?"

"Four," I said.

"Four?" Patch worked up a pouty face to rival a supermodel's. "How come I only got three?"

"I thought you didn't want any."

"I...I don't." He stammered and shrugged, bringing a smile to my face. "But it's the principle of the thing."

"Oooo, am I 'Attractive Friend of Varney?'" Trinnie asked, beaming.

"Yes." Trinnie certainly typecast as "Attractive Friend." I felt a pang of jealousy. Thousands of viewers would see how attractive Trinnie really is. What if one of those fans met her and swept her off her feet? My fantasy mushroomed. What if some director somewhere discovered Attractive Trinnie, offered her a part in a movie, and she made it big? Would I be happy for her? Or envious?

I played my wishful thinking out in my head for the thousandth time. If I pursued things with Trinnie, trying to turn our best-friend status into something more, what would happen if I screwed things up? Would our friendship disintegrate? Would things then be awkward between us *forever*? I'm not sure I could live with that.

I took a deep breath and banished those thoughts.

"Then here it is." Trinnie stabbed her finger at a page in the script. "'You should steer clear of those losers.'" Then she closed her eyes and repeated it.

"Brava!" I clapped. "And with such feeling."

She moved on to her next line. "'You're better than that, Homer. Don't let those guys get to you.'"

This time, both Patch and I clapped, while Trinnie bowed. She raised her head, then spoke to Patch. "What are your lines?"

He shrugged. "Something about bad dudes. Or bad news. Which I think will be my review."

"I think we need to celebrate," Trinnie said, ignoring Patch.

"I think what we *need* to do is learn our lines." I had a lot to memorize in two days. Nothing looked worse than an actor who was supposed to be off book walking around with a script in his hand.

"I already know my lines. Anyone can learn a handful of

lines in two days. You have to eat anyway, so why don't we go out for dinner?" She nodded at me. "Then you can go home and learn your lines while Patch and I hang out."

"I'm in," Patch said.

"Okay. But dinner only. I've got a lot of work to do."

We hit the mall's food court. Patch wanted Chinese, I wanted Mexican, and Trinnie wanted a salad. So naturally, we all ended up at the pizza place. Wasn't the entire purpose of the food court to allow each person to get whatever they wanted? I guessed the stomach craved what the stomach craved, and the call of pepperoni too great.

We decided to split a large—double meat—so we took our pizza and found an isolated corner, far away from a family with two screaming toddlers.

"I'm so excited." Trinnie's eyes gleamed, as Patch started on his second slice. "This is my first big break, you know. You're a pro, Dalton, but for me..." She fluttered her eyelids and fanned her face with her hand. "This is my cinematic debut." She troweled on a southern accent.

"Just don't blow it with one of your terrible accents." Patch talked around the wad of pizza in his mouth.

"Terrible?"

"Okay. Not terrible. Just bad."

"I was being artistic. And ironic. I can't help it if I'm so excited about—"

I held up my hand. "Guys. Enough. Being in a show is really cool. Or it would be, if I didn't have so many lines to learn."

"Oh, poor Dalton has too many lines as the star of a TV show." Trinnie scoffed.

My face flushed. "I didn't mean it like that. You'll do great." I noticed Patch's face flush. "*Both* of you will do great."

Patch reached for another piece of pizza, and I checked out the food court. Other high-school-aged kids I didn't recognize, a few couples, two old guys arguing about something. Another family with a baby in a stroller. A creepy guy in a Yankees baseball cap and sunglasses staring at us. A mom and three—

Wait, what? I turned back to the creepy guy in the cap.

He wore dark, dark glasses and his cap was pulled low on his forehead. Couldn't really see his face. Beneath the table, I got a glimpse of jeans and sneakers. He sat at a table for two, facing us, calmly eating a sub.

Could it be him?

I didn't want to stare, so I put my head on a slow swivel, turning back and forth, pretending to scan the entire area, just another guy people-watching. But I kept my peripheral vision glued to the guy in the Yankees cap.

"Dalton?" Trinnie nudged me.

"Hm?" I spun around. "What?"

"You okay?" Patch seemed concerned. Concerned enough to stop eating, which was saying something. "You spaced out there."

"Oh. Sorry." I thought back to what Ms. Z said about the stalker, and..."I was trying to recall some of my lines."

"You're hardcore," Patch said. "I guess that's why you're the star and we're the extras."

Patch's response didn't register. "Uh, yeah. Okay." I'd turned back toward the creep, but he was gone. Vanished like he hadn't even been there. A wave of panic rippled through me. I whipped my head around in case he'd circled behind us. Nobody there. I jumped to my feet, glancing in every direction, eyes wide, focusing on every human in the area for a split-second, trying to spot...what? A looming attack, maybe? What did he want from me?

"What the hell is going on?" Trinnie grabbed me. "Calm down."

My father always said my emotions were one of the qualities that made me a good actor. Heightened as they were now though, I wished I could just shut them off. I sucked in a deep breath, and then another. While I settled down, Trinnie held on tight.

"You're okay, Dalton. Sit down." Gently, she eased me back down into my chair.

"You look like you've seen a ghost," Patch said.

"Worse." I swallowed. "I think I just saw my stalker. A guy in jeans wearing a blue Yankees cap and sunglasses."

Patch and Trinnie popped out of their seats and scanned the food court, for anyone matching his description.

"He's gone now. I think he—"

"Stay here," Patch said. "Both of you."

Before I could tell him to sit down, Patch took off and circled the entire food court, searching for the guy. While he did, Trinnie patted my back. I felt like a three-year-old who'd been frightened by a big dog.

But I didn't tell her to stop, either. Sometimes I thought Trinnie's habit of always touching people was annoying. Now, though, I was thankful she was a hugger. A guy—me, specifically—could get used to it.

When Patch returned, he slid into his seat. "Gone. I did spot a guy wearing a Yankees cap, but he was about fifty years old. Nobody else."

"I didn't imagine it." At least I was pretty sure I hadn't.

"I'm sure you didn't," Trinnie said. "But it was probably some random dude. I mean, how would your stalker know you were here?"

I shook my head. "No idea."

"This is getting out of hand. You've got to get a hold of yourself," she said. "There's no reason someone would want to come after you."

Next to her, Patch nodded.

I nodded, too. What Trinnie said made complete sense. But, then why did I have the feeling I was being stalked by a madman?

We decided to get the hell out of the mall, and Patch scooped up the last piece of pizza as we left. But as we neared the exit, we saw someone worse than a mad stalker heading our way.

Gavin Grady.

Chapter Nine

Drama kids were a special breed. Extroverted, creative, attention-starved. I think I can safely speak for all of us and say that while we stood out, we liked it that way.

Unfortunately, a lot of kids *didn't* like us that way.

Sometimes we got shunned. Sometimes we got harassed. The self-described cool kids bullied us from time-to-time, shouting crap at us from their safe little cliques, mostly when they got bored of standing around trying to look cool. Showing off for their friends, I guessed.

While not exactly pleasant, I could live with all the harassment. I didn't really mind the cracks about being a drama *geek*. Hell, I knew firsthand how great most drama kids were.

But I did get pissed when guys like Gavin Grady started harassing me and Patch and Trinnie about being members of Club Diversity. Truth was, we *did* have many "diverse" boxes checked. I was White and Male and Jewish. Patch was Hispanic and Male and Catholic. Trinnie was African-American and Female and some kind of Christian denomination I could never remember. Of course, we didn't set out to be friends simply so we could please the Census Bureau. Just happened that way.

And really, so fucking what?

Gavin Grady was everything we weren't. A jock. Popular. Tall. Muscular. Egotistical. And most telling, a mega-dick. I'd known him since he started picking on me in fourth grade. He hadn't stopped since. I had to give him props for perseverance, if for nothing else.

"Well, if it isn't the United Nations of Drama Nerds." He bowed and swept his arms in a grand gesture, mugging for his three-member crew standing behind him. "We come in peace. Please don't monologue us to death."

We didn't say a word.

He turned to his gang. "See, I knew he'd be here. He's so famous, he tweets where he's going, so his fans can fawn over him."

I'd tweeted, *hitting the mall*, before we'd left. Not to attract any so-called fans, but if any friends happened to be there, we could meet up. I was a little surprised Grady was a follower.

"We were just leaving," Trinnie said. "Have fun in the kiddie's play area. I hear there's a ball pit you can jump around in."

Grady planted his feet and smirked at me. "Mr. TV Star, is this the best you can do for an entourage?" He turned to Trinnie. "And a question for you. How can someone like you hang with guys like...them?"

Grady's buddies snickered in the background.

Trinnie kept her mouth shut, lips pressed together. But it only lasted a second. Which was a second longer than she usually kept quiet when facing down someone like Grady. I sort of pitied him. "I've got a question for you," she said. "Which one of your semi-literate friends writes your lines? 'Cause they need some work."

"Seriously, you could do so much better than these two."

Trinnie was ready to drop another bomb on Grady when one of his goons snatched Patch's hat right off his head.

"Hey," Patch said, but he didn't go after the guy with his hat, just stood there, arms at his side.

Grady's pals started tossing it around Frisbee-style as we watched. I noticed Patch tense, but knew if he tried to make a move to intercept his hat, things would only get worse.

"We've got stuff to do. So...see you later." I held my hands out, palms up.

"What, too good for us regular people? Afraid one of your fans might see you talking to someone like me?"

"Yeah, right. We're out of here." I started to move around him, but he stepped into my path. "Come on, man."

Grady eyed me, probably wondering if he should keep at it, or give up and go look for some other people to hassle.

He glared for a few more seconds. "Okay, guys. Let's go. We've got better things to do than waste our time with these losers."

One of Grady's friends tossed Patch's hat back to him, and then they turned tail and left.

When they were out of earshot, Trinnie said, "Assholes!"

Patch and I nodded. They were assholes, but we'd gotten used to how they treated us. Not that we liked it, but we'd gotten good at moving on.

"Forget them," Trinnie said. "*They're* not going to be on TV, are they?"

In the TV business, imitation certainly is the sincerest form of flattery, especially when ratings are concerned. And given the popularity of the TV show *Cops*, it wasn't a surprise that the number of crime reenactment shows over the past few years had exploded. Now, *entire* cable networks offered them, and you could binge-watch people committing every type of terrible crime imaginable, all day, every day.

Typically, these shows sported low budgets and catchy names, like *Deadly Divas*, *Maniacal Motel Murderers*, and *Terror at the Rest Stop*. And although I was biased, I thought "High School Hitman" was pretty damn clever. They didn't pay the actors much, and the producers relied heavily on voiceovers so they didn't need to invest in a lot of retakes and fancy sound recording equipment. And every show cast no-name actors who were looking to get some exposure in the hope of catching a bigger break.

I didn't know what the fascination was for the viewing public to see all these crimes reenacted. Maybe in some weird way it helped people make sense out of some truly horrific deeds. *Whatever.* Crime reenactment shows needed actors, and the more shows, the more available roles. Put me down for being in the I-Love-Them group.

Low pay? Rushed production? Cheesy sets? Count me in!

I had a great time doing "High School Hitman," and I was looking for more of the same with the sequel.

Ranjay had emailed us the shoot details last night, as promised, but the instructions weren't very detailed. *Time, location, come dressed like you dress every day.*

Although, technically, it was against the law—teen-driver restrictions—to have more than one passenger in my car, I picked Trinnie and Patch up for the drive to the shoot. Every kid I knew ignored the law, and since I never heard of anyone *ever* getting a ticket for it, I assumed most of the cops ignored it, too. Just to be safe, anytime we spotted a police car, whoever was in the back seat ducked until the coast was clear.

Tonight, we arrived at the Windom Heights Academy—a private school—at about seven forty-five, giving us enough time to find a parking spot and catch our breath before our eight o'clock call time.

For many TV gigs, the makeup process took a while, an hour or more, depending on what was required. Foundation, blush, eyeliner, whatever. For these crime reenactment shows, however, makeup rarely lasted more than ten minutes. Barely enough time for someone to make sure your hair was combed.

Two folding chairs were set up facing the mirrors in one of the faculty bathrooms. Patch and Trinnie went first, while I leaned against the wall in the hall outside, trying to get centered.

I'd spent all last night in my room, memorizing lines. I did it on my own at first, then asked my dad to run lines with me. After camp this afternoon, I had gone back over the shaky spots until I felt comfortable with my role. I was as off-book as I was going to get. Of course, that didn't mean everything would come out perfectly, but that's what multiple takes were for. The beauty of working on film.

The plan was to shoot some indoor scenes here, tonight, then continue tomorrow for a handful of outdoor daylight scenes. Again, because of the limited budget—even with the increase—Ranjay had to be creative when it came to shooting locales.

Trinnie and Patch emerged from the makeup restroom together, five minutes after they went in. To my eye, they looked the same.

"I feel pretty." Trinnie fluffed her hair.

"Oh, so pretty," Patch sang in a falsetto as he fluffed his hair too. "Pretty and witty and bright."

Drama kids never passed up an opportunity to break out a show tune. "My turn to get pretty," I said.

"Good luck with that," Trinnie said.

I blew her a kiss and went into the bathroom to get prettier.

Ranjay gathered everyone in the school's cafeteria before the actual shooting began. He stood on a chair and addressed the crowd, which included the actors, the crew, and a couple of extra-large security guards hired by TCN. The guards helped put me at ease. Unlikely my stalker would make an appearance with those guys around. "Welcome, everybody. I'm thrilled we have the opportunity to continue our story on Homer Lee Varney. I also want to thank everybody for juggling their schedules to make this happen. This was a terrible crime that affected a lot of people, and I think it's important for us to present the facts as we know them. An uneducated public is a susceptible public."

A few people cheered.

"A couple of introductions. Many of you remember our technical consultant, Bronson Kennedy, from the first shoot. He was the supervising detective during the investigation of Will Ogden's death. We're lucky enough to have him back to make sure we don't commit any errors regarding the crime stuff."

There was some polite applause as a bald guy with a Van Dyke beard raised his hand and half-saluted. He was tall and broad, and a diamond stud twinkled in one ear. If I had to guess his profession by the way he carried himself, I would have guessed musician—he had that street-cool vibe. But cop would have been my second choice. "Hey everyone. If you have any questions, let me know, okay? Our goal is to make sure we get all the details correct. And please, I don't want to hear any *Detective* Kennedy. Just plain *Kennedy* is fine."

"Thanks, Kennedy." Ranjay stepped forward again, gesturing to a woman beside him. "And this is our new assistant director, Emily Petrucci."

More polite applause.

"She'll be my right-hand woman, so if she says something, it goes, same as if it came right out of my mouth."

Emily nodded and offered a tentative smile.

Ranjay continued. "On an operational note. TCN wants to rush this to air and they've given us a super-tight schedule, both for shooting and editing. So I'd absolutely love it if we could focus, focus, focus! Hit your marks, deliver your lines, then pick up and move on to the next scene. Wouldn't it be great if we could top the last episode?"

A few more people cheered.

Ranjay started to get down from his perch, then straightened. "One more thing. If protestors somehow get wind of our location and show up, I hope we can try very hard to ignore them. We're all professionals here, and I'd like to think we wouldn't let any distractions derail us. They don't want us to give more attention to a murderer, and I can see their point. But I feel it's our duty to report on important stories, those affecting the members of our communities. Our families and friends. That's what free speech is all about!"

Now everyone in the cafeteria applauded. Next to me, Trinnie and Patch were clapping loudest of all.

After Ranjay's rallying cry, he called for those scheduled in the first scene, which included me, but not Trinnie or Patch. Emily herded off all the other actors to prepare for the next scene.

I followed Ranjay as he led us through the school hallways. Charcoal portraits lined one entire wall; the students attending this school seemed to be a lot more artistic than those at mine. Inspirational messages were posted on another wall. Yet another wall was painted with a neon-colored mural. A cheerful place. Seemed a little weird we were going to shoot a show about a murderer here.

Our procession stopped at the gym. Two guys with shoulder-mounted cameras chatted with each other near a section of roll-out bleachers. In this scene, I was supposed to be bullying another kid, trying to get him to buy me some weed from the local dealer.

"Okay, everyone. Come over here, and I'll go over the blocking. Real simple on this one." Ranjay stepped over to the bleachers and gestured me over. "Okay, Varney, I want you to stand here, maybe put one foot up on the seat. Les, you come over here and sit down."

A skinny kid who I'd never met—Les, in the script—took a seat on the bleacher next to my foot.

"Okay. Dalton, you don't like this kid, but you need him to do you a solid. So you want to be half intimidating, half coercing, half friendly." Ranjay laughed. "Yeah, I know that's three halves. You get the idea. Any questions?"

Les and I shook our heads.

"Great. Let's run through it once, okay?" He stepped back and the two camera guys moved in. I tried to ignore them as I got ready to deliver my lines. One of the hardest things about film work was not looking at the cameras. You had to know where they were so you didn't turn your back—or your face—to them, but you couldn't look directly at them. Even a furtive glance would be caught on tape.

"And action!"

I spit out my first line, and Les answered, and we managed to wrap up the scene with only a couple of retakes. Ranjay and the rest of the crew seemed pleased.

So far, so good.

After we finished our scene in the gym, we traipsed through the school again, following Ranjay, pied piper-style, until we reached a classroom at the back of the school. About twenty kids were already there, seated, ready for our next scene, while Emily perched on the edge of the teacher's desk. Trinnie and Patch sat next to each other in the back row, and when they saw me, Trinnie smiled and Patch frowned. Typical.

Because of logistics, scenes were usually not shot in the order in which they appeared in the final cut of a show or movie, so even though this classroom scene occurred relatively late in the episode, we were shooting it now.

Ranjay consulted his clipboard, then pointed to an open seat right in front of Trinnie. "Dalton, you sit there. Les, you sit up front."

I took my seat, and Ranjay addressed the class. "Okay, everybody. This is before the teacher arrives, and there's a conversation between Varney and his two friends. Murmur to your neighbor or look at your phones or do whatever you'd normally do while you're waiting for your history teacher to show up. Of course, make sure your phones are really off. We don't want any extraneous noise." He pointed to the windows and the gathering darkness beyond. "This scene takes place during the day, so let's try not to get the windows in the shots. If we do, keep rolling. We can take care of it in post-production, but let's not make this any harder than we have to, okay? Any questions?"

No one raised their hands, so Ranjay clapped his. "Okay, then. Places, everyone." He stepped out of the way and the two camera guys got themselves situated. One behind Trinnie and Patch, at an angle, and the other over one of my shoulders, with a view of them.

Emily slated the scene, then backed out of the way.

"And action!"

I sneered. "Who do those guys think I am, anyway? Some lightweight they can just push around?"

"You should steer clear of those losers," Trinnie said, a little too fast. I could tell she was excited. "You're better than that, Homer. Don't let those guys get to you."

"Those guys are, um, bad dudes, for real," Patch said, not quite nailing it.

You always kept going until the director yelled cut. "I'm going to kick their asses. They'll be sorry they ever met me." I squinted like I meant business.

Patch swallowed, then said, "Homer, listen to yourself, Homer. You really need to listen to yourself, Homer."

"Cut." Ranjay flashed us a tight smile as he stepped in. "Got an extra Homer or two in there. Take a minute to go over your lines, please. No room for ad-libbing in this scene."

Patch's pupils jiggled when he was nervous. Right now, they were doing the two-step.

"Sorry."

"Just relax, you'll be fine," Ranjay said. Then he consulted his clipboard, flipping a few pages to give us a moment to collect ourselves.

Patch closed his eyes and recited his lines to himself, lips moving as he did.

Trinnie simply shook her head.

I leaned toward them and whispered. "Not bad, guys. Just take a deep breath and say the line. Nice and slow. Don't worry about having the right expression on your face or anything, okay? You both look fine." I smiled at Patch. "Remember, you only say my name once."

He nodded. "Got it."

Ranjay cleared his throat. "Everybody ready? Good. Take two." He pointed at the camera guys, then he pointed at me. "And...action."

We ran through another take, and then another. Each time, Patch couldn't quite pull off his lines without stumbling.

"Getting better, but...," Ranjay sighed. "Let's try one more time, okay? Everybody ready? And ...action."

I worked up my sneer again, then opened my mouth to speak. Before I could say a word, a loud yell from outside interrupted things.

"Cut!" Ranjay said. "What's going on?"

A voice from outside screamed, "They're in here. Over here, over here!"

We all turned toward the windows. Outside, a woman carrying a sign was screaming her head off and jumping up and down. "Over here! Over here!"

"Oh shit." Ranjay whipped out his phone and texted somebody. Then he said, "Just relax everyone. Don't be afraid. Only a few protestors. Please stay where you are while we get this straightened out. And whatever you do, don't engage with them! Emily, try to keep things together here." He rushed out, but not before telling the camera guys to make sure they caught whatever happened on tape.

"What's going on?" Patch asked. "Who's protesting what?"

"They don't want any more attention given to Varney. They want him behind bars."

"So do I," Trinnie said.

"Me too, but that's beside the point. We have a right to shoot whatever show we want, as long as we obey the laws when we do it."

"Just as they have the right to protest," Patch said.

"True. As long as they obey the law, too." I kept my gaze out the windows at the angry protestors, and I flashed back to a riot I saw on the news a few weeks ago where a protest went sideways and people got hurt.

Obviously, someone had leaked the shoot's location, and I bet Ranjay was super pissed.

More protestors had gathered at the windows. It was dark outside, so we could barely make out their faces from the light escaping the classroom. They held signs and shouted random things—obscenities and threats and trite sayings. Every so often someone would try to start some kind of chant. A few others would join in for a round or two, but it would peter out quickly. This group of protestors wasn't as cohesive as the ones I'd seen on TV. I wasn't an expert demonstrator, but I think they needed something catchier. Maybe something that rhymed, like *Keep Varney Locked Away, In Prison He Should Stay.*

One guy with a full beard started banging on the window with the end of the wooden stick holding his sign. "Stop trying to make a buck off of a murderer. He should be in jail, not roaming the streets," he yelled. "You should be ashamed of yourselves. Do your parents know what you're doing?"

"We've got nothing to do with Varney being on the street," Trinnie said to us. "He's scary."

"I don't think logic matters to that guy." Patch shook his head. "He's going ballistic."

Patch had a point. Now the deranged guy had picked up a rock and was tapping it against the glass. Taunting us. With a little more force, he could shatter the window, and he wanted all of us to know it.

Behind the guy with the rock, I caught a glimpse of a guy in his twenties. Wearing a hoodie. Was it? Could it be my stalker? My heartbeat sped up. This was getting ugly quickly.

Some of the kids sitting in the seats closest to the windows got up and moved to the other side of the classroom. Most of the kids had their phones out, taking video or snapping pictures, but we didn't do anything, just watched, heeding Ranjay's words not to get involved.

Emily had moved closer to the window, and it looked to me like she was thinking about talking to the protestors. Bad idea.

Even though we were sitting there peacefully, the protestors seemed to be getting more riled up. I estimated there were twenty-five or thirty outside our window, but for all I knew, there might have been a hundred outside the school's main entrance and another fifty picketing the cafeteria.

Another guy began banging on the window with a brick. Instinctively, I checked our possible routes of escape, and there was only one feasible way out—through the classroom door.

One of the kids jumped out of her seat. "They're going to get in!"

"Try to remain calm, everybody," Emily said, but the students weren't really listening to her, too focused on the action outside.

Another kid got up. And another. Pretty soon, everyone was scrambling for the door.

The glass window shattered, and the shouts got louder. A whole lot louder. What had been an orderly evacuation became a mini-stampede. Protesters started climbing in through the broken window.

I grabbed Trinnie and Patch by the sleeves of their shirts. "Come on!"

Chapter Ten

We all streamed out of the room as the amped-up protestors poured in through the windows. I'm not sure exactly what they thought they were going to accomplish except disrupt our shooting. Of course, maybe that was the point.

We burst into the hall, riding on a sea of people, only to find ourselves in the midst of more bedlam. Both of the security guards were holding protestors in their burly arms, but other demonstrators were running through the halls shouting at everyone who wasn't carrying a sign.

I kept my eyes peeled for the guy in the hoodie, but the scene was too crazy, and I didn't spot him again. Which was worse, because I just knew he was still there. Somewhere.

Off to one side, I noticed Emily standing there in the middle of the fray, frown on her face, hands on her hips. One of the protestors approached her, and she ripped into him, screaming until he backed away.

I grabbed Trinnie's hand, and she grabbed Patch's hand, and the three of us snaked toward the cafeteria, hugging the wall the whole way. We'd almost made it when the deranged guy with the beard stepped in front of us, blocking our path. Our little train pulled to a stop.

"You!" He pointed his fat forefinger directly at my nose. "You! You're the one playing Varney, aren't you? You should be ashamed of yourself!"

I was pretty sure he didn't want my autograph. "Look, man, we're just actors, trying to do our jobs. We don't think Varney should be out of jail, either. But what am I supposed to do about it?" I shrugged, trying to hammer home the point that I was as powerless as he was.

"Don't underestimate the position you're in. Lots of people watched that episode, especially around here. It's your duty to use your fame to speak out against what's happening, to demand our officials put him back into prison." He stepped closer and grabbed my shirt. His breath could have melted plastic. He pulled me closer. "Are you listening to me?" The way he lowered his voice, it was scarier than if he'd yelled at me.

Just then, a couple of protestors came flying down the hall and one of them knocked into the guy holding me. He lost his grip, and I grabbed Trinnie's hand again. "Come on, let's move."

We bolted, racing down the hallway, dodging a wandering protestor here and there. As we neared the front of the school and the cafeteria, we heard sirens, getting louder.

Reinforcements.

Ranjay stood right outside the cafeteria, directing traffic and yelling instructions to his cast and crew. When he saw us, he came running over. "You guys all okay?"

"Yeah." We all nodded as we caught our breath.

"Good. If it's not obvious, tonight's shoot is postponed. Trinnie, Patch, we'll figure out something with your scene later. Dalton, we'll try again tomorrow at a different place. I'll email details in the morning. For now, get home safely." He bent over and picked up a discarded protest sign reading, *Varney Belongs In Prison.* "Here, carry this and pretend you're one of them. They won't bother you." He thrust the sign into Patch's hand. "Feel free to chant something, too. How about *Kapoor is Evil*?"

Patch clutched the sign, and we started off, but Ranjay called us back. "Hey, one more thing." A worried expression crossed his face. "Someone said they saw a guy who looked a lot like Varney skulking around. I can't confirm it, but if it's true..."

Someone called Ranjay's name and he drifted away.

My feet felt like they were encased in cement—I couldn't move. The air whooshed from my lungs as I struggled to put things together in my head. Could Varney be my stalker?

Ridiculous.

But...

Why would a stone-cold killer be after me? To thank me for my on-point depiction?

I replayed the "High School Hitman" performance in my head, at four times fast-forward speed. Had I done anything that would have pissed him off? Did I play him being a jerk? I tried to be true to the facts. I'd done my research. I thought I gave an excellent nuanced performance, taking into account his various quirks and—

Shit. Who was I kidding? I portrayed Homer Lee Varney as a deranged psycho killing machine. Then Ranjay had wanted me to ramp things up, playing it even *more* over-the-top, and I'd done so eagerly.

In real life, Varney had killed Ogden in response to the smallest of perceived slights. Something that would never drive a reasonable, rational person to violence. But Varney had taken revenge to a whole new level. Like using a nuclear bomb to punish a shoplifter, he'd butchered Ogden for practically no reason at all.

And if Varney was looking for me...if he found me...

Pain shot through my arm. I looked down and saw Trinnie's fingernails digging into my skin. "Varney's here?" she said, voice trembling.

With my other hand, I gently removed her hand from my arm. "Okay, guys. Let's not panic. The Varney sighting is probably some rumor the protestors are spreading. Or something. Let's get out of here, as quickly as possible." I paused for effect. "Without attracting attention to ourselves." I didn't voice my belief that Varney could be my stalker. No sense agitating Trinnie and Patch any more than they already were.

With Patch taking point, sign bobbing as he walked, we hustled toward the exit and out of the school building.

And if we thought things were crazy inside, we didn't know the half of crazy.

Outside, it was like the Fourth of July on the National Mall, sans fireworks.

People everywhere, shouting and running around.

We held onto each other as we weaved through the crowd like some kind of three-headed beast looking to escape the zoo.

Four or five patrol cars had pulled into the parking lot at weird angles, their light bars creating colorful patterns on the school's outside walls and casting weird shadows on the throngs of people milling around. Something about a disturbance brought people out, like staring at a car crash instead of driving right on by.

Some people clustered together, talking, while others rushed this way or that. It seemed most of the protestors had congregated at one end of the lot. Lined up. Chanting. In unison. *Homer Lee Varney, Throw Away the Key-Key. Homer Lee Varney, Throw Away the Key-Key.*

Four police officers stood in front of them, watching. Hands on their holsters, maybe, but at the moment, all they were doing was observing. Making sure nothing happened here like what had happened inside.

A NewsChannelSix van screeched to a stop nearby, and a man and a woman jumped out. They grabbed some gear and jogged over to where the protestors had amassed, coming elbow-to-elbow with the cops. One of the camera guys turned on a very bright light and aimed it at the line of demonstrators.

Of course, with the cameras on, they chanted that much louder.

We'd halted in our tracks, taking in the whole spectacle. But nothing good would come of us hanging around. "We need to keep moving." I was on high alert, watching out for my stalker, watching out for Varney. Hell, I was watching out for anyone who looked like they might have it in for me. I wiped some sweat off my forehead as we pushed on.

We headed for the car, then the three of us stopped short, as if we were being controlled by a single brain. A guy with a hoodie was leaning against the side of an SUV, a few parking spots away from my car.

He seemed to be staring right at us.

A chill rippled through my body, right down my spine into my legs.

Was it the same guy from the food court? From school? More importantly, was it Varney?

"Is that him?" Trinnie said. "Varney?"

The guy wasn't very old, in his twenties, *possibly*, and he might have looked a little like the pictures on the news, *maybe*. In the darkness and at this distance, it was virtually impossible to make a positive ID. "I have no idea, but I don't really want to find out. If we run, he'll be sure to spot us. Just follow me. Slow and steady. And Patch, keep waving that sign."

I willed my racing heartbeat to calm, but that was like asking a squirrel to stop twitching.

We veered left, toward the line of protestors. I took the lead, and as much as I wanted to race away, to put as much real estate between Varney and us as we could, as fast as we could, I knew that was a bad idea. So I forced myself to walk slowly and concentrated on putting one foot in front of the other. A terrible thought entered my mind—what would it feel like to get shot in the back?

Trinnie held my hand in a deathgrip. I waited until we'd gone twenty feet before risking a glance over my shoulder. The guy in the hoodie had disappeared. I stopped abruptly, causing Patch and Trinnie to stop short, too. "Shit. He's not there anymore."

"Where'd he go?" Trinnie scanned the parking lot.

"There he is!" Patch pointed to our left. Hoodie Guy was strolling along the edge of the parking lot, on the grass border, and he seemed to be coming in our direction, but whether he was actually following us was hard to tell.

I wasn't going to take any chances.

"This way." I dodged us around a group of onlookers, circled wide to the right of the reporters and the cops, and wound up behind the group of demonstrators. "Blend in," I whispered.

We raised our fists. We shouted stuff. We chanted along with the crowd.

All the while, I kept my eyes peeled for any sign of him.

The TV crew stuck around for another fifteen minutes, but as soon as they left, the protest fell apart. Without an audience, what was the point?

A fair number of people still wandered around the school grounds. Patch tossed his sign into a dumpster, and we headed for the car, still ultra-wary. Now would be the perfect time for Varney to attack.

My car came into view. No Varney. Relief.

I turned my gaze to the left, and he materialized, out of thin air, like a ghost from a Dickens story. The guy in the hoodie was leaning against a tree, shielded from the closest parking lot light.

My heart raced as I tried to think what to do. "Stop."

Both Trinnie and Patch tensed up next to me. "What?" Trinnie whispered.

"Under that tree. At ten o'clock."

"Crap," Patch said.

"This way." I did an about-face and led us out through a gap in a hedge at the far end of the parking lot, behind where the protestors had been lined up. We didn't want to call attention to ourselves, so we didn't put it into top gear—but we sure walked fast. When we'd gone two blocks, I turned around, afraid I'd see him in pursuit, but the coast was clear. I finally took a relaxed breath. "We're safe. For now, anyway."

"But your car is back there. And we're about five miles from home." Trinnie wasn't quite right. We were more like ten miles away. "No way am I walking."

"He's not going to stick around forever. We'll just wait him out."

"Good times," Patch said. "Good times."

We wandered around for a while until we found a nearby 7-Eleven, then hung out by the magazine rack, under the very watchful eye of the store clerk, for about half an hour, until he shooed us out. A few blocks away, we found a shopping center and settled on a bench to wait. We were too depressed to talk.

Finally, after about forty-five minutes, I'd had enough. "Okay. He's got to be gone by now."

Neither Trinnie nor Patch argued with me; I knew both were bored silly waiting around. We walked back toward where I'd parked the car, stopping just as it came into view in the school's lot.

"Let's scope things out for a bit to make sure he's not lurking around," I said, ignoring Trinnie's sigh. We waited another ten minutes, just to make me feel a little better.

"Okay. He's gone. Let's make a run for it." The three of us dashed across the street, through the parking lot, and practically dove into the car.

No one sprang out of the shadows.

It wasn't until we were on the road that anyone exhaled.

I dropped Trinnie and Patch off at their homes, then glanced at the clock. A sinking thought hit me: If I went straight home now, so early, my parents would know something bad had happened. At the very least, they'd pepper me with questions I certainly didn't want to answer. So I did the only logical thing—I pulled over and waited in my car for another two hours, alternately killing time by playing on my phone and trying to come up with a reason why Varney *wasn't* my stalker, and failing.

When I arrived home, four minutes before my midnight curfew, I'd barely closed the door before Mom—and Dad, too, a bad sign—met me in the foyer. As usual, Mom spoke first. "Where have you been?"

"At the shoot."

"Don't play coy with me. I know what happened."

I adopted my best innocent expression. "What happened?"

Mom pointed to Dad. "We saw your friend Miguel. On TV. At the riot. He was holding a sign, in fact."

Riot? "On TV?"

"That's enough, Sport." Dad stepped forward. "Let's go into the kitchen and you can explain what happened. I hope no one got hurt."

Mom's face burned crimson, but she just said, "I'll put some tea on."

Five minutes later, we were seated around the kitchen table, Mom with her mug of tea, Dad with a bottle of Snapple, and me with a tall glass of the *oh-shits*.

"So, what exactly happened tonight?" Mom had calmed down to a level of merely being royally pissed. "And don't even bother trying to step around the truth. We saw the report on the news."

I took a deep breath. "There was a little commotion at the shoot."

"A little commotion. That was a riot!"

"Mom, it wasn't a riot. Just a bunch of protestors. They were angry about Varney being released."

"If I had any inkling of this, you never would have been permitted to be in this show." Mom was heating up again. Dad placed a hand on her arm.

"I didn't know either. But they're not mad at *us*. Not really. I think we just happened to be an easy target. A convenient way for them to get exposure for their cause."

"Their cause? Seems to me you and your friends jumped right in. I'm sure they didn't have a permit. You could have been arrested. My son, the inmate." Mom's lawyerly concerns had kicked in.

"Come on, no one's going to jail," Dad said. I couldn't tell whose side he was on, but if I knew my father, he'd try to play the role of peacemaker and seem like he was on both our sides.

"Was anyone hurt?"

"I don't think so."

"Was anyone arrested, that you saw?"

"No. The police were mostly standing around, preventing things from getting out of hand."

"So maybe this was an example of democracy in action." My dad sipped from his bottle of Snapple.

Mom swiveled her head and *snappled* at Dad. "Democracy? It seemed more like anarchy. Next time, someone could get injured. Or worse."

Now I flashed back to Varney lurking in the shadows, waiting for us. The feeling of dread I had experienced earlier threatened to resurface, so I exhaled very slowly, tried to get centered.

Dad set his bottle down. "Now—"

Mom turned her entire shoulder to me and faced Dad. "Surely you can't believe David should continue with this nonsense, can you? Especially in light of what happened tonight."

My dad tried again. "Well..."

"Richard, David was involved in a riot. He could have been killed. He's portraying a murderer. Is that something we should allow?"

"You can't be serious." I stood. "I can't quit. People are depending on me. You know, I'm only acting. I'm not really a murderer! For Christ sakes, I just play one on TV!"

"Please sit down, David," Mom said.

I remained standing. "Please call me Dalton."

We stared at each other for what seemed like an hour.

"I have half a mind to forbid you from being in that show," Mom said, finally.

Half a mind is right. "Forbid me? I signed a contract. You're a lawyer. You want me to break the law?" My breathing revved up. "This is what I do. This is what makes me happy. And you want to stop me from doing it? Because you're uncomfortable with a few protestors? You can't make me quit."

"You're a minor. I *can* make you quit."

Dad rose. “Okay. Let’s take a little break here. Before someone says something they’ll regret later.”

Mom and I glared at each other. Then she calmly raised her mug of tea to her lips, took a sip, and stared across the kitchen.

I stood there, fuming. She wanted to *forbid* me? “You can’t tell me what to do, not about this, you know. You agreed to let me act. You agreed to let me shoot ‘High School Hitman.’” My eyes watered. “You can’t do this. My career will be ruined. No one’s going to want to hire me if I quit now. No one’s going to want to hire a kid with a mother like you.”

I felt hands on my shoulders and I was vaguely aware of my father saying something. My mother stared into the distance, cradling her mug of tea, oblivious to my feelings. I opened my mouth to speak, to shout, but nothing came out. My father slowly steered me from the room, down the hall, and into the family room. He eased me down onto the couch.

I could barely feel my fingertips or my toes.

“Close your eyes and take a deep breath.”

It took a few seconds for my dad’s words to make sense, but when they registered, I did what he suggested. Closed my eyes. Took a deep breath. Tried to think of something—anything—except how pissed I was at my mother.

Didn’t she get how important all this was to me?

My dad put his arm around me, and I rested my head on his shoulder. I was aware of my mother going up the stairs, but otherwise we sat in silence.

For a good long while.

Chapter Eleven

I woke up early the next morning. Blazed through the quickest shower in history, threw on some clothes, and escaped the house before either of my parents was awake.

Without a more official declaration from my mother concerning the shoot, I chose to interpret her words as merely a strong suggestion—and not an actual *forbidment.* I mean, she'd said *half her mind* wanted me to stop. Which meant the other half didn't. A tie.

Usually after one of her unreasonable dictates, she'd soften and walk back her threats. I could only hope that would be the case now.

Either way, I was planning on going to today's shoot, as soon as I found out when and where it was. My safest course of action? Getting gone before any further argument—or irrational parental orders—could happen.

I left them a note on the kitchen counter, and gone I got.

It was a little after eight, too early to text Patch, so I wandered over to the elementary school near my house and sat on one of the playground swings.

I figured I was safe there. The swing set was in the middle of an open field, and I could see about one hundred yards in every direction. If I saw a stranger matching Ms. Z's description of the stalker—or Varney—coming toward me, I'd go sprinting off, with a ninety-five-yard head start. Even if I wasn't the fastest guy around, I could work with that.

But that wasn't the real reason I'd come there.

I'd met Patch here, years ago, right after my family moved to the neighborhood. We'd bonded quickly, and tightly, and no matter what shit was raining down on our heads, each of us knew the other had his back. Trinnie joined our little gang the year after, and we'd stuck together like siblings ever since.

When I got stressed out, sometimes I'd return to this playground, somehow drawing strength from it.

Now, I needed to think.

How could my mother be mad that I was playing a murderer? Actors played all sorts of roles and it didn't mean that's who they were. That's why they called it acting. I knew it wasn't that simple though. I tried to imagine what it would be like to see someone I loved playing the part of a criminal.

Was she worried her friends would somehow put me in the same category as Varney? Was she worried I was putting the family in a negative light? Was she concerned I was treating the whole murder episode lightly? Or that I could be seen as capitalizing on other people's tragedies?

There might be a whiff of truth in all of the above, but of course, the real reason was that she worried something bad might happen to me.

I thought about the protestors I'd seen last night. Without exception, they were committed to something they believed in. Hell, I believed in it, too—at least the part about keeping a murderer behind bars. I guessed what I didn't believe in was disrupting our shoot. We were trying to bring the facts to light, in the hopes viewers might learn something—the warning signs of a killer, perhaps—to prevent things like that from happening in the future.

In my opinion, censorship was never the answer.

I thought about being stalked. I wasn't sure it was Varney, but I wasn't sure you could explain his presence last night—if he indeed was there—as a coincidence. But I wasn't sure that mattered; it was pretty clear that *someone* was stalking me. What should I do about that?

Should I continue to tiptoe around on eggshells, scared he could pop out from every sewer grate?

Or should I tell someone—Ms. Z., the cops, my parents? What would they do if I did tell them? I tried to put aside my emotions and predict what would happen. If I told Ms. Z, she'd have to tell my parents, wouldn't she? I mean, my safety was at stake and to withhold that information would get her fired, for sure.

If I told the cops, they'd also have to tell my parents. And I wasn't sure I had enough concrete evidence for them to take action. My stalker had only contacted me once—maybe. I had no actual proof that the person searching for me at school and the Twitter message were connected. Someone—someone who wasn't in my shoes—could explain this all away by accusing me of being paranoid. But it wasn't paranoia if someone really was following you! Without tangible evidence, the police wouldn't be able to do much. They'd probably just tell me not to go anywhere in public and never to be alone.

And what about my parents? No matter who I told, they'd find out, so if I told anyone, it made sense to start with them.

I twirled in the swing until the chains were tightly wound, then I let go and twirled in the other direction as the chains unwound. Back and forth, back and forth.

What would happen if I marched back home and told my parents?

After my dad and I peeled my mother off the ceiling, I knew exactly what she'd say. "You are done acting, young man. *David*. You are so done acting." And then she'd give me her plastic lawyerly smile and say, "Don't be sad. You're better off anyway. Actors struggle to make ends meet. Now, why don't you take a coding class? Learn a valuable skill that will land you an excellent job."

Yeah, and why don't I stab myself in the eyes with a steak

knife while I'm at it?

Plain and simple, if I told my parents, I could kiss my acting career goodbye. Forever. Because if I gave up now, in the middle of a shoot, my reputation would be ruined and nobody would ever want to work with me again. I'd be the guy who flaked out. The guy who couldn't hack it.

I felt my face flush. No way was I going to be that guy. I'd worked too hard to give up now. That stalker—Varney or whoever—would have to do something drastic before I was going to quit. No way was I going to let my fear control me.

No way.

No way was I going to tell anyone in a position of authority.

On the other hand, if I *didn't* tell my parents, and they ever found out I thought a stalker was after me, I'd be in deep, deep shit.

Like the deepest shit ever. Like never getting to do any acting until I was thirty. I could hear my mother now: "If you're so irresponsible, and your judgment is so poor that you don't even recognize when you're in danger, then, young man, you most certainly are not allowed to"—fill in the blank.

I shook my head. The logical part of my brain was battling with the emotional side, and neither side would win in this lose-lose situation.

If only there was a way to tell my parents, alert the authorities, and *still* get to act in "High School Hitman II."

If only...

Even though it wasn't quite nine o'clock, I texted Patch.

> Me: You awake?
> Patch: Now I am. What up?
> Me: Meet me at the playground?
> Patch: Now?
> Me: Yes.
> Patch: You okay?
> Me: NO!

I stuffed the phone into my pocket and ignored the vibrations.

Fifteen minutes later, Patch rolled up. I watched him as he got out of his car, all the way across the fields on the other side of the school building, and bounded my way. Patch rarely jogged unless he had to. I felt bad about worrying him, but I guessed that's what friends were for. If Patch was in my shoes, I'd be the one jogging across the fields to make sure he wasn't melting down.

He arrived at the swing set breathing hard. "What's wrong?" He glanced around, as if maybe I'd called him while being held hostage by masked gunmen.

"My situation. That's what's wrong."

Patch nodded, and he seemed to relax once he realized my problem wasn't any kind of time-critical emergency. He leaned against the plastic fort that held the slide and crossed his arms. "Okay. I'm listening."

"You want all my thinking, or just the boiled-down version?" I asked.

"Hit me with the bottom line first. I can always ask questions."

"Okay." I sucked in a deep breath. "To recap. I'm pretty sure someone is stalking me. Not positive, but pretty sure. And after last night, there's a decent chance my stalker is none other than Varney. I don't know why, but that doesn't really matter. So, what would a normal person who's being stalked do? Well, a normal person—"

Patch interrupted. "I thought I was getting the short version."

I glared at him. "Trust me, you don't want to know all the mental gyrations I went through to arrive at my conclusion. This is the short version. And it will be shorter, if you just let me finish."

Patch rolled his eyes, and made a *get-on-with-it* gesture.

"Thank you. As I was saying, a normal person would tell someone. Like the cops, people with authority to do something." I paused. "But I can't do that."

"Because you're not a normal person?" Patch asked.

"No. Well, yes. I'm normal, but I can't tell the cops. Or Ms. Z. Or anyone except you and Trinnie."

"Why not?"

"Because if I did, my career would be over."

He cocked his head at me.

"Well, maybe not over forever, but over for the foreseeable future. Because if my parents found out I was being stalked because of this 'High School Hitman' gig, I'd never be allowed to act until I was married with kids. So I can't tell them. In fact—"

"May I speak now?" Patch uncrossed his arms.

"I'm not finished," I said. "But sure, go ahead."

"The police could provide protection. Your parents might be okay with that."

"Right now, there's not enough evidence. They wouldn't provide anything, protection or otherwise. And I'd be totally screwed. No, I can't tell anybody without something concrete."

"I've been thinking, too, after last night. In fact, it took me a while to get to sleep. Your life might be in danger, man. I know we don't have actual proof of this stalker, but someone did come by the school looking for you, you got that ominous message, and someone did say they saw Varney at the shoot last night, and well, that's enough evidence for me. This is one of those situations where it's better to be cautious—and alive—than to blow it off and be not so alive."

"Yeah, but—"

Patch held up his hand. "You know I'm right. Stalkers are twisted. No telling what one might do, given the opportunity. You need to tell someone. And I'd start with your parents."

"Look, if I—"

"You know I'm right."

I bit back tears. I couldn't tell if it was the fear of the stalker getting to me, or the fear of not acting. Or both. I knew Patch meant well. I also knew, again, that if our roles were reversed, I'd be saying the same exact thing, probably word for word.

And although Patch *thought* he knew how much acting meant to me, he wasn't even close. If my acting got shut down now, I was afraid of what might happen to me. Like a balloon getting popped with a pin, I'd spin out and end up lying on the floor, in tatters, lifeless. I had one chance, albeit a small one, of making everyone, if not happy, at least agreeable to me continuing this gig.

"What if we could prove Varney was there last night? Stalking me? And if it wasn't Varney stalking me, we'd know what the stalker looked like. We could take it to the cops, they could nab him, and I'd be home free. At the very least, we could get a restraining order or something. That might satisfy my parents."

"How are we going to do that?" Patch asked.

"Ranjay told the camera guys to keep rolling, right through the protests. Maybe they caught him on tape."

Patch turned slowly to face me, grin on his face. "You, sir, are a genius."

"And you, sir, are a genius for recognizing my genius." I pulled out my phone and texted Ranjay, asking him if we could review last night's extra footage. I also asked if he'd rescheduled the shoot.

He answered almost immediately: *Still working on shoot details. Might be delayed. As for the footage, sure. But not anytime soon. Plus you'll have to come here. Can't let that out, and files too large. Maybe next week? Or week after?*

I hadn't taken into account the logistics. I thought about telling him why I wanted to look, and about Varney actually being there, but I didn't want to further complicate things. I was bummed the shoot was on hold. I texted back a simple *okay.*

I told Patch what Ranjay had said.

"Delayed? What does that mean?"

"You don't know what delayed means?"

"I know what it means in English, but I don't know what it means in TV lingo."

"Delayed means we're screwed. With all the protests, we'll

never get it shot. It doesn't really matter. If we can't prove Varney is after me until next week, I'll be dead by then."

"Or..."

"Or what?"

"There might be other video of last night."

"Did you take some?" I couldn't remember either Trinnie or Patch taking video with their phones, but I was a bit distracted, like everyone else.

"No."

"What good are you then?"

"I didn't take any video." Patch paused. "But the TV stations did."

The TV stations. Of course. "Once again, your genius shows through."

He tipped his head. "And not just my genius. My talent, too. My dad saw me on the news. I'm a star, like you. Sort of."

Uh-huh. "How do you propose we get this video?"

Patch shrugged. "I'm just the idea man. I'll let you work out the specifics."

"Maybe it's posted online." To see every detail, though, we'd need a screen bigger than my phone's. "Let's go find a computer."

We drove over to Patch's—I wasn't ready to face my parents, maybe in a few weeks—and went straight up to his room.

Patch fired up his laptop and handed it over. I began with the local NBC affiliate, wanting to review the video they had posted. A few clicks later, I found what I was looking for and hit play. A news reporter stood in front of the line of protestors, talking into her mic, giving a live intro. Then they cut away to thirty seconds of the protesters themselves, with voice-over describing the scene. Patch hovered over my shoulder, breathing heavily. When a shot of Patch carrying his sign came on, he leaned closer, and his hot breath tickled my ears.

"Do you mind?" I said.

"Handsome guy." Patch didn't move back an inch, so I leaned closer to the screen. "Very handsome."

I checked the other local stations, ABC and CBS, and they also had stories posted, all similar. A reporter, some footage of the demonstrators. And Patch again with his sign.

"I wonder if I need an agent now."

"Sure. There's a lot of money in holding protest signs. I think that's how Ryan Gosling started, too." I pointed to the screen. "All the video was focused on the protestors. At least all the video that made it into the story. There's probably fifty times more they didn't use." Like with most shoots or news stories, only the best video was selected, leaving tons more on the proverbial cutting-room floor. "We need to see the raw footage. Unfortunately, I don't think we can just waltz into the TV station and ask to see all they've got."

Patch broke out a huge grin. "Unless..."

"What?"

"Unless you happen to know someone who works there."

"I don't. Do you?"

"As a matter of fact," Patch said, "I do."

I waited for him to tell me who, but he just stood there, grinning like a goof. "Well?"

He waited another five seconds before speaking. "Clarisse Rizzo's mom."

"Clarisse Rizzo? The new girl? The real quiet one?"

Patch nodded. "Her mom is the assistant news director at the local NBC station."

"Really?"

"Yeah, really."

"And how do you know this?" I eyed Patch.

"My mom and her mom are in book club together. They live a few blocks from me."

Made sense. "So do you think your mom will call her?"

Patch pulled out his phone. "Why don't I just text Clarisse? She's cool. I'm sure she'll ask her mom for us."

Before I could respond, Patch's thumbs were in motion. I didn't get a chance to ask how he got Clarisse's number, either.

Patch and I walked the two blocks to Clarisse's house, and she was waiting on the porch for us, curled up on a swing suspended from the ceiling, wearing black from head-to-toe. When she saw us, she sat up straight and smiled directly at Patch, who plopped down right next to her on the swing. My only choice? A rickety chair across from them. I lowered myself carefully.

"How's it going, Rizzo?" Patch said.

"Just another nice day in lovely Vienna, Virginia. How are you?"

"Good. Real good."

Clarisse touched Patch's knee. "I saw you on TV last night. Very cool."

"Thanks. It wasn't planned or anything." Patch had a sparkle in his eyes I hadn't seen for a while, and I had the distinct sense I was the third wheel here. Which surprised the heck out of me. I thought I knew pretty much everything Patch was up to.

Finally, Clarisse looked my way. "And how are you, Dalton?"

"Fine. I'm just fine." I smiled, but it was too late. Clarisse had turned her focus back to Patch.

"So, you wanted a favor?" Clarisse asked Patch.

"Yes, and it's about last night's piece, in fact. We'd like to see all the raw footage that was shot last night by your mom's station. At the demonstration."

"Why?"

Patch nodded at me to explain, but I nodded right back at him. "Go ahead." I knew who should do the talking to increase our chance of success. Patch proceeded to explain the whole Varney thing. Clarisse already knew the basics, having read about the case and by watching her mother's newscasts. On the walk over, though, Patch and I had decided we would leave out the *me-being-stalked* part of the story. We—*I*—didn't want to take even the smallest possible risk that word would get back to my parents.

"So if we can prove he was there at the shoot, maybe we can get the police to do something," Patch said, finishing up his explanation.

Clarisse sat back a little. "Wow, Miguel. That's kinda scary. I'm glad you..." She glanced at me. "Both of you are okay."

Miguel? *Miguel*? I'd talk to him later about getting Miguelled by Clarisse. I caught Patch's attention and nodded at her. *Ask*.

He got the hint. "So what do you think? Would you help us out and ask your mom?

"Of course," she said, touching Patch's arm again and not letting go. "For you, sure. She's already at work. Hang on." She took out her phone and texted her mom. A moment later, her phone rang and she answered it. Five minutes later, she had everything arranged for a little trip to the station to talk to her mom.

"Cool," Patch said. "Thanks!"

"My pleasure. I hope things work out for you guys."

Patch looked hurt. "You're not coming?"

She smiled, patted his knee again, as if she'd been patting his knee for months. "Unfortunately, I can't. Got some chores to do. But you don't need me. My mom doesn't bite."

Chapter Twelve

"Where are we going?" Patch drove, and Trinnie rode shotgun. Trinnie always got shotgun without having to call it. Who wanted to argue with her?

"Field trip," I said from the back seat.

"What kind of field trip?"

"I thought you liked surprises."

"Only ones involving chocolate." She turned her head to stare at me. "Spill."

I knew when I was defeated. "We're going to a TV station. Our friend Patch got his friend, Clarisse, to get us set up there. Her mom is the assistant news director."

"Clarisse? As in Clarisse Rizzo?" Trinnie asked, with a healthy dose of amazement. She swiveled in her seat toward Patch. "Since when are you tight with her?"

Patch met her gaze for a second, then refocused on the road. "Since a while. She's cool."

"So many questions," Trinnie said. "First, why is this the first we're—"

I made a game-show buzzer noise, stopping the inquisition before it really got rolling. "Why don't we concentrate on the task at hand, okay? To answer your question about the field trip, we're going to the station to review their footage of last night's protest. Hopefully, we can spot Varney lurking about."

Trinnie whipped around front, flipped the sun visor down

and started examining herself in the little mirror.

"We're not going to be *on* TV, you know."

"It pays to be prepared."

I was going to give her grief when my phone rang. *Agent Alf.*

"Hello, Alf."

"Hello, my boy. I heard what happened yesterday. Are you all right?"

"I'm fine."

"And your friends?"

"They're okay, too. In fact, I'm in the car with them now."

"Ah. Then why don't you put us on speaker. I have news that affects you all."

I put the call on speaker. Even though they had listened in on a previous call, I introduced them as if it was the first time they'd talked with Alf. "Guys, this is Alfred McMaster, my manager."

Patch and Trinnie said, "Hello."

"Greetings, young thespians. I'm glad you weathered last night's storm. Unfortunately, I have some bad news regarding things moving forward. I spoke with your esteemed director, Mr. Ranjay Kapoor, and he informed me the project is on hold for the moment."

"Did he say for how long?" I guessed that *might be* delayed had turned into *definitely* delayed.

"Indeterminate. He's having a hard time finding an alternate shooting location, what with all those high-minded demonstrators."

I pictured them bashing the windows with rocks. Not so high-minded.

"So we just wait around?" I asked.

"I'm afraid so. I was once in the hot tub with none other than the charismatic Christopher Walken, and he leaned over to me and said, 'Sometimes you have to know when to hold your horses in the barn.' Hell of a guy, that Christoph. One thing I do know. Things change in the blink of an eye in this business. I'll keep you posted, lads and lassie. Ta-ta!"

I ended the call.

"Christopher Walken, huh?" Patch said.

"He's creepy," Trinnie added, still preening in the mirror. "But not as creepy as Varney."

Although it was Saturday and there were, theoretically, fewer cars on the road, traffic still sucked. Traffic always seemed to suck. But Patch did a great job of getting us to the TV station with a minimum of fuss. And we didn't hit anybody or anything, so I figured we were ahead of the game.

We entered the lobby and marched straight up to the receptionist's counter. A young guy in a blue blazer sat there, gaze locked onto a security monitor.

I cleared my throat, and his head snapped up. He had a dark, neatly-trimmed beard and intense brown eyes. "How can I help you?"

"We'd like to talk to Ms. Rizzo."

"What might this be regarding?" he said in a stick-up-his-butt way.

I straightened. "Well, it might be about—"

I got shoved aside, and all of a sudden Trinnie was standing in my place. "This *is* about a murderer. You may have heard of him, Homer Lee Varney?" She leaned over the counter and the receptionist leaned back so they wouldn't bump heads.

"Uh, what about him?"

I tried to nudge Trinnie out of the way but she wasn't having any of it.

"He's stalking us, and we thought that might be the kind of news you'd like to report. If not, we'll go over to Channel Six and see what they think. I understand they're a very professional station." Trinnie raised one eyebrow. "By the way, Ms. Rizzo is expecting us."

The man stared at Trinnie, pursed his lips, unpursed his lips, then squinted at both me and Patch. Finally, he sighed. "Okay, hold on." He picked up the phone, punched in a number, then swiveled in his seat so his back faced us while he talked. I tried to overhear his conversation, but all I could make out were the words *teens*, *obnoxious*, and *Varney*.

He swiveled back around and forced the lamest smile I'd ever seen. "Have a seat. Ms. Rizzo will be out shortly to talk with you." He went back to scrutinizing the security monitor.

There were two dozen chairs in the lobby, but we wandered around examining the photos on the wall. They'd been enlarged to poster size, and framed, and they displayed various newsmaking events and newsmakers. Some photos had national importance. A reporter at 9/11 Ground Zero. President Reagan getting shot. The space shuttle explosion.

Other pictures held local interest. Panda bears frolicking at the National Zoo. Washington football players hoisting the Super Bowl trophy. And plenty of politicians we'd never seen before.

I pulled Trinnie aside. "You know, you didn't have to push me aside up there."

"You didn't seem to be getting anywhere, so I stepped in. You're welcome, by the way."

"Thank you, but I could have handled it myself if you'd—"

She patted my shoulder. "Face it, Dalton, we each have our strengths. If I ever have a jar I can't open, I'll call on you." She drifted away to look at more pictures as I stared after her with my mouth open.

Twenty minutes later, after we'd been sitting for a while, a lady, clearly dressed for work in a nice skirt and blouse, came over to us in the lobby. "Hello, Miguel. How are you?"

"Fine, Ms. Rizzo. Thanks for meeting with us."

"Of course."

"These are my friends, Trinnie and Dalton."

"Nice to meet you. Why don't we go back to my office?"

She badged us through the door and led us down a long, long hallway. We passed offices and editing rooms and even a studio with the On-Air light illuminated. We hooked a left down another corridor, then she ushered us into a bullpen full of cubicles. A few people glanced up as we passed, but nobody seemed to care who we were or what we were doing there.

I guessed they didn't recognize me from "High School Hitman."

We ended up in the corner office, and the nameplate by the door read, Hannah Rizzo, Assistant News Director.

"Have a seat." She gestured to a couple of plastic chairs in front of her desk, as she sat in her big swivel chair. "Well, two of you, at least."

Trinnie took one chair right away, while Patch and I stared each other down. "Go ahead," I said.

"So, what's this about Varney stalking you?" Ms. Rizzo pointed at Trinnie with a pen. Why did everyone always think she was in charge?

I spoke, quickly, before Trinnie could get on a roll. "I think he's stalking *me*."

Ms. Rizzo aimed her pen at me. "Okay. Why do you think he's stalking *you*?"

"I, uh, I played him in the TV episode 'High School Hitman' on a show called *Teen Killers* on the True Crime Network. I was Varney as a teenager. For some reason, I think he's after me."

A flicker of recognition in her eyes. "I knew you looked familiar. We watched that show a few times, for background. I bet that was fun, huh?" She turned serious. "But why would he be after you?"

"I have absolutely no idea."

"Has he tried to speak to you?"

"No."

Patch and Trinnie both shook their heads, as if my statement needed confirmation.

"When was the last time you saw him?"

"Well...here's the thing. We're not *absolutely* positive he's after me."

Ms. Rizzo scooted her chair back. "This some kind of game? A prank? Very funny. Clarisse always did have an interesting sense of humor." She stood. "Time to go. I've got real work to do."

"Wait! This isn't a joke. Varney is after me. We saw him last night, at the shoot. You know, the one with the protestors."

Ms. Rizzo eyed us and slowly lowered herself back into her chair. "He was there last night?"

I nodded, and Trinnie chimed in. "We think so. That's why we're here. We were hoping to look at the footage you shot to see if we can tell for sure."

Ms. Rizzo tapped her pen against her chin.

"If he was, it would make a great story," Trinnie added, knowing how to put the cherry on top.

"Just to be clear. You want to go through the footage and see if you can spot him? Then what?"

I spoke up. "Then we'll know for sure. And we'll call the police, too. I think they might be interested if Varney is after me."

Ms. Rizzo tilted her chair back and stared at the ceiling for so long, I thought maybe she'd fallen asleep. Abruptly, she sat up straight. "Any of you eighteen?"

Three heads shook no.

"Promise you won't sue me, and I'll get you set up so you can review the footage we took."

Three heads nodded yes.

"Okay, then. Come on."

Back in the bullpen, Ms. Rizzo crooked her finger at a guy on the phone. He told whoever he was talking to he'd call them back, then hung up and stood.

"Do me a favor. Take these three and show them last night's footage—every last second—of the Varney demonstrators." Ms. Rizzo turned to us. "Thanks for coming forth with this. Please leave your contact info with Dan here, in case we need to follow up with you. And Miguel, I'll see you for dinner in a couple of days, right?" She shook our hands, gave Patch an extra hearty smile, then spun on her heels and returned to her office.

I mouthed *dinner* at Patch, but he just shrugged noncommittally.

Dan nodded his head. "This way."

We ended up in a dark editing room, and Dan dragged a couple of chairs from another room so we all could sit. "Gather around this monitor and I'll get it set up."

Dan got busy and it took him a while to get the right video queued up. While he worked, Patch, Trinnie, and I sat in silence.

"Okay. Here we go. What exactly are you looking for?"

We told him about Varney and his stalking. He didn't react beyond a nod. "Okay. Why don't I run it straight through at regular speed? If you see something of interest, we can slow it down and you can watch it in slo-mo."

He hit play and the footage rolled by. The beginning was like the spot I'd seen on TV. The reporter, Mary Ann Wilson, doing her stand-up. Then it cut to the demonstrators. But where the TV report only contained twenty or thirty seconds, this footage went on for minutes. Ten minutes in, three familiar faces came into view for about one second, in the back row of protestors.

"There we are," Patch said.

Dan hit stop. "See something?"

"No. Just us. Keep going."

Dan started up the video again.

Trinnie clapped when the close-up of Patch holding the sign appeared. At one point, the camera shifted from the line of protestors to people milling about the parking lot.

"Hold it." I rose, pointing to the screen.

Dan froze the video. "See something?"

"Right there. Behind that lady." A guy in a dark hoodie. *Our* guy in a dark hoodie. I moved my finger closer to the screen, almost touching it. "I think that's him."

Varney—or at least the guy we thought was Varney—was pretty far from the camera, and he was partially obscured. But it sure looked like the guy who seemed to be waiting to ambush us.

Patch nodded. "Yeah. Could be him, all right."

I turned to Trinnie. "What do you think?"

Trinnie stood too. Put her hands on her hips. Tilted her head this way and that. "Can you go forward in slo-mo?"

Before, Dan had been checking out his phone while the video ran. Now he paid close attention as he set the video playing in slow motion.

In the footage, Varney took a few steps and emerged from behind the woman, but his face was in the shadows from his hood. You couldn't tell it was him at all.

The video crawled forward, and Varney seemed to stand around, facing vaguely toward the camera, which was located right in front of the demonstrators. In other words, he had been looking in our direction.

We tracked Varney for a few more seconds, then the camera abruptly shifted again to focus on the real action: the demonstrators.

Dan hit pause. "So? Was that him?"

"I dunno. Looked like him, but we couldn't see his face."

"Yeah," Patch said. "It could have been any old stalker."

"I think it was him. I know we aren't sure, but I have a feeling it's him." Trinnie touched my arm, held on.

"I don't think your feeling is going to persuade anybody I'm in danger." I sighed.

"Sorry, guys," Dan said. "Want me to run the rest of it?"

"I guess."

We watched the rest of the footage at regular speed but there were no more Varney sightings. When we finished, Dan asked if we'd like to see it again.

Three disappointed head shakes.

He flicked the lights on. "Sorry you didn't find what you're looking for, but if you see him again, please be sure to let us know. It would have made a great story."

Chapter Thirteen

I'd hoped we'd be able to identify Varney from the TV footage. Then—in my feverish daydream—we'd call the cops or the FBI or whoever was in charge of capturing ex-con stalkers. They'd devise a clever way to trap him, and he'd be behind bars by dinnertime. No more stalker would mean no more ammunition my mother could use against me in her quest to get me to drop my drama pursuits.

Unfortunately, daydreams seldom came true. We weren't any closer now than we were before we watched the video.

And, in the far, far back corner of my brain—the logical, rational part—I knew that maybe, just maybe, I was making the whole thing up. Maybe there was no guy in a hoodie, no killer out for revenge.

Maybe I was a little crazy and was imagining the entire thing.

Maybe I'd gotten carried away from my part in the show, building up my self-importance like some kind of prima donna.

After all, I was just a kid who got lucky to get a part in a second-rate show on a third-rate network. A cable network, to boot.

As we left the TV station, my mood was lower than an infomercial's ratings.

The three of us ended up back at Patch's, downstairs in his workout room, which, I had to admit, was better suited for us than my house—for obvious reasons—or Trinnie's. Her parents kept their home way too neat—we had to remove our shoes at the door and use coasters whenever we wanted to drink anything.

"So now what?" Patch sat on an old rowing machine, holding the oars but not moving.

"I wish I knew." With all the media attention and public outcry, the sequel to "High School Hitman" would have gone through the roof, ratings-wise. But now, because of that same attention, it seemed my big chance in the spotlight—fifteen more minutes—was in severe jeopardy. Being an actor meant having your dreams dashed on a daily basis, but it was still hard to take.

Trinnie seemed to sense my despair, because she came over and started massaging the back of my shoulders. "You're tight. You need to relax."

My career had stalled, right before a big launch, and a madman might be gunning for me. Easy for her to tell me to relax. "I know you're right, but..."

"Want to go hang out at the mall?" Patch's cure for everything.

"Not really." I didn't want to bump into Grady again.

"Want to go swimming?" Trinnie asked.

"Not really."

"Want to visit a couple of hot supermodels dying to meet a suave and handsome young TV star?" Patch asked.

"Not really." I hung my head. "I think I'll go see what the campers are up to. Except I'll probably mess up somehow." A bunch of them—under the supervision of Ms. Z and her wife—were building sets. They'd gotten a little behind and needed the extra weekend time to catch up.

"See you guys later."

"Later."

I was sorta hoping one of them would beg me to stay, but I guessed they didn't want to. Didn't blame them a bit.

I walked to school, although it was probably more of a trudge than a walk. I glanced over my shoulder every few steps, on high alert, almost hoping Varney would jump out from behind a parked car.

No such luck.

I made it to school without any incident and the closer I got to the auditorium, the louder the bangs of the hammers and whirs of the saws. I opened the door and stepped into a haze of sawdust.

About twenty kids and a smattering of parents were busy working. Some constructed sets from plywood and two-by-fours, while others painted backdrops of the Emerald City. A group sat on the floor in the corner, drawing plans for something on an oversized piece of paper. Ms. Z wore a carpenter's belt and a painter's hat, ready to help whoever needed it. She saw me and motioned me over.

"Hey Ms. Z."

"Glad you could make it. We can always use more hands."

"Yeah," I said without much enthusiasm.

She eyed me. "I saw the protest on the news last night. You okay?"

"I guess so." I debated telling her my troubles. She was much easier to talk to than my mom, especially when it came to drama stuff. She got me. Even so, I didn't want to get into it. Not there, not then.

"Dalton, none of that was your fault. You're just playing a role. Don't let all of the negativity get you down. Your performance in the first episode was fantastic. If you get a chance, you'll do even better this time around."

"I hope so."

"Sure, I'm a little biased, but you have to remember: I've seen a fair number of drama students come through here, and you have a rare talent. Keep improving your craft, work hard, never surrender, and you'll go far."

"Thanks, Ms. Z. I'm not planning on quitting."

"Good." She smiled. "By the way, you and the other counselors can have the day off when we visit the Shakespeare Theatre this week. They're requesting adult chaperones. Sorry."

"No big deal." I could use the day off to perfect my moping.

"Now, do you want to build or paint? Or..." She leaned in. "Do you want to sew?"

I was in the mood to take out my frustrations, big time. "Build. Specifically, hammer."

Ms. Z nodded in a way that meant she understood.

I joined up with the construction crew and pounded nails for a while, working up a sweat while smashing away the frustration, until my phone buzzed with a text from a number I didn't recognize.

My heart raced. Lots of people I didn't really know followed me on Twitter and Instagram, but I didn't give my phone number out to strangers. Could my stalker—or Varney—have gotten it? My phone buzzed again, and I almost dropped it like it was on fire.

I moved to the side so I didn't get whacked by some kid wielding a hammer with a little too much excitement.

With shaking hands, I read the text.

Great news. Shoot is back on. Kapoor wants to film a few scenes, principals only. This afternoon (sorry for short notice). Please meet in abandoned ZMart building at 3 pm—only place we could find suitable space. Entrance in rear, look for red ribbon. Please park elsewhere and walk and don't tell anyone else—can't let word get out like last nite! Pls respond. Thx, Asst. Dir. Em.

The text was from Emily, Kapoor's assistant director. Mystery solved. My breathing returned to normal.

I reread the text. We're back on? Awesome!

I texted Emily back: *I'll be there!*

It was two-thirty now, and the ZMart building wasn't very far. The huge store had gone out of business about eight months ago, and I'd heard recently it was going to be subdivided into a few fast-food restaurants. Ranjay must have figured that since it was empty, he could shoot a couple of scenes there without anyone caring. It was a big space inside, yet out of the public's eye. Knowing how tight a budget these types of shows were on, I bet Ranjay didn't even bother to clear it with the building's owners.

The details were just that—details. We were back in business! The show must go on!

I found the crew leader and excused myself, said goodbye to Ms. Z, and left the auditorium, practically skipping. Ducked into the boys' room to check myself in the mirror. A little grimy, but I didn't have time to go home and shower, so I ran my hands through my hair to get rid of the sawdust, then brushed off my shirt. Not too bad. I was playing a killer, so I guessed it would be okay if I didn't look perfectly groomed. The younger Varney was no Abercrombie model.

Satisfied with my appearance, I left the school building, and headed toward the old ZMart, right down Maple Avenue, walking fast, ready to break into a sprint if I saw any sign of my stalker.

I passed the same old stores, the same old restaurants, the same old boring hair salons and drugstores. How could people live in the same town their entire lives? New York or Chicago or L.A., maybe. But Vienna, Virginia? I didn't care if it did make the Best Small Towns In America list year after year. Boring was boring.

Maybe this gig, or the one after, or the one after that, would be my ticket out of here. I bet Hollywood wasn't boring.

I felt bad about Patch and Trinnie. They were excited to get a small part in the shoot—even if Patch said otherwise—and I was afraid Ranjay might rewrite the script to reduce the number of people involved. If I got the chance, I'd do what I could to make sure Ranjay didn't cut their scene.

I also felt bad not texting them what was going on—it felt like I was keeping a dirty little secret. They were going to find out eventually, and they wouldn't be happy. I tried to imagine how I would feel if I was in their position.

I wouldn't be happy either.

Some things were beyond my control. I knew they would understand.

I reached the ZMart site, with five minutes to spare. The place had been in business forever, according to my dad, and it served as the Vienna version of Walmart or Kmart. The kind of store that had everything you needed in one place. Products that weren't too fancy or too expensive. The store's layout was designed for function, not beauty. In the couple of years before its demise, again according to Dad, a vocal group of residents had wanted it torn down or remodeled, claiming it was an eyesore.

They were probably right. And they probably were afraid it threatened Vienna's status as a Best Small Town in America.

Someone had removed the ZMart signage, so now it looked exactly like what it was, an ugly, hulking, empty shell of a building. To call it an eyesore would be insulting to eyesores.

Naturally, it was the perfect location for a secret film shoot.

I angled through the empty parking lot. No cars were parked in the front, which made sense, considering Ranjay wanted to keep things on the down low.

I passed through the lot and veered left along the side of the building. A row of small windows ran the length of the wall, twenty feet off the ground, and every single one had been busted. Probably by kids—junior residents of a Best Small Town in America—throwing rocks.

No sign of any stalkers. No sign of anyone at all.

Around the back corner, I came to a loading dock, then a small parking area. No cars there either. Maybe Ranjay had asked everyone to park a few blocks away so they wouldn't arouse any suspicions.

My pulse quickened.

The entire back portion of the building had been roped off with yellow caution tape, the same kind that surrounded all the crime scenes on *Law & Order*. I ducked under it and walked closer to the building.

According to my instructions, I was looking for a red ribbon.

The store's façade, fronting Maple Avenue, was neat and tidy, with two sets of neat and tidy doors. The rear of the store was a complete mess. Three rusty dumpsters overflowed with construction debris, creating a mountain of trash on the surrounding asphalt. I waded through some of it so I could peek behind the dumpsters, in case there was a door hidden back there.

No door. No red ribbon.

I moved on, past the mountain of trash, searching for a way in.

A large back door was locked, and a heavy chain—secured by the biggest padlock I'd ever seen—encircled the handles.

I walked away from the building until I could see the entire rear wall, and what looked like another set of doors at the far end. Unfortunately, it appeared heavy chains had that door locked, too.

I pulled out my phone and rechecked the text to be sure I was in the right place at the right time. Yep, and yep.

Part of me was thinking that something didn't seem quite right. Another part of me was excited about the prospect of filming in an abandoned store, putting one over on those protestors in the name of art.

I jogged down to the doors, and when I got near, I spotted a red ribbon tied around the door handle. I slowed and looked around. It would ruin everything if someone saw me enter the building and called the cops. Ranjay wouldn't be happy, and I didn't want to take any chances losing my role.

The coast was clear. Upon closer inspection, I realized someone had cut the chain on the door handles and draped an unattached length of it on each handle. The doors opened, no problem. I left the ribbon alone, in case someone was arriving after me.

I stepped into the building, and it was like stepping into a cavern, except it was warmer. The air was still, and it was eerily quiet, and the only light filtered in from another series of broken windows on this side of the building. I could make out dark shapes and piles of debris here and there, but I didn't see any people. Or any evidence there was going to be a shoot.

Resisting the urge to turn and run, I called out. "Hello? Ranjay? Emily?"

Only a faint echo.

I walked deeper into the building, treading carefully as I crunched along the floor. Dust motes rose in the shafts of light, and I felt as if I'd stepped into another dimension. A scurrying noise on the floor caught my attention, but whatever it was—squirrel, rat, or something even worse—skittered off in the other direction.

"Hello?" I crept farther into the building. The insides hadn't been entirely demolished; the whole place seemed like a bombed-out building in some war-torn part of the world.

With all the shadows and piles of debris, I couldn't see more than fifteen feet in front of me.

Hard to believe Ranjay knew what this place looked like when he decided to shoot here. I'd had enough. Time to get back outside—to civilization—and text Ranjay to see what was going on. I turned to retrace my steps when I heard a voice calling from somewhere across the vast space. "Dalton, is that you? We're over here. At the front of the building."

I exhaled. I set off in the direction of the voice, careful not to step on any sharp pieces of metal—or anything else that might hurt. As I rounded the end of what used to be a shopping aisle, the space opened up a bit, and the trash had been cleared away enough for someone to have set up a couple of chairs.

But I didn't see a soul.

"Hello?"

Nobody answered this time.

I took a few steps closer to the chairs.

Scuffling noises behind me. I whirled around, heart hammering.

A man stood there, silhouetted against the light streaming in from a broken window high on the wall.

He wore a hoodie.

Chapter Fourteen

"Dalton? I need to talk to you." The shadowy figure approached.

I took a few steps backward.

He took a few more steps forward.

"Who are you? What do you want?" My throat constricted and it was a challenge to get the words out.

"I think you know who I am."

I did. I sure did. I recognized the voice from the TV interview he did when he got out of prison. "I've got nothing to say to you, Varney. My friends will be here any minute."

"Your friends aren't coming."

Shit. "So, *you* sent the text? How did you get my number?"

"I swiped your director's cast sheet at the shoot the other night. During the chaos. Sorry about that." Varney shrugged.

"I knew you were there."

"You were correct. Sorry to deceive you with the text, but I needed to talk to you. Alone. I won't hurt you." He inched closer. "Promise."

As if a promise from a murderer meant something. Varney blocked my path out. I figured if I turned around and ran, I might be able to somehow worm my way to the back door where I'd come in. But he'd been in the building a while, casing the place. For all I knew, he'd set a trap and was waiting for me to take the bait.

"You want to talk to me, go ahead. Talk." I shuffled

backward, squinting through the dim light, glancing this way and that, searching for an opening I could dash through. But it seemed the renovation contractors were using the front of the store as a staging area to keep waiting-to-be-used building materials. Panels of wallboard, metal frames, and flooring had been stacked, floor to ceiling. I didn't see any obvious ways through the stuff.

"Why don't we sit and talk like two reasonable people?"

"If you try anything, I'm out of here." Of course, I had no intention of sitting down for a chat with Varney.

He pointed at the folding chairs, which seemed totally out of place. "Go ahead."

I headed toward the chairs, sideways, like a crab, to keep him in view, and he trailed behind. We walked slowly, as if any second one of us was going to make a move.

Which I was.

I waited until I'd reached the first folding chair, then leaned over as if I was going to sit. I grabbed the chair, and spun around, flinging it at him, Frisbee-style. Then I took off.

I raced away from him, hooking a left behind a stack of empty plastic construction buckets. As I turned the corner, I grabbed the handle of one of the buckets and pulled hard, causing it, and a few others, to topple behind me.

"Goddamn it, Dalton!" Varney yelled as he chased me. "I didn't kill Ogden! I need to talk to you!"

Of course he was going to say he didn't kill Ogden. But why in the world would he need to talk to me? I wasn't sticking around to find out. I tore through the building, down aisles that once held packages of underwear, beach towels, shampoo, toasters, basketballs, and motor oil. You could find anything—everything—at the ZMart.

Now I was trying to find the exit.

Behind me, Varney tripped over something and started cursing. I ventured a glance backward, and he was up on his feet, charging at me. *Gaining* on me. He knew exactly where the back door was, and I didn't. When I reached an area of darkness, I cut quickly to my right, ducked under a fallen beam, then crawled into a corner and pulled a flattened cardboard box over my head like a blanket.

Unless he'd seen me shimmy into my hidey-hole, he'd have a tough time knowing where I'd gone. I held my breath, listening. Nothing. Complete silence. I pictured Varney, ten paces away, holding his breath, too, waiting for me to make a sound.

I thought about pulling my phone out and calling Patch—or better yet, 9-1-1—but with Varney so close, I didn't want to risk making a sound and giving up my location. I huddled there and slowly exhaled.

The seconds crawled by. I kept waiting for my heart to stop pummeling the inside of my chest, but it didn't. If anything, it sped up. I prayed Varney couldn't hear my nerves jangling.

I was trapped alone with a killer waiting for me to emerge from my hiding place. If he wasn't right within spitting distance, then he was probably next to the exit, ready to nab me there. That's where I'd be if I were him.

Eventually, I'd have to leave. If I didn't show up by bedtime, my parents would be in a panic. They'd start calling all my friends, alerting the authorities. But even then, it might be days before they'd find me here. I'd be passed out due to hunger—or worse, I'd fall asleep and snore or cough and Varney would find me.

I bet he could wait me out. I doubted he had parents who were expecting him home.

I took a deep breath of hot, recirculated air—my own—and tried to get a grip. My stupid imagination was running amok. Some plan would come to me. Some sound, logical—safe—plan for escaping would materialize.

I just needed to remain calm and patient.

I closed my eyes and sucked in another hot, stale breath.

"Come on, Dalton. I know you're still in here." Varney didn't sound like he was ten paces away—he sounded closer.

My eyelids sprang open, and I prayed they didn't make any noise.

"I swear I just need to talk to you. Please come out. I won't hurt you."

I'd ended up in a tight space and didn't have room to stretch my legs, so I'd been sitting on them. And they were starting to cramp. My fears about being stuck here for days evaporated. I wouldn't be able to last two more minutes without screaming out in pain. I bit the inside of my cheek to distract myself from the torture in my right calf.

"Dalton, please listen to me." Varney's voice got softer, as if he were moving away. The agony in my leg intensified.

I remained still. I heard a sound, something metallic falling, halfway across the space. I couldn't stand it any longer; I had my opening. I shoved the cardboard blanket aside, slithered out of my hole and sprinted for the exit—or at least where I though the exit was. The cramp in my leg still hurt, but at least it wasn't getting worse, and it wasn't going to prevent me from running as fast as I could. I'd deal with the pain later.

I raced down one aisle, then zigzagged down another. Leaped over a pile of trash, sped right, then straight, then left, and before I knew it, I'd hit the back wall. Now all I had to do was follow along to my left until I found the door. No sign of Varney. He must have heard me tearing through the place, but maybe he was disoriented.

Or maybe he'd left.

I didn't let myself dwell on that possibility. I could do that when I was back home on the couch.

I moved as swiftly as I could, while still maintaining some measure of quiet. If he hadn't heard me yet, no sense announcing my position. I was so close...

But when I saw the crack of light coming through the gap between the back doors, I skidded to a stop and crouched behind a stack of boxes. If Varney was anywhere, this is where he'd be.

I waited. Freedom so near. Yet...

Squinting into the darkness, I tried to spot him hiding behind something. Looked for a foot sticking out, or an elbow, or the tip of his hoodie peeking over the top of an old display case.

Nothing.

I swallowed, and my pulse went bonkers again. How could Varney not hear my heart thundering in my chest?

Waiting around wouldn't gain me anything. If Varney was waiting to pounce, he'd continue to wait. If he was in another part of the store, then now was my chance, before he wised up.

I visualized my escape, focusing my full attention on the door twenty feet away. When I reached it, I wouldn't even slow down, I'd simply go flying right through the door's crash bar, out into the back alley, then I'd rocket across the asphalt patch and into the neighborhood. If Varney was on my butt—and I had every reason to suspect he would be—I'd leap a few fences and cut through some back yards.

This was my town, and I had it memorized like my lines for "High School Hitman"—thoroughly. I'd grown up here, played hide-and-seek here, ridden my bike here. I was confident I could outmaneuver him on my turf. Plus, I was terrified. That spike in adrenaline could only help.

Now or never.

I counted to myself.

One.

Two.

Three.

I launched myself at the door as if the starter's pistol had just sounded in the Olympic one-hundred-meter dash. Eyes glued to the crash bar.

Fifteen feet.

Ten feet.

Then my view of the door was blocked.

Varney stepped in my way, shielding his body with his hands. Said something, but it didn't register. Too late to try to evade him, I had only one choice. Barrel right through him.

I put my shoulder down and charged dead ahead.

We collided and although I didn't quite see stars, my world shook. Through the pain, I was vaguely aware of falling to the floor and banging my head. Varney fell on top of me and for a millisecond, we both seemed frozen.

Then we started scrambling. I tried to get up, but dizziness overwhelmed me and I toppled over again. Varney pawed at my leg. I shook him off, smacking into a wall as I did.

My world spun, as if I'd just gotten off a high-speed merry-go-round. I tried to concentrate on one spot, but I felt myself tipping over. A moment later, I was on my knees.

A hand grabbed my wrist in a stranglehold. "Dalton, I need to talk to you."

I mustered my last bit of energy and tried to yank my arm away, but Varney was too strong. I swung my other arm at him, but he caught it, and now held both my hands. As I struggled, we shifted out of the shadows into a pool of light near a broken window.

I aimed a few kicks at his shins but he dodged them easily.

"Calm down," he said. "I'm not going to hurt you."

I pictured Will Ogden, throat sliced from ear-to-ear. I struggled harder, kicking wildly and jerking my upper body around, trying to make him lose his grip. No sense yelling at him to let me go. I was pretty sure he knew how I felt. My wooziness was making my stomach queasy.

"I need to talk to you. Please." He had leverage and somehow managed to wrap me up like a pretzel, him behind me now, holding both of my arms wrapped around me. "If you listen to me for five minutes, calmly, I promise to let you go." He was directly behind me, and his breath tickled the back of my ear.

I stopped struggling. Closed my eyes. Tried to regain some sense of balance. Not much I could do at this point, except listen.

"You okay?" Varney asked.

I nodded and managed to say, "Yeah. Okay."

"And you'll listen, without trying to run off?"

I nodded again.

"Fine." He let go of one wrist and unwound me so I faced him. Then he led me back to where he'd set up the chairs and gently sat me down on one. "I'm going to pull my chair over there." He pointed to a spot ten feet away, in the direction opposite the door. "That way, you'll be free to go any time you wish. I won't chase you. All I ask is that you hear me out. I think what I have to say might help you, too." He let go of my other wrist. "Sound fair?"

My head hurt from banging into the floor. My shoulder ached from banging into the wall. My pride hurt from getting suckered here in the first place. If Varney had wanted to really hurt me—or worse—he'd already had his chance. I might as well listen to what he had to say. He must think it was extremely important to go to all this trouble. Kidnapping was a crime, after all.

"Okay. I'll listen."

"Thank you." He dragged his chair across the small open space and set it down. Then he perched on the edge and looked at me, earnestly. Either he really was sincere, or he was a damn fine actor himself.

"I didn't kill Ogden. I was framed."

You and everybody else who was ever in prison. I glanced over my shoulder, toward freedom. I could bolt right now, and might be able to escape even if Varney didn't keep his promise to let me go. But my curiosity was piqued.

"Why do you care?" I asked. "You're free."

He laughed, but it didn't sound like he was amused. "People think I'm guilty, that I'm only out on a technicality. Everywhere I go, for the rest of my life, people will point and whisper, 'Murderer.' I won't be able to get a decent job. Or a girlfriend. Or anything. I got screwed, big-time, and I'm telling you, the injustice of it all is crippling. If I don't clear my name, my life might as well be over."

"Can you prove you're innocent?"

"Now, I think I can," Varney said. "With your help."

"*My* help? How can I help *you*?" My dizziness was fading.

"I watched your episode. And something caught my eye."

"What?"

Varney stood. "Okay, bear with me. I went to the shoot to see if you were right-handed or left-handed. It didn't take long to discover you're a natural righty."

"So?"

"So, in the episode, you held the knife in your left hand, as if the murderer was left-handed."

I nodded to myself. I'd been thorough in my research for the role, digging into the police reports and other stuff given to me by Ranjay and our show's crime consultant, who'd wanted to make sure that everything was as accurate as possible. The medical examiner—the guy who conducted the autopsy—had concluded that Ogden had been killed by a lefty, based on the angle of the stab wounds.

"Right." I nodded. "According to my info, the killer was left-handed, so that's how I played him."

Varney stared me right in the eyes. "I'm right-handed. I can't be the killer."

Chapter Fifteen

Varney was right-handed? I thought it through for a moment. "Why didn't that come up at trial?"

"Because I was the very first case assigned to a rookie public defender, one who didn't even know what he didn't know. Because we never saw the report. Because the public wanted the crime solved fast." Varney's bitterness shone through.

"Maybe you used your left hand anyway," I said. "Some people are ambidextrous."

"I didn't, and I'm not. Besides, I think most people have a dominant hand, regardless, and if you're going to knife someone, I don't think you take any chances using your weaker hand." He glared at me for a beat. "There's so much more that's bullshit with the evidence. They planted my fingerprints on the knife, and they must have smeared Ogden's blood on one of my old T-shirts. They said they found one of my baseball caps, also spattered with blood. But if I was wearing a hoodie—as the witnesses said the murderer was—why would I also be wearing a cap? Not my style. And that crap about me having a piece of paper with Ogden's address on it? Nope. Someone had it in for me. Plain and simple—I was framed."

Varney had five years in prison to weave together a plausible alternate scenario. Probably ninety percent of convicts claimed to have been framed. How could I know if anything he said was accurate? "If what you're saying is true, what do you expect me to do about it?"

"Show me the research you had access to. Then I can go to the police, the courts, and explain the facts. If they don't believe me, if they just dismiss me as a desperate ex-con, you can speak in my defense. If I can get you—and whoever else knows the truth—to tell what they know, then the cops will be much more likely to believe me. One thing is true: I am desperate."

"I don't know if I'd be any help."

Varney shook his head and his emotions bubbled to the surface. "Haven't you ever been unfairly accused of something?"

In eighth grade, a teacher accused me of cheating because I got a ninety-nine on an exam, and she called my parents. My mom reamed me out, not believing I'd aced the test because I busted my ass studying. I was pissed for a week. And that wasn't anywhere close to the same as being locked up for five years and accused of a murder you didn't commit.

"Proving your innocence seems like a longshot." I shook my head. "I mean, a jury convicted you."

"All I ask is that you keep an open mind and help me out." The expression of hope on Varney's face touched something inside me. More acting? I didn't think so. "Look, I wasn't an angel back then. Got into a few scrapes. But I didn't *kill* anyone. And I've changed. For the better."

"You said this will help me, too, but I don't see how."

"Are you kidding? Helping to exonerate an innocent man? You'll be all over the news, and what a great story it will be: 'Actor helps clear innocent man—the same man he portrayed as a killer.' You'll have every director and producer in America knocking on your door. You'll be known as Dalton Black, good actor, better person." He held his hands out, eyes pleading. "So what do you say? Will you help me?"

"I...I don't know."

"I'm a desperate man, Dalton. And I've got nowhere else to turn. Please, you've got to help me."

I stared at him, trying to see all the way down to his soul.

He stared back at me, waiting for my response.

A lot to consider. "Can I think about this?"

His face sagged with disappointment. "Sure, but if that sequel you're filming comes out before I speak up, it will be that much harder to sway public opinion. You have to make your mind up fast, Dalton. My life depends on it."

Acting on a TV show was filled with pressure, but nobody's life was at stake. I felt my chest tighten. "I'll let you know as soon as I can."

"Thanks, Dalton. I really mean it." Varney fixed me with a look so pathetic, I almost teared up.

"Okay. Gotta go now. I'll text you with my answer."

Varney just nodded a single time as I left him.

I kept glancing over my shoulder as I walked—quickly—away from the ZMart, but he didn't follow me.

A million thoughts tumbled through my mind.

I replayed and analyzed everything Varney said, and everything he communicated non-verbally, too. For an actor, being a good judge of people helped immensely, and reading someone's expressions and movements was an excellent way to get a better understanding of the entire person.

What I'd seen of Varney, even in this stressful situation, led me to believe he was telling the truth. That he really needed my help. How would I feel if I was the only thing standing between Varney enduring a terrible life, unfairly marked as a murderer, and exoneration, especially if I didn't even *try* to get at the truth? I knew exactly how I'd feel. Like a worthless piece of shit.

What downside was there to offering my help? If he'd wanted to hurt me, he just passed up his golden opportunity. Me, alone, in an abandoned warehouse. He could have done whatever he wanted and disappeared. Hell, my body might not have been found for days.

He didn't want to hurt me.

I felt I had to take him at face value—he simply wanted my help in clearing his name.

Worst case, this would all be for nothing, and I'd be wasting my time.

Best case, I'd be able to make a huge difference in a wrongly accused guy's life.

I turned the situation on its head. What if I was in Varney's situation? I'd be grateful for any help I could get.

I sighed. Too big a decision to make on my own. I needed some help.

Instead of going straight home, I headed for Patch's.

Five minutes later, I was on Patch's porch and ringing the bell. After thirty seconds, the door swung open.

"Dude. What are you doing here? And why didn't you text me?"

"Can you come out now?"

"I'm halfway through dinner. Come on in. You can join us, there's plenty. Mom made apple pie."

"Tell your mom you need to go."

"Didn't you hear me? Homemade apple pie." He waved me in, but I stood my ground.

"It's important. You can eat your pie later."

"Seriously?" He lowered his voice and finally seemed to notice my filthy, ripped T-shirt. "What happened? You look like you've been rolling around in an alley. A dirty one."

"Not here." I glanced around, as if maybe the FBI was on my tail. "Come on."

"Just a sec." He ducked back into his house, and I heard him call out to his mother, "Gotta go."

She was yelling something back at him about apple pie when he reappeared at the door. "Bye," he shouted over his shoulder. Then, to me, "What's so important?"

"Come on, I need to burn up some energy." Getting kidnapped had gotten my motor revved. I motioned for him to follow and started walking away at a pretty good clip.

He fell in next to me, and we didn't speak until we were half a block away from his house.

"Okay. Here's the thing. I just had a conversation with Varney, and he—"

"Varney? Jesus, how did he find you? And, seriously, what happened? Did you get into a fight?" Patch grabbed me, spun me around, and began checking me out, top to bottom.

"I'm okay. Really. If you let go, I'll fill you in."

Patch's neighborhood was a diverse collection of homes. Some were old and small, while others had been renovated into extra-large mini-mansions. The fancy and the mundane existed, side-by-side, and I thought it gave character to the neighborhood. It wasn't as cookie-cutter as other neighborhoods, and I guessed that's what gave Vienna its charm. And its high ranking in the Best Town listing.

As we strolled along the sidewalk, I proceeded to tell Patch everything that had just happened.

"Are you sure you're okay?"

"I'm fine."

"Have you called the cops yet?"

"Wasn't planning to."

"Are you insane? He probably just committed ten crimes! You can put him back in prison for good!"

"Look, I believe him. I think he was framed."

"Oh, you believe him?" Patch rolled his eyes. "Well, if Human Lie Detector Dalton Black believes him, then it's got to be true."

"I think we should consider helping him."

"Are you doing this of your own free will? Or has he threatened to kill your family—or your friends—if you don't cooperate? Like, come on Dalton. This is ridiculous." I could feel anxiety radiating off of him.

I tried pleading my case again. "I really believe him. I don't think he killed Ogden. It's the least we can do to help him prove his innocence, don't you think? I mean, we are trying to exploit his story. It would be nice if we could depict what really happened."

"We?"

"You have a role in the show, too," I said.

"You fell on your head during your fight with Varney, didn't you? We should call a doctor. And then we're calling the cops."

"You're not hearing me. I'm good. Under no duress." I stopped walking and grabbed Patch by his shoulders. "Listen to me. If my parents find out about this, my career is over. My life is over. You know how much this means to me. And now that we know Varney wants to work with me and not harm me, what danger am I in?" My voice cracked, and I wasn't even acting.

Patch shook his head.

"Come on, what danger am I in? If he'd wanted to hurt me, he just threw away a golden chance."

"I understand what you're saying, bro. Have you thought about what your parents might do if they find out you're helping Varney?"

I let go of Patch. "They won't find out. They can't find out."

Patch sighed. "I hope you know what you're doing."

"I do." My dad always said to Go With Your Gut, and my gut had decided. "I'm helping him. Are you in?"

Patch stared at me, poker-faced, and shrugged. "You know I always have your back And there's no way I'm going to let you do this alone. So, if you're sure, I'm in, too."

"Oh, I'm not sure. But it's the right thing to do. I mean, if we were in his shoes, we'd want someone to help us." I held out my fist, and he bumped it. "One more thing. We're *not* telling Trinnie until we find out for sure Varney's not going to kill us. I had enough trouble convincing you that what I'm going to do isn't crazy. And she's a lot more stubborn than you are."

"Amen, brother."

"Plus..."

"What?" Patch cocked his head.

"Plus, it might be dangerous, and there's no need to expose

Trinnie to that."

"But it's okay to expose me to danger?"

"You know what I mean," I said.

"Yeah, I think I do." Patch smiled.

"Give me a break, okay?" I stared at him a beat. We had more important things to take care of. "Let me text Varney and tell him we can meet him tonight."

"Tonight?"

"Why wait? The sooner we get started, the sooner we can clear his name. And the sooner I can stop worrying about my acting career getting cut short."

I texted Varney and told him we were willing to help, and we could meet him in an hour. He replied with a simple, *Thank God*.

"Okay, we're all set with Varney, but we need to swing by my house and pick up some stuff."

By the time we got to my house, my parents had already finished dinner and were sitting on the couch watching the news. Mom hit the mute button. "Hello, David. Hello, Miguel." She made a face at me. "What happened to your shirt?"

I looked down and pretended I'd just noticed the tear. Shrugged. "Must have snagged it on something."

Mom stared at me an extra beat. "If you two are hungry, there are leftovers in the fridge."

Patch opened his mouth, but I elbowed him before he could take my mom up on her offer. "No thanks, we're good."

"Where have you been all day?"

Getting abducted in an abandoned building. "No place. Around. We're heading out in a few minutes. Just need to pick up something."

"Okay. Have fun," Mom said. "Nice seeing you, Miguel."

"You too, Mrs. Berglund."

"Be back before curfew," Dad added, unmuting the TV.

We took the stairs two-at-a-time and went straight to my room. Patch flopped onto the bed. "Your parents are pretty cool."

"You caught them on their best behavior." I opened the bottom drawer of my desk, the one that held files, and started flipping through the tabs. Most of my important stuff was kept on my computer—or stored on thumb drives—but the research I had collected for this role came mostly in the form of paper.

Patch watched as I searched my files. "You're the most organized person I know. And my dad is a CPA."

What could I say? I hated misplacing stuff and spending hours looking for it, a trait I inherited from my mother. I found what I was looking for, right where it was supposed to be. I pulled out a thin folder and put it on the desk. "Bingo."

"That's it?" Patch asked.

"Nope. This is only the latest stuff, some clippings about Varney's release. There's tons more I compiled months ago."

I went to my closet, pulled out a storage bin full of bits and pieces of old costumes. This is where I'd hidden the research I'd done on Varney for the original episode of "High School Hitman," mostly so Mom wouldn't find it when she cleaned. I was afraid she'd jump to some wild conclusion—about how I was bonding with a crazed murderer—and put a permanent halt to my acting career before it really got started. Keeping it all hidden had just seemed safer.

I dug beneath the jazz dance shoes and the tights and removed the two thick folders held together with big green rubber bands. I stuffed all the research into a backpack.

"I was thinking we probably need a code word. You know, in case we're with Varney and things don't seem right, we'll say the code word and know to abort our mission," Patch said.

"This isn't a Jason Bourne movie."

Patch ignored me. "It needs to be something that wouldn't ordinarily come up in conversation. How about 'Jean Valjean'?"

"Well, it'll take a lot of effort, but I can try not to use that in everyday conversation." I shook my head. "I've got what we need. Come on, let's go."

"Aren't you going to change your shirt?" Patch asked.

"Are you my mother?" I shot him a dirty look, then changed my shirt.

We said goodbye to my parents and managed to escape without having to answer a bunch of nosy questions. On the way out the door, Patch asked me again, "Are you sure you know what you're doing?"

I didn't answer. Didn't want to lie.

Chapter Sixteen

When Patch and I got to our rendezvous point—an all-night IHOP—Varney was standing inside, near the hostess stand, partially hidden by a family waiting to be seated. He hadn't seen us come in, and he was staring out the window, shifting from foot to foot.

This was our last chance to change our minds; we could turn around, run to the car, and roar off, leaving Varney to fend for himself. And not just in the IHOP, in the world at large.

Patch knew it, too, because he stopped and whispered to me. "You sure about this?"

He'd been asking that question every few minutes during the drive over. I gave him the same answer. "Yeah. Let's do it. If our roles were reversed—"

"You'd want someone to help you, too," Patch said. "I get it. Let's do it, then."

We excused ourselves past the waiting family, and I tapped Varney on the shoulder. "Hey."

He jumped back, startled. "Oh, hey."

"I brought a friend with me. Patch, this is, uh..." I didn't know what to call him. After all, we hadn't been formally introduced when I was kidnapped. "Well, this is Patch."

Varney stood still for a moment, blinking, taking us in. Then he held a fist out to Patch, who hesitated before lightly bumping fists. "You guys can call me Homer, or you can call me Varney.

People call me both. Either is better than most of what they called me in prison."

In prison. Those two words echoed in my brain. I'd never known anyone who had been in prison.

Patch eyed him warily. I'd seen that look before, from time to time, usually when some creep was coming on to Trinnie. Patch as Uberprotective Poppa. This time, I was okay with it, although I was fairly sure Varney was telling the truth. Of course, *fairly sure* wasn't the same as *positive.*

"Before we even get started, I want to thank you—both—for offering to help me out. And for believing in me. It means a lot."

I nodded, but Patch didn't say a word.

"Come on," I said. "Might as well get started."

We asked for a booth in the back, and the hostess led us through the restaurant, past a few elderly people and a group of loud high school-aged kids on a group date. Luckily, Patch and I didn't know them.

In the waiting area, Varney had seemed uptight, but as we slid into the booth, he finally forced a smile and took off his hoodie. The hostess left us menus, and Patch opened his up right away—*natch.* Varney, on the other hand, kept his closed. "Listen guys," he said. "I really, really appreciate this. It means a lot, helping me out. And even if nothing comes of it, I still want to thank you."

Patch put his menu down. Stared at Varney, stone-faced. Sometimes, Patch was a hard nut to crack.

"It's the right thing to do. But let's not act defeated yet, okay?" I said.

"Sure." He picked up his menu. "All of a sudden, I'm starving."

Kidnapping a guy is hard work. "Me, too."

"I'm always starving," Patch added.

We ordered our food—pancakes all around—and we didn't discuss our mission, or even open the backpack, until the dishes had been cleared. The place wasn't crowded so it didn't seem like a bad idea to hang out for a while.

I emptied the backpack onto the table, and I expected Varney to dive right in. But he restrained himself—at least physically. His eyes seemed to glisten. "That's a lot of stuff, isn't it? And to think, the key to reviving my good name is in there somewhere."

"Then let's find it."

I opened the thick file and removed the top sheaf of papers. Handed it to Varney. "This is the report I got from the technical consultant, Bronson Kennedy. He was in charge of the detectives who worked the case at the time. Somewhere in there you'll find the medical examiner's report indicating the murderer was left-handed." I figured Varney would want to read it for himself, first.

"I remember the detectives, all right," Varney said. "But I don't think I ever met their boss." The knuckles on the hand holding the file were white. His entire life depended on what we found in these documents. I didn't blame him at all for being nervous.

I passed Patch another stack of papers. "These are transcripts from the trial. I figured you should look at these, because he—uh, Homer—was..." I clammed up, mid-sentence.

Varney smiled. "Because I already know what was said. I was there."

Awkward.

"Um, sorry to remind you."

"Dalton, I think about what happened to me every hour of every day. There's nothing you can say to make that worse. Don't even worry about hurting my feelings. They've been hardened, trust me." He wiped the smile off his face. "Let's get to work, shall we?"

I flipped through the rest of the file. I'd already gone through it five months ago, but when I had, I was trying to get a handle on his frame of mind, his physical characteristics, and anything else I believed might be able to help me portray him. Back then, I'd thought Varney was guilty. It wouldn't hurt to reread everything with a different perspective. Now, I was looking for evidence to get Varney cleared.

I picked up a stack of subject interviews—people who knew Ogden or Varney—and read through them. Based on their statements, there were plenty of Ogden-haters. Evidently, he was an asshole who thought that being on the football team made him God's gift—above the rules. He bullied other kids, both verbally and physically, and he pretty much did as he pleased with little regard for other people's feelings.

Nothing useful jumped out at me, and my attention kept drifting back to Varney. He reclined in the booth and even though he was seven or eight years older than me, he sorta seemed like he belonged with us. Maybe like an older brother, or a friend of a friend.

Outwardly, he didn't seem like he'd been in prison for five years. He seemed more like a recent college graduate, maybe, simply downing a stack of pancakes at the local IHOP. I tried to imagine what it had been like for him in prison. I guessed the first year or so—until he'd turned eighteen—had been easier. He'd been in a juvenile detention center with people his own age. But when he got transferred to general population, the regular prison, he'd been thrown in with a whole other crowd.

Hardcore criminals. Murderers. Rapists. Child abusers. Drug dealers.

What did that do to a person?

I'd done research on Varney. As he himself said, he wasn't a saint. He'd been brought in a couple of times for lesser offenses—assault, petty theft. But there was a big difference between stealing a bicycle and killing someone. A few of the interviewees had corroborated this, detailing various illegal activities they'd heard Varney had been involved with.

And several of those interviewed hadn't been surprised by what happened, seeming to think it was only a matter of time before Varney graduated to felonies. But they'd also been interviewed *after* Varney had been arrested. *After* he'd been accused of murder. Of course people would say it didn't surprise them, given what they now thought they knew. Human nature.

Varney pounded the table, and my head snapped up. His eyes blazed and his nostrils flared like you'd see on a second-rate cartoon. "Shit! I knew it was too good to be true."

"Dude, come on." I glanced over my shoulder to see if anyone had heard Varney's outburst. The last thing we needed was for the cops to arrive. Nobody seemed to notice. I turned back to Varney and whispered, trying to model appropriate behavior. "What's the matter?"

"This report." He held up some stapled papers. "It clearly states the killer was right-handed." Varney tossed the report across the table at me. "Thanks a lot for getting my hopes up."

My face became warm as I grabbed the report and started reading. Two-thirds of the way down the second page, and there it was: "...based on the angle and depth of the wound, the killer was most likely right-handed." I reread it, feeling as if someone had knocked the wind out of my lungs. Had I messed up? Had I somehow gotten my right and left hands mixed-up?

I tried to remember. I was a detail-oriented guy. And I was a righty myself, so I would only have switched to my left hand if I'd seen it specified someplace.

Across the table, Varney held his head in his hands, staring down at the tabletop. "Homer," I said, gently.

He slowly raised his head, despair practically oozing from his pores.

"I don't think I screwed up. Somewhere I read or heard the killer was left-handed." I swept my arm over the table, now covered in paper. "I'm not leaving here until I find it, even if that means I'll be ordering breakfast."

"Hey," Patch said. "I think I just saw Jean Valjean going into the restroom."

"What?"

He spoke through clenched teeth. "Jean Valjean. You know, from the show we did a couple of years ago."

"You saw Jean? Here?" I said. "Now?" We'd barely begun

with Varney and Patch wanted to give up? *Christ.*

"In the restroom. Come on." Patch slid out of the booth and headed to the back of the restaurant where the restrooms were located.

"Back in a sec," I said to Varney, who barely looked up from his reading.

I met Patch in the bathroom. "We just got started. Why do you want to quit now?"

He held his hands up. "Relax. I don't want to stop. I think you made the right call. I think Varney was framed, too. He seems so earnest, yet broken. And the stuff I'm reading. Well, I don't understand a lot of it, but what I do understand makes me think he didn't get a fair shot."

Nice to know Patch's gut agreed with mine. "You could have told me this later, you know. Without the code words. Without dragging me in here."

"I know. I just needed to take a leak."

I left Patch to do his business and returned to the table, and Patch reappeared a minute later. We continued poring over the documentation, passing each report to the next guy when we were finished with it. I made a few notes of things to follow up on, but it was tough work, reading all the interviews, analyses, lists, action items, and other background information I'd collected from a variety of sources.

As I was about to tackle a new set of reports, my phone buzzed with a text from Trinnie. "Uh-oh, it's Trinnie."

"Just be cool," Patch said. "And lie like a rug."

> Trinnie: What's up?
> Me: Nothing.
> Trinnie: Want to hang out?
> Me: Too tired. Tomorrow maybe?
> Trinnie: Sure. I'll see what Patch is up to. Bye.

I felt like shit lying to her, but it was for her own good. At least that's what I told myself. "Dude, you're about to get a text."

"I'll just ignore it. She'll believe that I've left my phone someplace. Besides, I can't lie to her."

"You just told me to lie."

Patch shrugged. "Sorry. I wasn't being literal."

Whatever. We all ignored Patch's phone buzzing as we kept plowing through the files.

Several times I spotted our server giving us the stink-eye, and each time her expression was slightly different. The place wasn't crowded, and it wasn't like we were keeping them from closing or anything. I just think she was practicing making ridiculous faces.

Unless she'd recognized Varney from the news reports. But if that were true, she'd probably tell all the other servers and we'd have a whole army of face-making servers glaring at us. And a police car in the parking lot, too.

I turned back to my reading.

At eleven twenty-three, I found what I'd been looking for, evidence that meant I wasn't crazy. Evidence that might give Varney a new life. "Guys, I've got something."

Chapter Seventeen

Patch and Varney both put down the reports they were examining.

"Here it is. And I quote, '...based on the angle and depth of the wound, the killer was most likely left-handed.' It's identical to the description in the other report, except the words 'left' and 'right' are interchanged."

"What report are you reading from?" Varney asked.

"The medical examiner's report."

"So it wasn't part of the evidence the judge threw out?" Patch asked.

"No. That was only the stuff processed through the crime lab. The medical examiner's office wasn't affected," I said.

"I was reading from the M.E.'s report, too," Varney said. "Same report. Different words. Let's compare the entire report."

I found the original M.E.'s report and placed it beside the other M.E.'s report. Both reports were identical, except for one single word. *Right* instead of *left*. Or left instead of right, depending on which was actually correct.

"Where did you get that report, the left-handed one?" Varney asked.

"It came from documents Ranjay Kapoor received from True Crime Network. From a confidential source within the police department." TCN liked to get their reports straight from the original sources, whenever possible, to avoid any chance of censorship. According to Ranjay, they paid a modest sum for that privilege.

"And the right-handed report came from court testimony." Varney shook his head. "Obviously, something doesn't add up."

"Which one is correct?" Patch asked.

I looked at Varney. He looked at me. We both shrugged.

For Varney's sake, I hoped the one claiming the killer had been left-handed was correct. I wasn't sure it would be enough to get his name cleared, but it would be a start. If the right-handed report was correct, his hopes, while not completely dashed, would be dealt a near-fatal blow.

"I guess we'll have to try to figure that out."

"How do you propose we do that?" Patch asked.

"Ask a few of the right people a few of the right questions," I said. All we had to do was find those people and come up with those questions.

When I woke up the next morning, I wondered if I'd been dreaming. My nightmare included getting kidnapped in an abandoned store by a murderer, then spinning one hundred and eighty degrees to start helping him prove his innocence. Pie also was involved.

I glanced at the backpack on my desk. No dream.

I hopped out of bed, showered, downed a package of Pop-Tarts, brown sugar. My parents liked to sleep in on Sunday mornings, but we'd often sit down to a late breakfast of waffles and bacon, so I left a note saying I wouldn't be joining them.

I'd texted Trinnie when I'd gotten up and asked her to meet me at the amphitheater park in the center of town. It was a warm morning, and we could sit there and goof on people as they walked to the church adjoining the park.

Also, I needed to fill her in on the latest developments, and I figured if we were in public, in the great outdoors, her shrieking wouldn't attract as much attention as it might in an enclosed space.

Being Sunday, Patch was out of commission, relegated to helping his father catch up on chores around the house in the morning, then off to visit aging relatives in the afternoon.

Informing Trinnie was all on my shoulders. I just hoped she wouldn't be too upset with me because we hadn't invited her to join us last night.

I made it to the amphitheater before she did, so I texted Varney. Told him I had an idea, but needed some time, so he should sit tight.

He texted back: *You mean, like I did in prison?*

I didn't respond.

I was about to text Patch to see how the gutter cleaning was going when I received a text from Ranjay.

Ranjay: *We're back on. This evening. Can you make it?*

My heart skipped a beat, then my memory kicked in. Not again. This time, I thought I should confirm that Ranjay had actually sent the text, so I called him. "Ranjay? This is Dalton."

"You're responding to my text?"

"Yep. Tonight is great. Where and when?"

He gave me the details and said he was going to email me a few last-minute changes to the scenes we were planning to shoot tonight. I told him I'd be ready.

"Great. See you then."

We hung up. A family of six—mother, father, and four little girls—walked hand-in-hand past where I sat, heading to church. The girls wore identical yellow bows in their hair, and they reminded me of a family of ducks crossing the street. Cute ducks.

I snapped a picture and put it on Instagram with a clever caption, then watched as people liked my post.

Trinnie came bouncing along a few minutes later. "Good morning, Dalton." She sat down beside me on the bench.

"Back atcha, Trinnie."

"So where were you guys last night?"

"Um, about that..." I closed my mouth.

"What?"

"Here's the thing. I'm going to tell you what happened yesterday, but you have to promise you're not going to flip out. Or be pissed at me. Or at Patch. Okay?"

I could tell by how tightly her jaw clenched that she knew I was about to hit her with a bombshell. Tough to get anything by her.

"Oh my God. What did you guys do?" Her fingernails dug crescents into my forearm. "Was anyone or anything hurt? Set on fire?"

I shook my head no. "Promise you won't get mad?"

"Dalton, if you don't tell me what happened this instant, you'll know what mad is. And there might be screaming involved."

I knew it. I sucked in a deep breath and quickly—before the screaming could commence—started talking. I decided to lead with the shocker.

"Varney attacked me yesterday."

Her eyes grew to the size of dinner plates. Her mouth opened and closed a couple of times. She blinked once, twice, and after a few "Oh my Gods," the questions started, rapid-fire.

"Are you okay? What did he want? What did you do? Did you call the cops?" She stopped and glared at me. "How come you didn't tell me until now?"

"I, uh. Why don't you let me go through it all, from the start?"

"Just get on with it!" She grabbed my forearm and held on tight.

I told her about the fake text from the assistant director, and about going to the abandoned ZMart store. I told her about entering the creepy building and about how it looked like a post-apocalyptic scene and about seeing Varney silhouetted in his hoodie.

I told her about him chasing me and about me hiding until my legs cramped up so badly I had to escape.

With every word, her grip on my arm tightened.

"Varney claims he didn't kill Ogden. That he was set up," I

said. "And I believe him."

"You believe a murderer? Are you insane? Of course he's going to say he didn't do it. Once you've killed someone, lying is a piece of cake. I'd prefer not to have my best friend carved up like a Thanksgiving turkey."

"I appreciate that. Look, if he'd wanted to hurt me, he had his chance. He gave me some good reasons why he says he's innocent. Besides, he's already out of prison. He could just go on his way. Move somewhere else and get a new identity. Start fresh. But he wants to clear his name." I shrugged. "I believe him."

"Okay, then. For the sake of argument, let's say he's telling the truth. What does he think you can do to help him? No offense, Dalton, but you're just a guy who played him on TV. Not some kind of fancy lawyer."

"Somewhere in all my research, it said the killer was left-handed. So that's how I played him. But Varney is right-handed. We found two reports with conflicting information in the files. At the very least, it's worth looking into."

Trinnie pressed her lips together.

"What?" I asked.

"You said 'we.' Who's the *we*?"

"Me and Varney," I said. "And, uh, Patch, too. We met Varney at the IHOP to go through all my research."

Trinnie let go of my arm and her expression shifted.

"Trin—"

"So you and *Patch* helped Varney?" she snapped. "You and Patch? *You* and Patch."

"Yes."

"You and Patch. Know who's missing from you and Patch?"

I opened my mouth to answer.

"Me," she said, before I could get a word in. Then she punched me in the arm. "Me! Why didn't you let me help you go through the reports? Why are you such a jerk?"

"We—Patch and I agreed, by the way—thought it might be

dangerous. You know, given that Varney had been convicted of killing someone. We were looking out for your safety."

She punched me again.

"I'm perfectly capable of looking out for my own safety. And you lied to me. Too tired, my ass."

"Sorry. Won't happen again."

"Better not."

"Please don't hit me again."

"I'm not sorry." Trinnie glared at me.

"Really though, I'm sorry for not including you."

"Okay, you're forgiven." She smiled. "So now what are we going to do?"

"We need to figure out what happened with that M.E.'s report. Whether the killer is right-handed or left-handed."

"I figured. I meant *how* are we going to do that?"

I flashed her a grin. "As it turns out, the shoot is back on. Tonight."

"How do I look? Is my hair okay?"

Her hair always looked great. "Sorry, girl. Your scene isn't called."

"But it will be, right? It hasn't been cut, has it?"

"I don't think so."

"Well, I hope not." She plumped her hair anyway. "How does the shoot help us solve our problem?"

"Kennedy, the tech consultant, is usually around. I can ask him about it. Maybe he's got a clue why there's a difference between the two reports."

Trinnie jumped off the bench and paced, tapping her chin as she did. I'd seen her act like this before, and it often preceded the delivery of some kind of theory of life. I readied myself.

After a dozen back-and-forths, she stopped and faced me. "You know, even if we determine the real killer is left-handed, I'm not sure that's good enough."

"What do you mean?"

"People think Varney's guilty, right? He was convicted by a

jury of his peers, and he spent years in prison. Just because someone now says the killer used his left hand doesn't mean people are going to change their minds."

Trinnie had a point. Once people believed something, you had to put up some pretty strong evidence to change their minds. My Great Uncle Herschel believed stuff made in Japan was junk, and even when my parents told him we'd been driving Japanese cars for years without any problems, he still balked at going for a ride in our Lexus, afraid it might disintegrate underneath his not-so-scrawny butt.

"Maybe we'll find another piece of evidence, while we're digging, that will help Varney's case."

"Maybe..." Trinnie shook her head. "But still, a large percentage of the population won't believe Varney's innocent."

"So what do you suggest? That we just give up? His life is totally ruined. If he has been unfairly convicted, then doesn't he deserve to have his name cleared?"

She sat next to me. Put her arm around my shoulders. Pulled me tight.

Her hair smelled good, real good. And her body so close felt damn good, too. Words were coming out of her mouth, but I couldn't make sense of them. I was too caught up in trying to put together my own words, to tell her how I really felt, that I really cared for her and that I wanted something more than being best friends. I opened my mouth to blurt out something, and—

"Dalton! Are you listening?"

"Huh? Yes, of course." I took a couple of quick breaths and tried to focus.

"I was saying that we shouldn't give up."

"Give up?"

"Trying to help Varney." She looked at me funny. "You okay?"

"Yeah, sure. Sorry." I snapped out of it. "Okay. We shouldn't give up. Then what do you suggest?"

She tapped the side of her head. "Think. What's the best way to prove Varney didn't kill Ogden?"

I thought for a moment but nothing new came to me.

Trinnie rapped the side of my head with a knuckle. Hard. "Come on, dude. Think!"

Finally, a light bulb lit up over my head. And not a measly refrigerator bulb. A thousand-watt spotlight. "Prove that somebody else did!"

"I knew you'd get it. Eventually."

"Okay," I said. "How are we going to do that?"

She laughed, waved her hand in the air. "Puh-*leez*, you don't expect me to have *all* the answers, do you?"

Trinnie offered to help me review my lines for tonight's shoot, but I actually had to *learn* them, so I politely declined. Plus my brain was a little scrambled from what I'd *almost* said to her. I went home, enjoyed a waffle with my parents as I reluctantly exchanged obligatory pleasantries, then locked myself in my room to get busy, without distraction. I had even passed up a chance to tease my sister Annie about the suitcase-sized bags under her eyes.

I flopped onto the bed and stretched out, script in my hand.

According to the schedule Ranjay sent, we were going to shoot four scenes tonight, two of which seemed relatively easy, and two of which didn't. I started with an easy one, just to get warmed up. Read and memorized the first few lines. But I couldn't concentrate.

My mind kept wandering back to Trinnie's solution: Find the real killer. It made perfect sense, of course, but it was sort of like saying all you needed for a perfect game in bowling was to roll twelve strikes in a row. *Oh, is that all?*

How in the world were we going to catch Ogden's real killer? The murder happened years ago; there wasn't a fresh trail of clues to follow. No witnesses to interview. No crime scene to examine. We couldn't very well put an ad on Craigslist, asking for the killer to turn himself in.

All we had to go on at the moment were the reports and statements in the files we'd been poring through. The same reports and statements the cops and lawyers had probably been through a million times. And they hadn't caught Ogden's killer.

I got up and began pacing. My room wasn't very big, so it was three steps one way, spin, three steps the other.

As I'd read the reports last night at IHOP, something had been nipping at the edges of my mind. Something that didn't seem right, but I couldn't put my finger on it, probably because I'd been so focused on Varney—back when I'd researched him originally, and again last night. I'd only cared about his physical appearance, his mannerisms, events that could have affected his motivations. I'd been concentrating on the person I was going to be portraying and let everything else go.

I'd only skimmed the personal interviews. I'd only skimmed the forensic evidence that didn't pertain directly to Varney. I didn't even recall seeing anything more than a passing reference to any other possible suspects.

Because the police hadn't *considered* any other suspects. They'd found Varney quickly—he'd been in a recent fight with Ogden and witnesses had placed him near the scene. They'd picked him up and found a bloody T-shirt and baseball cap in his car trunk. They'd homed in on him and concentrated on proving their assumption, rather than considering that someone else might have been the killer.

Which made total sense.

If they thought they'd already nabbed Ogden's murderer—Varney—why in the world would they keep on searching? Well, they wouldn't. They'd stop following up leads, stop interviewing potential witnesses and other "persons of interest." They'd move from investigating the crime in a general sense—with an open mind—to helping the district attorney find evidence that would implicate only Varney.

Which meant the clues that could exonerate him might very

well be contained in those files. We just had to find them.

I sighed. So many reports. So much information. How were we to figure out what stuff mattered and what was just noise?

We had access to all the information the police had collected, thanks to Ranjay and TCN's inside connections. What we didn't have was any clout to conduct any further questioning ourselves. Which meant if the answer was hidden somewhere in our files, we had a chance. If it wasn't, we were screwed. *Varney* was screwed.

The whole situation reminded me of the plot of half the episodes of *Law & Order*. I used to watch that show with my father, and we'd exchange comments—about the "perps" and about the gaping plot holes and about how all attorneys were so good looking. Dad would always hold Mom up as an example of that. But Mom refused to watch the show, saying it was total baloney—her words—and real lawyers wouldn't work that way at all, bending and breaking rules every chance they could. No, real lawyers took the law seriously.

Whatever. I got to bond with my dad.

That show also came up once in a conversation with Alf. We were discussing shows filmed in New York, and he said it was sort of a joke that every up-and-coming actor got a guest spot on *Law & Order*, and if you didn't, there must be something wrong with you.

Thinking about Alf reminded me that I should call him and let him know the shoot had been rescheduled. I pulled out my phone and hit a couple of buttons. He answered almost immediately. That was one of the great things about Alf—he always took my calls, whatever time or whatever day. And if he couldn't, he was always quick to get back to me.

"Hello, my young friend," Alf said. "I trust you're having a wonderful day."

"Hi Alf. I am, and I hope you are, too." Politeness never hurt.

"Indeed I am. Just watching an old flick on the telly starring one of my dear friends, Denzel Hayes Washington, Jr. We used to tip a cold one together, now and then, Denz and I, and he always told me to 'Watch my peas and carrots.' A fine actor and a finer man." He paused, and I could imagine him staring off into the distance, into the past. "What can I do for you today?"

"I wanted to let you know the shoot is back on. Tonight, in fact."

"That's marvelous news. Splendid. I certainly hope those protestors won't be a nuisance anymore. You have constitutional rights to free speech."

As did they. "Thanks. The director is keeping things secret. Hopefully they won't find out." I wanted to fill Alf in on the whole Varney thing, but I was afraid he'd react the same way I was afraid my parents would. Badly. And if any of them ever found out I was actually helping Varney, I'd be locked in my room, for real.

"Be careful, Dalton. I know I say you should be allowed to pursue your craft, but if safety ever becomes an issue, you should think twice. Caution is the better part of valor, and all that."

I wasn't sure if Alf had gotten the quote exactly right, but I knew what he meant. "I'll be careful."

"I know you will. Let me know how the shoot goes. If we're lucky, maybe TCN will turn this whole thing into a ten-part mini-series! TTFN, my boy!"

I pushed thoughts of Varney and rowdy protestors and mini-series out of my mind as I forced myself to finish memorizing the lines in my last scene. Then I took a shower, found a fresh set of not-too-badly-wrinkled clothes, and got dressed. Went downstairs.

Mom was at the sink, peeling potatoes for dinner. "You're a lucky boy, David. I'm making your favorite. Meatloaf."

Crap. I'd forgotten to tell Mom I wouldn't be eating at home. "I'm sorry, something came up. I need to go now."

She pivoted, a slow burn building on her face. "What do you mean? What came up?"

"I, uh, Trinnie needs help with something. She didn't say

exactly what, just 'I'll die if you don't help me.'"

"Trinnie, huh?" Mom loved my friends—sometimes, it seemed, more than me.

She narrowed her eyes and stared at me, human polygraph. I struggled to keep my pupils from dancing around and my heart rate even. If I didn't, she'd spot the tell-tale pulse in my neck veins. I knew that from experience.

After a long minute, she sighed. "If Trinnie needs you..."

"Thanks, Mom. Can I take the car?" I didn't know what Annie's plans were, so calling dibs seemed like a good idea.

"Sure. Drive carefully." She smiled. "I'll leave a plate in the fridge you can microwave when you get home."

"Bye, Mom."

I waited until I was outside before I exhaled.

Chapter Eighteen

Having to help Trinnie wasn't a lie. Together with Patch, we were going to help Varney clear his name. Although I hadn't specifically asked Ranjay if I could bring Trinnie and Patch to the shoot, that was my plan. As many of my friends always said right before they did something impulsive—it's better to ask forgiveness than to seek permission.

I picked up Patch first, then Trinnie, and we made it to the shooting location—a twenty-minute drive—exactly at call time. It was in some random townhouse in Annandale, and I wasn't sure we were in the right place until we knocked on the door and Ranjay answered.

"Good, you're here." His features seemed tight.

"I hope it was okay to bring my friends."

"Sure. Just keep still and quiet. And watch. You can learn a lot simply by watching. Dalton, check in with makeup, although I think you're probably good the way you are." Someone called his name from inside, so he turned and left.

"I can be still and quiet," Patch said. "But I don't know about Trinnie."

Trinnie elbowed him. "Like a statue."

"I'll see you later." There were twenty people milling about the townhouse, all involved in various tasks. Some were setting up cameras, others were fiddling with mics, and a few were seated, scribbling on clipboards.

Several scenes were being shot here. One in a bedroom, one in the kitchen, and one in the basement, so people were running in all directions on all floors.

Chaotic.

I managed to locate the lady in charge of makeup, Sherry or Charlene or something like that.

"Oh there you are." Sherry/Charlene took hold of my shoulders and examined me at arm's length, clucking. "In the first scene, you're in the dirty and moldy basement, right?"

"Yep."

"Where you're supposed to look grungy? Maybe a little disheveled?" She tilted her head this way and that, sizing me up.

"I guess."

"Wearing a ratty T-shirt, even?"

"Seems right." I waited for her to muss my hair, smear some dirt on my face, and give me an old, holey T-shirt.

Instead, she just said, "Then you're perfect as is. Go on, now." She pushed me away and switched her attention to someone else who appeared in a later scene.

I tried not to take her approval as an insult.

I found Trinnie and Patch, almost exactly where I'd left them by the front door, and we headed downstairs.

"What's this scene about?" Patch asked.

"This takes place three months before the murder. Varney—me, as high school Varney—is making a pipe bomb in his basement."

Trinnie grabbed my arm and pulled us to a stop at the top of the stairs. "A pipe bomb? Really?"

"Well, this is a dramatization, so there's a little bit of creative license involved. But according to the police reports, they found materials that could have been used to make a pipe bomb in Varney's basement."

"Oh, the reports you wouldn't let me see?" She glared at me. Then at Patch, who shrugged.

"Sorry." I had a feeling Patch and I would be apologizing for that stupid decision for a long time.

"But they never actually found a bomb?"

"Not to my knowledge. I guess we can ask Varney about it when we see him."

Trinnie let go and we continued down the stairs. "When is that going to be?"

I shrugged. "When we get some information. Hopefully, we'll get it tonight." At the bottom of the stairs, a few chairs were set up facing a workbench. A camera on a tripod was aimed at the workbench, and Kennedy was showing Ranjay and assistant director Emily a few things on the workbench surface.

I whispered to Patch and Trinnie, "There's Kennedy. After the shoot, he's the one we need to talk to. Tactfully." We needed to be careful broaching the topic of the discrepancy in the two reports. The detectives on Varney's case worked for Kennedy, and we didn't want to accuse someone of messing up, figuring that might piss him off and he wouldn't want to help us.

Ranjay motioned me over.

"Okay guys. Be still. Be quiet. Be awesome," I said, winking at my friends before I went over to talk to Ranjay.

"Okay, kid," Kennedy said. "Let me show you what we've got. Now, remember, this doesn't have to be exact—we don't want to be showing folks how to make bombs." He pointed to the items on the workbench. "Here's a pipe. You'll want to thread the cap on one end, like this." He showed me how to screw the cap on. "We've already drilled a hole here." He pointed to the center of the pipe. "So all you need to do is thread this string—our fuse—through the hole. Then carefully pour this into the pipe." He pointed to a pile of black granules in a little container. "It's supposed to be gunpowder, but don't worry, it's only coffee. After that, put some of these nails in the pipe and screw the other cap on. You with me?"

"Got it."

"Don't worry about getting it exactly right," Ranjay said. "I'll edit it all together so it looks like you know what you're doing." He patted Kennedy on the shoulder. "And I won't give out any vital information. The last thing we need is more kids blowing stuff up. Although TCN might be happy—more terrible deeds to reenact."

Kennedy made a fist and pretended to punch Ranjay, who laughed. Then Ranjay clapped his hands together. "Okay everyone, places." He took a seat in one of the chairs, and Kennedy settled in next to him.

I perched on a stool in front of the workbench and tried to imagine how an angry teenager intent on making a bomb would act. With that image in mind, I contorted my face accordingly. I didn't have any lines in this scene—they were going to add voiceover during production. Right now, it was only me, my expressions, and my movements.

"Quiet on the set!"

Emily stepped out of the shadows and slated the scene with the clapperboard, then shrank away.

Ranjay pointed at me. "And...action."

I picked up the pipe and held it up. Hefted it. Peered through it. Satisfied, I screwed a cap on one end, exactly like Kennedy had showed me. Then I sorted through the junk on the workbench until I found the string that was supposed to be the fuse. I threaded it through the hole and held up my work again, admiring it. I stuck the narrow end of a funnel into the pipe, then tipped the container of coffee into it, jiggling the pipe to help the faux gunpowder fill in. I paused and nodded a few times, clearly proud of my work. With an evil grin, I dropped a handful of nails into the cylinder, then screwed the other cap on, then caressed the completed pipe bomb as if it were a newborn baby.

"Cut!" Ranjay said. "That looked great. We'll change the camera angle and do it again. That should be enough." He directed one of his assistants to disassemble the pipe bomb and lay out the parts as before. Then Ranjay turned to me. "Good job. Remember, our viewers like it hammy. Don't be afraid to really amp up that crazy grin."

In the back, leaning against a wall, Patch gave me a thumbs-up, while Trinnie blew me a kiss. I ignored them, trying to stay in character.

We ran through it again, and I did my best to seem like an unhinged lunatic. But part of me, after having met Varney, felt a little weird about the whole thing. I didn't get the vibe he was crazy, let alone guilty. But they hadn't hired me for my insight. Actors were supposed to play their roles, and if crazytown was what the role called for, I'd give it my best shot.

And when you got right down to it, I didn't *really* know what Varney was like seven years ago. By his own admission, he'd evolved from being a lowlife. Maybe once he got his name cleared, TCN would do an episode on that. For now, though, I'd do what Ranjay wanted.

"Okay, that's a wrap. Next scene is in the kitchen, people. Do what you need to, and we'll start in ten minutes." Ranjay stood and I overheard him saying goodbye to Kennedy.

I motioned Patch and Trinnie over and whispered, "He's leaving. Now's our chance."

After saying a few other goodbyes to the assistants, Kennedy headed upstairs. We followed and caught up to him in the foyer. "Excuse me, Kennedy?"

He spun around. A big man, he seemed bigger standing in the narrow foyer. "Yes?"

"Do you have a couple of minutes? We, uh, we had a few questions."

"Sure. You did a nice job making the bomb, by the way." He gave me a sly look. "You haven't done that before, have you?"

"No. Just a quick study, I guess."

"Sure. What can I do for you?" His head was only six inches from the hall light, and his bald scalp glistened.

"I like to do research for my roles, and I've collected a lot of information about Varney. There seems to be a discrepancy between two reports. I—we—were hoping you could help us sort it out."

"I'll do what I can, but it was a few years ago."

"Great."

From his back pocket, Patch pulled out folded copies of the two contradictory M.E. reports and handed them to Kennedy.

"Two identical reports from the M.E., except one says the killer was left-handed and one says right-handed." On each copy, we'd circled the sentence in question in red Sharpie to make it stand out.

Kennedy reached into his own pocket and removed a pair of reading glasses. Put them on and examined the two pieces of paper. After a moment, he lifted his head. "One is wrong, obviously. Varney is right-handed." He handed the papers back to Patch. "Can I ask why this matters? Varney was convicted, served some time, and is now on the streets. Unfortunately."

"When I portrayed Varney in the first episode, I held the knife in my left hand, because I'd read the report saying the killer was left-handed."

"Really?" He shook his head. "I don't think I was there during the filming of that scene. Damn. Damn, damn, damn. I hate screwing up." He gathered himself. "For this episode, please favor your right hand, okay? No sense compounding my error."

"But how do you know the report saying he was right-handed is the correct one? It seems the original report, the one in the detective's book, would be correct." Varney had made a compelling case, and I wanted to believe in him.

"I honestly don't know how the M.E. reports got mixed up, or conflated, or whatever. Unfortunately, stuff like that happens *all* the time. Drives me and my boys absolutely crazy. And the M.E. himself died two years ago, so we can't ask him. I suppose I can double-check at his office, go through the archives to be sure. But what's the point? All the evidence pointed to Varney. DNA evidence on Ogden's body. The cap and bloody T-shirt from Varney's trunk. Eyewitness accounts of the fight they'd had. Trust me, kids. Homer Lee Varney killed Will Ogden, as sure as I'm standing here. And if not for that massive screw up in the forensics lab, he'd still be in prison, rotting for his crime." Kennedy had worked up a lather. "If I find anything else saying he was left-handed, I'll let you know. But don't hold your breath."

Kennedy turned and banged out the front door, leaving me and Patch and Trinnie staring at each other. I felt as deflated as they looked. What had we been thinking, anyway? Believing a murderer as he grasped at straws to clear his name? He'd seen me mistakenly use my left hand, and he'd seized on it as a way to raise doubt in our minds. Varney probably thought if he could make us believe he was innocent, he could make others believe it too.

"So," Patch said. "Kennedy was positive Varney is guilty."

"Yeah," Trinnie mumbled. "Couldn't be *more* positive."

The energy and enthusiasm for righting a wrong, for saving a guy's life, had been flushed right down the drain.

"Mix-ups like that happen all the time? That doesn't give me much confidence in our justice system." Patch slowly shook his head.

"So now what?" Trinnie asked.

"I've still got a few more scenes to shoot," I said.

She slapped my chest with the back of her hand. "I meant with Varney."

"I dunno. What do you think?"

Trinnie and Patch both shrugged.

After a moment, Trinnie spoke. "We're probably wasting our time. Especially, if it's just a stupid mistake."

Patch jerked his thumb at Trinnie. "What she said."

"Agreed. But let's sleep on it. We don't need to tell Varney tonight. We can tell him in the morning."

"Dalton," Emily called from the kitchen, shrill voice echoing through the entire first floor of the townhouse. "We're ready for you in the kitchen."

"Time to get to work. See you in a few." I trudged off to the kitchen, definitely feeling like I'd just lost a battle—and the war.

***

Before the shoot, we'd talked about getting something to eat afterward to discuss our mission to clear Varney's name.

But after the shoot, after hearing what Kennedy thought about our discovery, the last thing we wanted to do was stuff our faces, so I drove Trinnie and Patch home, and it might have been the quietest ride the three of us had ever taken.

Trinnie managed a *goodbye* when I dropped her off, which was only slightly better than Patch's grunt.

I headed for home, trying to make sense of my feelings. Varney had shown up, begging me to hear him out. Then he'd presented a credible story proclaiming his innocence. But if Kennedy was to be believed—along with detectives who'd investigated the case, a jury who'd been at the trial, a judge presiding over the affair, and probably a hundred other people—Varney was stone-cold guilty. I'd wanted to believe his tale. I'd wanted for this to be a cause we could fight for. Free an innocent man! Battle injustice! Was it some kind of proxy for fighting other, larger, injustices in society?

Was I channeling my mother, the lawyer?

When I'd realized Varney was using me, feelings of disappointment and disillusionment and disgust rushed in where hope had taken root. Now that we had to tell Varney we were abandoning him and his wild goose chase, I recognized another feeling gnawing at my insides: Fear. He wasn't going to be a happy camper.

The light ahead turned red, and I stopped. Behind me, a car eased up to my rear bumper, high-beams blinding me in the mirror. Had I noticed that same car behind me, soon after we'd left the shoot?

Home was straight. When the light turned green, I turned right.

The car behind me turned right, too. It hadn't had its signal on. I hit the gas and opened up some distance between us. These were residential streets, and the speed limit was twenty-five miles an hour. But it was late and the streets were deserted, so I bumped it to forty-five. The car behind me sped up, too.

At the next intersection, I turned left.

The car on my tail also turned left.

I took the next right. He did, too.

Coincidence? Or had Varney somehow found out we'd talked to Kennedy and he'd set us straight? Did Varney know we were going to give up trying to prove his innocence? And, more importantly, was he going to take out his frustration on me?

I stomped on the gas.

Chapter Nineteen

We were on a main artery now, so I managed to get my car up to fifty-five. I kept hoping the guy behind me would turn away, tired of our little game of tag, and motor off to wherever he'd been going before starting to play.

He didn't. He increased his speed to match mine.

But this was *my* home field. I knew these streets.

At the next intersection, I jammed on the brakes and skidded into a right turn, almost taking out the street sign. Then I sped around the curve and took the first right, then a left, then stopped right in front of a narrow alley bordering Old Man Nesbit's house.

A terrible screeching made me wince as I squeezed the car into a space not quite big enough for a car. I'd worry about the passenger-side mirror later.

I killed the lights and slumped down in my seat. My pulse pounded, and I sucked in air so fast I was close to hyperventilating. After that wild ride, I think I could add *stunt driver* to my acting resume with complete honesty.

Hunched down, I couldn't see a thing. If Varney had spotted me ducking into the alley, he could be sneaking up on my car this very instant. I grabbed the keys out of the ignition and held the keyring in my palm. Then I poked the keys through the gaps between my fingers, making a Fist of Hurt, like I'd seen on a TV show once. If Varney attacked, I'd try to punch him in the face.

I shivered just thinking about that.

A swoosh of headlights painted the side wall of the alley with bright white light. I tensed, but the car passed, and I let out a small breath. False alarm. I'd been there five minutes or so. With each passing moment, I figured the odds were slimmer that he'd find me.

A rapping on the window almost caused me to jump through the roof. I dropped the keys in my fist, and I bent over to get them, scrambling, needing to get them back in place so I'd have a chance against the stronger—and crazier—Varney, but I couldn't find them and I shivered again, and my hands started shaking, and—

More rapping on the glass. Somebody held up a phone to light me up. Still bent over trying to retrieve my keys, I looked out the window.

Old Man Nesbit stood there, making the universal roll-down-the-window gesture.

I forced my hands to stop shaking long enough to hit the button, and the window opened.

"David Berglund? Is that you? Are you okay?"

"Uh, yeah, fine," I sputtered. A loud yapping, presumably coming from the other end of the leash Nesbit held, seemed to answer me.

"What are you doing here?" He turned away for a second. "Down, Dixie. Down!" The dog only barked louder.

"I had to...make a phone call, and I know it's dangerous to do that while driving so..." I shrugged.

Nesbit stared at me. He was just about the oldest person I knew who didn't live in a nursing home. He'd been ancient ever since I could remember. Gaunt and humorless. But he was still pretty sharp. "I don't believe that for a minute. You're not getting high out here, are you?"

"No sir."

"Uh-huh," Nesbit said as Dixie kept barking. And barking. Did dogs get sore throats?

"I don't—"

Nesbit scowled. "Move over."

"What?"

"Lean back. I'm going to stick my head in and smell."

I leaned over as far as I could to make sure we didn't bonk heads. He poked his nose in and took a deep breath with his eyes closed. If I didn't know better, I'd think he was hoping I *had* been smoking weed and he could suck in a lungful of secondhand smoke. He exhaled right into my face, and I was greeted by a bouquet of onions, garlic, and, weirdly, licorice.

"Okay. You're clean." He withdrew his head. "Be careful backing out. You're parked very close on the other side. Goodnight, David." He yanked on Dixie's leash, then circled the car, shuffled up his sidewalk, and disappeared into his house. Dixie yapped the entire time.

I flipped on the dome light and found my keys, which had gotten wedged between the seat and the center console. I started the car and, very carefully, backed out of the space. This time, the noise was less screechy and more crunchy. When I got clear of the side wall, I hopped out to inspect the damage.

The side mirror hung against the door, with only a thin black cable keeping it from falling off. *Shit.*

I drove home, keeping to the side roads and going about twenty, not wanting to lose the mirror entirely. Negotiating the numerous speed bumps turned out to be a challenge.

Some level of sanity had returned, and I reasoned it was very unlikely that Varney had been following me—how could he possibly have known we were going to ditch him in his quest to clear his name?

Obviously, my imagination was running away with me. I was seeing Varney around every corner. Tomorrow, I'd tell him—with Patch and Trinnie by my side—we were done. No matter how uncomfortable it might be, for him or for us.

I made it home, and being careful, I parked up the street with a view of my house and watched it for a while in case I hadn't imagined someone following me.

At five minutes before my midnight curfew, I figured it was clear. I parked the car across the street, facing the other way so my parents wouldn't see the destroyed mirror when they went to work in the morning.

Then I sprinted into my house as fast as I could run, again holding my keys in the Fist of Hurt.

Just in case.

Mom was at the kitchen table, in her pjs, sipping tea. "Hey, kiddo." Her eyes narrowed. "You okay? You look like you've seen a ghost."

I tried to control my breathing. "Fine. Fine."

She raised an eyebrow but didn't pursue the interrogation. "Care for some tea?"

"No, thanks." I was going to say goodnight, but something had been eating at me. I'd spent a lot of time reviewing and re-reviewing the evidence in Varney's case, generating more questions than answers, like I imagined a real lawyer doing. Most of what I knew about lawyering came from movies and TV shows, as well as those rare times when I paid attention to what my mother talked about at the dinner table. I knew there was a lot of strategizing and poring over the details and reading up on past cases, but I hadn't been aware of how emotionally invested someone could get fighting for another person's innocence. In some sense, being *emotionally invested* resonated a lot with me—actors had to understand our characters' emotions before we could deliver a convincing performance.

Was I more like my mother than I wanted to admit? Was that why we fought so much? *Because* we were so alike?

Instead of going up to bed, I decided to join Mom at the table. "No tea, but maybe we could talk?"

She smiled, as if I'd never sat down with her before, just to chat. Of course I had. Although the last time might have been three years ago.

"What's on your mind, honey?"

"Tell me what it's like to be a lawyer."

She laughed to herself, a soft chuckle. "That's a broad question. Is there a specific aspect of being a lawyer you're interested in?"

"You defended people once, right? A long time ago?"

"I spent a couple of years in the public defender's office when I was first starting out. And yes, it was a long time ago. Well before you came along." She set her mug down and gazed into it for a moment, as if she were dredging up old memories. Then she raised her head. "Eye-opening, for sure. So many disadvantaged people in the world. I felt like I was doing a good thing, providing them with legal services they couldn't afford. But there was a depressing flip side—it wasn't always easy defending people you knew were guilty. I mean, many of them did some pretty bad things."

"They weren't all guilty, though, were they?"

"No, they weren't. Now, I'm not saying I didn't try my absolute best for *all* my clients, but sometimes it was the innocent ones—or at least the ones I was convinced were innocent—who were even more difficult to defend. You wanted so, so badly to get that acquittal. And if it didn't work out..." Mom's eyes got moist. "Win or lose, I got to go home to my warm bed after the trial, but not everyone was as lucky. Sometimes life isn't fair. Which, of course, is one of the reasons I wanted to practice law in the first place. To make the world a fairer place for everyone."

"What about a real loser of a case? One where the evidence is stacked against you. Or maybe a case where you think you can win, then something changes drastically and you realize you can't." All the evidence pointed toward Varney's guilt. Was I grasping at smoke, wanting to believe he was innocent?

"Why do I get the feeling this isn't a hypothetical situation?"

I shrugged. "Uh, Patch and I were having a discussion, is all."

"A discussion, huh? Well, at the end of the day, you can only work hard and work smart. Do your best. Trust your gut. Sometimes you have to know when to cut your losses, and sometimes you have to know when to fight with everything you've got. Knowing one situation from the other comes from years of experience."

Years? I had about ten minutes of experience dealing with this stuff.

She finished her tea and set the mug on the table with a small thud. "I will say this. You'll find that opportunities to stand up and do the right thing, no matter the personal cost, don't arise very often. Grab hold of them and ride your hardest. You'll be able to sleep better at night." She rose. "And speaking of sleep, it's time for me to turn in. Thanks for keeping me company and chatting. You do know how much I love you, right?"

"I love you, too, Mom. Goodnight."

Chapter Twenty

When I got up the next morning, Mom was already gone, and Dad was heading out the door as I came down the stairs.

"Good morning, Sport." He stopped with his hand on the doorknob. "How are you?"

"Okay." The fewer words, the better.

"How come you parked across the street?"

"'A foolish consistency is the hobgoblin of little minds,'" I said, quoting Ralph Waldo Emerson.

"Well, hobgoblin or not, I think it's better if you park directly in front of our house. The Morgans always make a face at me when your car is parked over there."

"I'll move it."

"Great. Have a nice day. Stay out of trouble." He winked at me and left.

Annie was in the kitchen eating breakfast. Or more accurately, drinking breakfast. She had a huge glass of something green and murky in front of her, and she was staring at it.

"That is disgusting." I plopped down across from her, trying not to look at the noxious concoction.

"OMG, after sixteen years, it happened." She pretended like she was having a coronary.

"What?"

"You finally, finally, finally said something that makes sense." She made a face. "This *is* disgusting."

"So why are you drinking it?"

"To be healthy. Happy."

"How's that working for you?"

"I'll let you know if I can ever choke this down." She wrinkled her nose and raised the drink to her lips. But her mouth didn't open, and she slowly lowered the glass. "I'm only human, fuzzface. Only human." She got up, pushed the drink toward me. "Help yourself. And don't say I never gave you anything."

"You give me indigestion," I said, as she left the kitchen.

I scarfed down a waffle and skipped my shower, making sure I left before Annie had a chance to take the car. I needed to do something about the busted mirror before anyone found out.

My father was a firm believer in duct tape, so I took his cue and did my best to re-attach the mirror. I parked in a nearby shopping center lot and went to work with a silver roll and a box cutter. After about fifteen minutes—and half a roll of tape—it wasn't dangling anymore. It was a piss-poor job, to be sure, but I figured it would hold until I had a chance to get it done properly. I had more important things to do than fuss with the mirror.

I ignored the texts I got from Annie wanting to know when I was bringing the car back and went to pick up Patch and Trinnie. We'd all cleared our absences from camp with Ms. Z, and we'd arranged to meet Varney at noon, in a public place—the food court at the mall. We figured he'd be less likely to slit our throats in front of a hundred people eating burgers and pizza.

As my mom would say, sometimes you need to know when to cut your losses.

We batted around a few ideas about the best way to inform Varney we were ditching him, but in the end, we decided we would just be honest: we could no longer help him because our parents forbade it. Sometimes self-preservation won out over *complete* honesty.

Trinnie and I staked out a table in the center of the dining area, while Patch trotted off to forage something to eat. Even though it was lunchtime, I didn't have much of an appetite. Nor did Trinnie.

"You think he's going to be angry?" Trinnie asked for the twentieth time, as if she was going to get a different answer than the first nineteen times.

"Yes. Yes I do. But we'll be okay if we stick together, and make sure he leaves first. Then we'll sneak out a different exit."

"We'll be looking over our shoulders the rest of our lives, not knowing when or where he'll pounce."

"Let's just try to get through the next fifteen minutes, okay?"

Patch returned with two slices of pizza, an eggroll, a basket of cheese fries, and a roast beef sandwich.

"Only an appetizer?" Trinnie asked.

"That's right," Patch said. "I'm saving room for dessert."

"There he is." I pointed across the concourse and raised my hand. Gave a little wave. Varney spotted us and changed course, weaving through the maze of tables.

"Remember," I said. "Let me do the talking."

Varney wore his dark hoodie, hood up, same as he had at IHOP even though it was eighty degrees outside. As he pulled out a chair to join us, it screeched on the floor, a sound I had heard last night, when I destroyed the side mirror. I winced.

"Hey guys. Find out something good?"

I hadn't told Varney why we wanted to meet today, and now, seeing the hope reflected in his smile, I realized he assumed it meant we'd discovered something beneficial to his case. My nerves kicked up. "No. Not really."

The optimistic glow on his face dimmed. "Then what did you want to discuss?"

"Well, here's the thing."

A few tables away, a kid dumped over his soda, and his father, in trying to avoid getting soaked, managed to knock everyone's food on the floor.

"What? What's the thing?" Varney leaned forward, his tone

bordering on irritation. Or maybe more accurately, anger. I had a feeling he could tell from my hesitation he wasn't going to like the message.

"It's just that—"

"We can't help you anymore," Trinnie blurted out. "Our parents won't let us."

Varney jerked back, as if someone had socked him in the gut. "Your parents?"

I glared at Trinnie, then spoke. "That's right. Our parents don't think it's a good idea."

"You told your parents you're helping me? A convicted murderer?" He stared at me, challenging.

Evidently, we hadn't thought through our excuse very well. "Not exactly."

Varney balled up his fists, set them on the table. "I don't know what I expected. Why should you help me, anyway? You don't know me. You don't care about me. I thought maybe you cared about justice, but who wouldn't put themselves first, anyway?" He first shook his head no, then started nodding. "You were afraid I might go off or something, weren't you? That's why you wanted to meet here, in public, isn't it?"

I answered with a small, ashamed nod.

"I don't know what changed your mind about helping me, I really don't. But I swear I'm innocent. I was framed. I thought you believed me." He started to get up, then dropped back down in his seat. "Do you have any idea what my life is like now? No one, and I mean NO ONE, trusts me. I can't get a job. I can't get a date. I can't get an apartment. People think I'm a cold-blooded murderer." He tugged on his hood. "Do you know I've worn this hoodie every single time I've left the house? It's the middle of summer! I can't risk people recognizing me. They'll start pointing and running. Or worse. I'm afraid for my life. All it takes is one nutjob with a gun, bent on keeping the community safe, and I'm a goner. If I get shot in some incident, who do you think the cops will believe?"

I pictured Varney slinking around in his hoodie, with the hood pulled down as far as it would go. At the shoot. At IHOP. Today at the mall, like a social reject. I felt horrible for him. But Kennedy had declared Varney guilty with a capital G. And Kennedy had seen all the evidence, not just relied on a single messed-up report.

"I'm sorry."

"Yeah. Me too." He rose abruptly, sending his chair screeching again. A few people at nearby tables glanced over. "Thanks for nothing."

Varney turned on his heels and started to leave.

Something clicked in my mind. "Hey, just a minute."

He'd gotten three steps away, and he spun around, but he didn't step closer. "Yeah?"

Not wanting to shout, I motioned him over. He stood his ground for a moment, then shuffled back. "What is it?"

"You said you wear your hoodie whenever you go out?"

"Yeah. Quite a fashion statement, huh?"

"But when you came to my school looking for me, you weren't wearing it. At least not according to my teacher." I eyed him. "How did you know to look for me there, anyway?"

Varney wore a blank expression. "I don't have a clue what you're talking about."

"When you came to my school and asked the drama teacher about me. How come you weren't wearing your hoodie?" I thought it was a simple question.

"I never went to your school."

Chapter Twenty-One

Something bucked in my gut. "Yes, you did. You were looking for me."

"No. I didn't. I would know." Varney sank into his chair.

"What about that message on Twitter?"

"What message? I'm not even on Twitter," Varney said.

I tried to come up with a reason why Varney would lie to me now. *Nada.* "If it wasn't you, who was it?"

Patch and Trinnie looked puzzled, and I thought maybe they were waiting for me to deliver a punch line. But there was nothing funny about this.

Varney nodded gravely, and his features tightened as some sort of realization seemed to dawn on him. "I have an idea. But you're not going to like it. Not one bit."

I swallowed. Nothing good ever happened when someone said that. *Ever.* "What?"

Varney put his elbows on the able and tented his hands together. "Let's assume, for the sake of my theory, that the killer really was left-handed—as the original report stated. What if someone else noticed the discrepancy on the TV show, just like I did?"

"I guess they'd realize you weren't the killer," I said.

"Correct. And who might be most threatened if that fact came to light?"

It only took a few seconds before the implication of Varney's theory hit me.

"Oh shit," I said.

"Oh shit," Trinnie said.

"Oh shit," Patch said.

"Oh shit, indeed," Varney said. "What if the real killer watched the episode, too? That's a safe assumption, right? After all, it's about him. When he saw you stab Ogden with your left hand, he must have gotten worried, because the truth had leaked out somehow. The truth that could put him behind bars for life. Now he's afraid a sharp D.A. somewhere also noticed and might reopen the case."

My chest got tight. Varney's theory was entirely plausible.

He continued, "With his freedom in jeopardy, he'd do what I did. Try to find out where you got that information and see if there's more damning evidence. Here's the big difference: I want that information to become public to prove my innocence, but he doesn't. Quite the opposite. If that information becomes public, he'll go to prison for life." Varney raised an eyebrow in my direction. "Who knows how far he'll go to keep the truth buried?"

I didn't know for certain how far someone that desperate might go, but I sure could imagine it, as I recalled the car chasing me last night. Every cell in my body vibrated. I closed my eyes, hoping that when I opened them, I'd be in Europe or Australia or South Africa, somewhere very far away.

But when I opened them, I was staring right into Varney's smiling face. "Why are you so happy about this? Someone may be trying to silence me. Permanently, if your theory is right." What was I missing?

"Yeah, why are you so happy?" Trinnie raised her voice. "My friend is being stalked and you look like you're at Disney World."

"Please keep it down." Varney put his finger in front of his lips, then his broad smile widened. "Don't you see? This is my chance to prove my innocence."

Another jolt of understanding hit me. Varney was borrowing a page from Trinnie's playbook. "You want to prove my stalker killed Ogden."

"Now you've got it," Varney said.

"That's what I told him the other day." A moment ago, Trinnie's face was painted with worry. Now she was beaming. How quickly she'd gone from yelling at Varney to being his cheerleader. "If we prove this other guy is the murderer, then everybody wins."

"And how are we going to do that?"

Trinnie practically bubbled over. "Don't you see, Dalton? When I mentioned that all we had to do is prove someone else killed Ogden, I had no idea how to actually do it. Didn't know where this guy would be. For all we knew, he could have been halfway across the country. But now we know he's right here. Which will make things oh so much easier."

Patch had been quiet through all this, soaking it in. He finally broke his silence. "Trinnie's right. We need to lure him in." He chucked me on the shoulder. "And we have the perfect bait."

Now everyone—except for me, Mr. Perfect Bait—was grinning like a six-year-old eating a hot fudge sundae.

One thought ran through my mind: Was this the rare opportunity to do right, like Mom was talking about last night?

I guessed I was about to find out.

We left the mall and headed to a local park for privacy while we brainstormed ideas. Simply saying we needed to use me for bait wouldn't cut it—we needed an actual plan. Trinnie and I parked ourselves on one side of a picnic table. Varney and Patch sat on the other side, facing us. We all wore serious expressions, and if anyone spotted us, they'd think we were having the most unpleasant picnic ever.

I started our little meeting by asking Varney the same question I'd asked him forty times already. "Do you have any idea who this guy might be? Someone from school? Someone from your neighborhood?"

Varney glared at me. "I told you, I have no idea who this guy might be."

"This guy. This guy. This guy!" With each word, Trinnie's voice rose. "I can't visualize an unnamed killer. We need to give *this guy* a name. We need to make things *personal*."

Once again, Trinnie was getting dramatic.

"He reminds me of Sweeney Todd," Patch said.

"Who's Sweeney Todd?" Varney asked.

"A character from a musical. He's a barber who slits people's throats," Patch said.

"Sounds like a fun musical," Varney said.

Trinnie snapped her fingers. "Perfect. We'll call him Sweeney."

"We can call him Pinocchio for all I care," Varney said. "We just have to catch him."

We all nodded, but now that the easy part was done, no one spoke. We sat in silence for thirty seconds before I realized they were waiting for me to say something.

"So, I guess now we need a plan," I said. "A good one."

"Why don't we leave you here, in the park? Sweeney will think you're alone, and then when he attacks, we'll jump out from behind the bushes and grab him?" Trinnie said.

"No, the park's too creepy. How about we strand Dalton in the mall's parking lot, after hours? Then when Sweeney tries to kill Dalton, we jump out from behind a van and nail him?"

"That's not creepy?" I said.

Varney held up his hand. "Guys, please, we need to be serious. This is my life we're talking about."

He had a point. "Sorry. It's just that we've never been in this situation before."

"You think I have?" Varney glared at me, then shook his head. "I'm sorry, too. It's...never mind. Let's figure this out."

"You know, simply flushing him out would be helpful," Trinnie said. "If we can identify him, then maybe we can figure out his motive. And it will steer us in the right direction to look for clues."

Simply flush him out. Twenty yards away, one squirrel chased another, spiraling up a tree, chattering like monkeys. I pictured Sweeney chasing me, spouting obscenities as the knife glinted.

"So all we need to do is think of a plan that doesn't put anyone at risk, a plan that exposes who the killer is, and while we're at it, one that proves he actually killed Ogden." Patch stretched his arm behind his head. "Piece of cake."

Something was coming together in the far reaches of my brain.

"What if we let *him* know that *we* know he's after Dalton, and that Dalton needs to speak to him? I'm sure he'll be curious. Then we can control the time and place. No leaving anyone in a dangerous spot." Trinnie nodded my way. "We'll do it in public, where you can talk to him. Then we can see what's going through his mind."

"Why in the world would he want to do that?" Patch asked. "I'm sure he'd just think we were trying to trap him. Which we are."

The idea in my head started to gel a little more.

Varney had put down his hood—nobody else was in our corner of the park—and he ran his hand through his hair. "I have a feeling Ogden's killer—Sweeney—isn't interested in conversation. He saw what I saw on 'High School Hitman.' Evidence I'm *not* the killer and he *is*. He's going to do whatever he can to eliminate that evidence. And that starts with getting to Dalton and silencing him, I'm afraid."

"High School Hitman." Click! The idea that had been forming smacked me in the forehead. I pulled out my phone, retrieved Ranjay's latest email to confirm what I remembered. "How does this sound? We're shooting a promo tonight. I could slip something in, some kind of message to him. According to Ranjay, it will start airing immediately."

"A promo?" Varney asked.

I answered him. "You know, one of those 'coming attractions'-type ads. In it, I'm portraying you right as you're released from prison." I appraised the real Varney sitting across the table. Very, very weird to think I was playing him on TV. We shared a basic physical resemblance, but I knew they'd have to do a damn good job with the makeup so I would seem older. Our age difference was only about seven years, but Varney had a certain world-weary sheen I assumed he'd acquired in prison. Not very attractive.

"You're doing what?" Varney said, in a harsh tone. "You're playing me? As I am now?"

If Varney minded that I'd played him as a high school kid, he hadn't shown it. But now he seemed pissed. "I'm playing you being interviewed right after you were released."

"All you want to do is exploit me. All of you. Make me look bad so you can get ratings. That's BULLSHIT." Anger burned on his face, and he slammed his palms on the top of the picnic table. The sound echoed off the nearby trees.

Patch froze, while Trinnie yanked her hands off the picnic table and leaned back. The bugs and birds and squirrels in the park had gone quiet. For a moment, I simply sat there. Then I gathered myself. "First of all, I had no idea you were innocent when I took the gig. Second of all, I know the director, and if you truly are innocent, he'd want to tell that story, too."

"So tell him I'm innocent." Varney all but snarled.

"It's not that simple. He'll need to see proof."

"Show him the goddamn reports."

"Look, Homer, I know how badly you want this. But we'll probably only get one chance, and we've got to make it count. If I bring up those reports, Kennedy, the tech consultant, will tell Ranjay what he told me. Simply a clerical error. They'll dismiss you—and us, too—as being desperate. We need to catch the real killer. Then TCN will run a show about that, I guarantee, and the entire country will know you're innocent."

A few tears welled up in Varney's eyes. He didn't say anything, just nodded.

"But the show you hate? The promo for it is going to help save you."

"How's that?" Varney asked.

"I'll slip something in to get Sweeney's attention."

"Like, 'Hey, dude who's stalking Dalton Black, we know who you are.'?" Patch said.

I ignored him. "Let's figure something out. Something subtle, something only he will know."

The four of us spent the next hour testing possible lines on each other. Unfortunately, nothing hit the mark directly. Some were too subtle. Some too overt. Some were downright confusing. Finally, I couldn't take it anymore. "Enough! I've taken plenty of improv classes. In the spur of the moment, it'll become clear to me. I work better under pressure, anyway."

Patch snorted.

"Sure you do," Trinnie said. "Sure you do."

The promo shoot was being held in the community room of Ranjay's condo building, in what my grandmother always called the "party room." Tonight, though, no party, only half a dozen people getting ready to cut a promo for "High School Hitman II."

The scene was a simple one. As the recently-released Varney, I was being interviewed by a news reporter. Two chairs were set up in one corner of the large room, against a pure white backdrop. A short square table was positioned between the chairs, and two mugs had been set upon it. As if we were having a friendly little chat.

I had to arrive early to get made up, and I spent an hour in the chair, getting powdered and creamed and eyelined. Which was kind of ironic, considering the promo was only going to last thirty seconds, tops.

On low budget productions, people often pulled double duty. Today, the makeup person was also in charge of hair. Ranjay and Emily thought changing my hairstyle would be the best way to indicate I'd aged, but we couldn't cut it because I still had scenes to shoot for the sequel as high-school Varney. So the stylist slopped on a half-gallon of hair product and sculpted my hair into a completely unrealistic—and unfashionable—hairdo. I guessed it could have looked like something I'd had done in prison by a fellow inmate, but if Varney really had hair like that while he was in prison, he would have gotten abused.

When I finished in makeup, Emily introduced me to the woman who would be my interviewer in the spot. Roxy was in her thirties, blond, and attractive in that TV interviewer way. She looked vaguely familiar, and for all I knew, I'd seen her in dozens of pet food and cleaning products commercials. "Nice to meet you, Dalton. Just relax, and we'll be out of here in no time."

Usually, I was fairly relaxed, but tonight, the butterflies in my stomach had butterflies.

"Everybody ready? Quiet on the set!" Ranjay shouted, trying to get things rolling. "Places!"

Roxy and I settled into our chairs, and because this was supposed to be an interview for a TV news show, I clipped a mic onto my shirt and she affixed one to her blouse. Roxy was lucky—she got to read her lines off a clipboard, exactly like a regular interviewer might. I'd had to memorize mine.

Two camera operators—the same ones who had been at the townhouse shoot the other night—maneuvered into position. One focused on the two-shot, while the other had close-up duty, ready to switch to whoever was talking. For a big budget production there would have been more stationary cameras, but for our purposes, more herky-jerky camera movement would give a sense of docudrama to the proceedings.

Bronson Kennedy lingered in the background, ready to make sure we got all the crime-related details correct. For some things, we had plenty of artistic freedom. For other things, especially in areas where someone might want to sue us, we needed to stay a little closer to the facts.

I'd seen what Ranjay did with the first episode, and I had complete confidence he knew what he was doing. Whether I knew what I was doing was another story.

Ranjay stepped up to us. "Okay, guys. Let's take it from the top. Remember, Dalton, you've just gotten out of prison and you're declaring your innocence. You've seen the actual interview, right? That's the same tone we're going to use here. Righteous indignation."

I nodded.

"Good. Let's do it."

Emily stepped in and slated, then Ranjay yelled, "Action!"

Roxy cleared her throat, removed her glasses, and fixed me with a serious expression. "Mr. Varney, you've just been released from prison on what many in the public are calling a technicality. How do you feel about being free, under these circumstances?"

I tried to adopt an air of righteous indignation. "Of course it's great to be out," I said, regurgitating the lines I'd memorized. "But I'm innocent, and for the last five years, I've been incarcerated unfairly. I demand that my name be cleared."

Roxy acted taken aback. "That's quite a charge. Do you have any evidence?"

I swallowed. My line was supposed to be, "No. But it's out there. I just need to find it." Instead, I said, "As a matter of fact, I do. A young man—"

"Cut!" Ranjay leaped out of his chair. "Dalton, your line is 'No. But it's out there. I just need to find it.' Let's save our ad-libbing for another time, okay?"

"Sorry."

"Okay. From the top," Ranjay said, sitting back down. "Action!"

Roxy asked her question about me having any evidence, and I answered, "As bizarre as this sounds, the young actor portraying me in a TV show—"

"Cut!"

"—was doing research on this case and came to me with evidence that completely exonerates—"

"Cut! Cut! Cut!"

I clammed up. Roxy looked confused as Ranjay walked over with Kennedy on his heels. Emily scowled in the background, and even the camera guys seemed torqued.

"What's going on?" Ranjay asked.

"I thought my line would be a better cliffhanger for the promo. You know, to pique people's interests more."

"Now you want to be a writer? Can we please—"

Kennedy interrupted. "This is about the M.E.'s report, isn't it?"

"Well, I thought—"

"What about the M.E.'s report?" Ranjay asked.

"Evidently, two copies of the report surfaced. One had a mistake on it, a mistake that was corrected before trial." Kennedy jutted his chin at me. "Junior Columbo here thinks foul play is afoot."

"Could there be any truth to what he says?" Ranjay asked Kennedy, as if I wasn't even sitting there.

"Ninety-nine percent no. All the evidence pointed toward Varney, and the jury and judge agreed. Case closed."

"Except for Varney is walking around, out of jail. Like an innocent person. Which he might be," I said.

"I assure you that's a technicality. The forensics lab was a disaster. A dozen cases were affected, and the judges used a very broad brush, tossing out verdicts right and left. All that doesn't mean Varney's not guilty. Just that he wormed out of prison." Kennedy scowled at me.

"Still," I said. "There's enough doubt to reopen the investigation, isn't there?"

They both glared at me. Ranjay tapped the clipboard in his hand with a knuckle. "Look, Dalton. This is the script. It's been vetted by our lawyers. If anything changes with the evidence, *officially*, we'll address it then. For now, please deliver your lines as written. This isn't a game." He held my gaze an extra beat. "Got it?"

"Yes, sir."

I delivered the lines as written, fighting the urge to interject something that would flush out Sweeney. When we finished shooting the promo, Ranjay called everybody over. "Tonight, I'll send the shooting schedule for the remaining scenes. Our goal is to wrap things up by the day after tomorrow. Then we're going to bust our butts turning it around in production so it can be ready for air Sunday night." He clapped his hands. "This is exciting, everyone. A few more days of hard work, then we can relax."

Relax? Easy for him to say.

I left Ranjay's party room feeling as if I'd been to the worst party ever. I'd been unable to say what I'd wanted in the promo, and now, instead of us being able to control the situation, we were at the mercy of Sweeney. And in danger. For all I knew, he could be waiting around the next corner.

With that image in mind, I turned the corner of the building, heading toward the parking lot.

"Hey, Dalton."

I spun around, heart threatening to burst through my chest.

Chapter Twenty-Two

It wasn't Sweeney calling my name; it was Bronson Kennedy.

My heartbeat slowed to something approaching normal, but it took a moment.

"Sorry if I startled you. Got a few minutes?" he asked, pushing off the wall he'd been leaning against. "How about some ice cream?"

Ice cream? I wasn't old enough to drink, so did Kennedy think this was like asking me out for a beer? And what did he want to talk to me about? Had he somehow found out I'd been working with Varney? I shuddered, thinking about what a burly ex-cop could do to me if I got on his bad side. So I accepted. At least I'd get some ice cream out of the deal.

We drove separately over to Dreamery Creamery, three blocks away. I ordered a triple scooper in a chocolate-dipped waffle cone: Funky Fudge Forever, Atomic Apocalypse, and Would You Lime to Me? The over-the-top creation was slathered with hot fudge, which in turn was blanketed with shredded coconut. Three cherries topped everything off.

Kennedy ordered a single kid-sized scoop of plain vanilla in a dish.

We sat at a rickety table in the back, next to a water fountain that wouldn't stop gurgling. Kennedy caught me gawking at his pathetic choice. "Yeah, I used to be able to eat like you. Now that I'm old, my metabolism has slowed to a crawl." He patted his ample gut. "Too many slices of pizza and bottles of beer."

I didn't comment, just began attacking my ice cream mountain with fervor. This was Kennedy's idea, so I figured I'd let him steer.

I didn't have to wait long. "Listen, Dalton. I appreciate the fact you're following up on something that looks...out of the ordinary. But mistakes like the error on the coroner's report happen all the time. Unfortunately. A lot of people are involved in an investigation, and sometimes wires get crossed. I'm sure I don't have to tell you it would be better for the show—and really, that's what you should be caring about right now—if you dropped this whole thing."

I swallowed my mouthful of ice cream. "It just seems that this particular mistake could be important. I mean, if the killer was really left-handed, then Varney would be innocent."

"You know, just because someone is right-handed doesn't mean they can't use a knife with their left hand." He switched his plastic spoon from his right to his left hand and stabbed the air.

I'd had the same thought—many times. "I know. But all the evidence was circumstantial. It could have been planted. Plus there were other inconsistencies."

Kennedy carved a small chunk of ice cream off his scoop and slid it into his mouth, as if he were savoring the most exquisite delicacy ever. "I was there, Dalton. Those were my guys running the investigation. You're right, there were no eyewitnesses to the actual murder, but everything—and I mean everything—lined up against Varney. He's guilty." He narrowed his eyes. "Is there something else going on here? More than idle curiosity?"

I concentrated on the mound of ice cream before me. I could come clean and tell him I'd been working with Varney. But every time I envisioned my mouth opening and saying those words, I gagged. I gave him a secondary reason, still true. "I'd feel terrible if I was portraying a murderer who wasn't really guilty. I'd feel that I was somehow doing him an injustice."

"I can see that. So let me put your mind at ease. Varney's

guilty." He spooned another miniature bite into his mouth. I felt as if I was eating with the anti-Patch.

"I wish I could believe you, but..." I shrugged.

"You're not going to drop this, are you?"

I didn't see how. Not until the real killer was brought to justice. "I don't think so."

Kennedy sighed. "Okay. Tell you what I'll do. I'll dig around a bit. Talk to the detectives again. Go through the murder book. See if I can find something that might ease your mind, one way or the other." He pointed his little white spoon at me. "What do you say?"

I smiled. "Sure." I knew it was a super long shot that Kennedy would find something to change his mind about Varney, considering what he already thought about the case, but it felt better than getting totally shot down.

"Good. If you've discovered anything else besides those reports that's relevant, let me know. No sense re-re-reinventing the wheel here."

"I have other stuff, but I'm not sure it's really worth much."

"What kind of stuff?"

"Honestly, I don't even know what I've got." I'd made some notes, based on stuff Varney had told us—other people who hated Ogden, more details about his alibi, and a few other tidbits. Nothing was rock-solid, and, of course, I had no intention of telling Kennedy where I'd gotten this information. Before giving him anything else, I wanted to run everything by Varney again, as well as see if he had anything more to add now that Kennedy was going to take another look at things.

"Well, I should probably go over it all again. Maybe I can make sense of it," Kennedy said.

"Sure. I'll pull it together for you."

Kennedy ate his last bite of ice cream and licked the spoon clean, just as I was finishing up. Even though I'd had roughly ten times as much food, we finished at the same time.

"I'll say it one more time," Kennedy said. "You really should leave the investigating to the professionals. This isn't a game."

I nodded, knowing how right Kennedy was.

We parted ways, and my phone rang as I arrived at the car. *Agent Alf.*

"Hello, Alf."

"Hello, my favorite young thespian. How art thou?"

"Fine," I said.

"Good, good. How's the shoot progressing?"

"We're almost done. They want to rush it to air this weekend. We just shot a promo."

"Yes, I just got off the phone with Ranjay. He was a little worried about you."

"Oh? Did he say why?"

"Something about losing your focus. I assured him you would regain it soon. Very soon. I am correct, aren't I?"

"Yes, sure. Sorry if I—"

"You know, I once worked with an actress you might have heard of. Jenifer Lawrence? Sweet gal. Terrific performer. Wise, too. Jen-Jen told me that, every morning, she looks into the mirror and tells herself that today is going to be the best day of her life. Then she goes out and acts like it *is* the best day of her life. Art imitates life, or life imitates art, or something like that. Great sense of humor, too. Did you know she can make up a limerick, right on the spot? Clean or dirty, doesn't matter."

A limerick? "I'll step up my game. We're only shooting a couple more days."

"Indeed. And I'll be there."

"What?"

"It's been too long since I've seen my grandson—my daughter lives in Reston. So I'm coming down for a visit. Taking the train, I am. I'm going to pop in on your shoot. You know how I always like to support my actors."

I wondered if Ranjay's comments worried Alf so much he felt the need to visit to make sure I didn't screw things up. "That's, uh, great."

"Maybe we can go out for a meal after the filming? My treat."

"Well, I don't—"

"I won't take no for an answer. Here's something else Jen-Jen always said. 'Aim for the stars. That way, if you miss, you'll end up dying and your body will float forever in a cold, infinite vacuum.' She really is a card. TTFN, my boy!"

Alf hung up before I could say goodbye.

Ranjay was disappointed with my effort? Crap. Success in the business often relied on good word-of-mouth. One director finds an actor who's good to work with, and he tells another who happens to be looking for someone. And so on. I'd have to hit it out of the park during the rest of the shoot if I wanted to stay on Ranjay's good side. I knew ad-libbing during the promo had been a risk, and it hadn't paid off at all.

I drove around for a while, first to be sure I wasn't being followed, then just to clear my head, thinking about all the things that had gone wrong. Number one, I hadn't been able to send a message to Sweeney through the promo, which meant he was out there, somewhere, still stalking me.

Number two, if something drastic didn't happen, Varney's name would never be cleared, and he'd always be a "murderer" in the eyes of the public, unable to have a worthwhile career or sustain any meaningful relationships.

Number three, my director thought my behavior was so unprofessional that he contacted my agent, who was now on his way to come babysit me. If that got out—and it would—my acting career would be over before it even really got started.

And, finally, what was going on with *my* relationship? I still didn't know what I really wanted with Trinnie. Including Patch, the three of us were best friends, confidants, partners-in-crime. We did everything together. If I ruined that bond, I was afraid I'd never recover. *We'd* never recover.

Yet...weren't my parents always telling me how they were so lucky to have married their best friend?

My head felt like it was about to explode. I couldn't control what happened with Sweeney. I couldn't control what happened with Varney. Much of my acting career also was out of my control—a huge amount of luck was involved when it came to auditioning and landing gigs.

But there was one thing I could control.

I pulled over to the side of the road. Picked up my phone. Texted Trinnie.

> Me: You home?
> Trinnie: Yes
> Me: See you soon.

I didn't wait for her response. I tossed my phone on the passenger seat, slapped the car into gear, and drove to her place.

I parked behind another car in her driveway, one I thought I'd seen before, but I couldn't quite place it. I bounded up her walkway to the porch and rang the bell.

Trinnie answered and before I could say what was on my mind, she blurted out, "Cam's here."

That's where I'd seen that car. The other day, when Cam had given me a ride back from the audition. My pulse quickened and I dry-swallowed. "Why is he here?"

"Please don't be all weird about it, okay?"

The way she said it, she was the one being weird.

I was more confused than weird. And a bit panicked. "What are you guys doing?"

"Watching a movie. Cam, Patch, and me."

"The three of you?" I stepped into the hallway, but she blocked me from going farther into the house. What was Cam really doing here? A million thoughts rushed through my mind, none of which was very kind. To anyone.

"Yeah, the three of us. You would have been invited too, if you hadn't been at the shoot." She arched an eyebrow. "How did that go?"

I gathered myself and explained my failed attempts to incorporate the ad-libbed lines. Her frown deepened with every word.

"You did your best. We'll just have to come up with another plan."

"Yeah." I started past her, but she placed her hand on my chest. Normally, I didn't mind when she touched me, but now it felt electric. And not in the usual Trinnie's-electric-touch-kind-of-way. Now it stung.

"Please don't be a jerk about Cam being here. I know how you feel about him, but I really think you'd like him better if you gave him a fair chance."

"Have you guys been hanging out with him?"

Her smile warped like a crayon left in the sun. "I have, a few times. He's seriously not a bad guy, you know, once you get to know him. And he's as passionate about drama as we are."

I'd sorta stopped listening after she admitted hanging out with Cam *a few times*. Were they...were they dating? For a flash, I pictured Cam kissing Trinnie, and I tried to shake the image from my head.

I wasn't sure what was worse, finding out Trinnie had been hanging out with him, or that she hadn't mentioned it to me.

"Dalton?"

"Huh?"

"You okay?"

"Yeah, sure." I was half a mile from okay, but damned if I was going to show it. "Just three best buds watching a movie."

"Dalton, I know that tone. Promise to behave?"

"Of course."

I started past her again, but this time she grabbed my arm to slow me down. "Listen Dalton, Cam Carter is my friend, and if you can't play nice then..." She pointedly looked at the front door.

I respected Trinnie too much to embarrass her by making a scene in her own home. I thought of myself as a true actor, able to take on a variety and breadth of roles. Really selling my characters.

So now, I'd simply take on the biggest challenge of my young career: portraying a guy who could play nice with his biggest rival. Academy Awards, here I come.

Two normal-sized living rooms would fit inside Trinnie's, with extra space for a bathroom. A big stone fireplace stood on one end, and a jumbo-sized flat-screen TV covered most of the opposite wall. At the back of the room, floor-to-ceiling windows looked out upon a park-like backyard, which was now illuminated by a dozen fancy landscaping lights.

In between the walls and windows were a couple of table-and-chair groupings. On one of the tables, a half-done jigsaw puzzle was laid out. We headed to the TV end of the room, where three couches formed a cozy U-shape. On the middle couch, Patch sat on one end, Cam on the other. Obviously, Trinnie had been sitting in the middle.

"What's up, bro?" Patch said, rolling his eyes a little at Cam. I'd grill Patch later to see if he knew Trinnie had been hanging out with Cam. He probably did—I was probably the last guy around to know.

"Hey, Dalton." Cam rose and gave me a fist bump. "How's it going?" He'd done something different with his hair since I'd seen him at the audition. Which wasn't too unusual for an actor. Whatever the part called for, and all that.

I was going to make some wise-ass remark when I remembered my promise to play nice. "Hey, whatever happened with the wireless company audition?"

"Booked it. We shoot in two weeks." He shrugged, sinking back onto the couch. "I guess I got lucky. I'm always surprised when I get picked."

Yeah, I'll bet.

"We're watching *Titanic.*" Trinnie settled back in her place between Patch and Cam. "I love this movie. Dalton, grab a seat and watch with us." Trinnie pointed to an adjacent couch. You can stretch out if you like."

"Yeah. A true Leonardo masterpiece." I'd seen the movie

half a dozen times, including, I believe, once with Trinnie.

They'd paused the movie, and on-screen, Leonardo was frozen making a weird face. For a brief moment, I sympathized with him. Then Trinnie hit Play, and Leonardo burst into motion, and he never looked so vulnerable yet in control.

As we watched the movie, every so often I'd glance over at Trinnie and Cam. They weren't holding hands or anything; they were just sitting there facing the screen, but their bodies were touching. I imagined all kinds of electricity flowing between them, their joint body heat making the temperature of the room rise by ten degrees. Once again, my actor's imagination was threatening to turn something nonexistent into something of importance.

Or was their chemistry really nonexistent?

I'd also noticed Patch texting someone whenever there was a lull in the action on-screen. I was here. And Trinnie was here. Who else could he be carrying on a conversation with?

Judging by his goofy smile, the answer was Rizzo.

I tried to drown my troubles in root beer, but all it gave me was gas.

The movie ended, and nobody made a move to get up. It was getting late, and I'd had a rough day—another in a series of rough days. I needed to get home and get to bed. "Gotta bounce, guys. Thanks for letting me crash your movie night."

"You're always welcome," Trinnie said.

"Catch you later," Cam said.

"Yeah, later."

Trinnie walked me to the door. "See? That wasn't so bad, was it?"

I think I'd have preferred going to the dentist. "I'll survive."

"Cam's just like the rest of us. Normal."

First of all, none of us was normal. We were drama kids. Second of all, the rest of us weren't seated next to Trinnie. "Sure. Listen, Varney's been texting me all night—and I've been ignoring him. I didn't want to tell him I failed and crush his dream. Tomorrow, though, we all need to meet and come up with a plan."

"Roger that. See you tomorrow." She engulfed me in a comfy hug.

I didn't want to let go.

It was almost midnight on a Monday, and the streets of Vienna were deserted as I headed home. Seeing Cam at Trinnie's burned me, but it wasn't as if I'd witnessed anything going on between the two.

Would I have felt like I did if it was some dude other than Cam? He beat me out—constantly—for gigs. He was a little taller. He was a little more muscular. He did get slightly better grades, if Trinnie could be believed. People did seem to gravitate toward him a little more than they did toward me. He'd always treated me fairly. Hard to spot any flaws.

Yet...

Was I jealous? That thought—that I could be jealous—bothered me.

I chewed on that until my thoughts turned to Varney and what he'd had to endure. If I got convicted of something, how would I fare in prison? The jealousy question was a puzzler, but the prison question was one I could answer easily: not well. I'd put the over/under on me surviving in prison at three hours.

Of course, maybe that told me something about myself. Maybe it was a *good* thing that I didn't have the tools necessary to survive overnight in prison.

With the rushed shooting schedule, camp, working with Varney, looking over my shoulder for Sweeney, and now, worrying that Cam was putting the moves on Trinnie, I had a lot on my plate. I wished I could call timeout in my life and try to catch my breath.

I turned the corner of my street and spotted a police car in my driveway. I stomped on the gas for half a block, then slammed on the brakes, coming to a screeching halt in front of the house. I jumped from the car and sprinted across the lawn, hurdling a couple of rose bushes. I yanked open the storm door, but it took way too long to fit my key into the lock, my hands were shaking so bad.

A terrible thought raced through my mind. Had Sweeney shown up looking for me and butchered my family as some kind of threat? Visions of my parents and Annie, sprawled across the kitchen floor, bodies lying in a pool of blood, floated before my teary eyes. If something had happened, it was all my fault. All my fault. Had my obsession with all things Dalton blinded me to any danger involving my family? Finally, I managed to insert the key, and I flung open the door. "Mom! Dad! Where are you?"

"We're in here, honey," my mother called from the kitchen.

I rushed in. No bloody bodies on the floor—thank God—but a Town of Vienna cop sat with my parents at the table. Mom wore a fancy dress, and my dad was rocking a tux, bowtie undone. They'd been out at one of my Mom's business functions. "What's going on?" I gulped for air as the tension in my body slowly dissipated.

"Relax, nothing's wrong," my father said. "False alarm."

He and Mom didn't seem panicked in the least, and if Mom thought even the slightest thing was wrong, I'd be able to see it on her face. She was a lousy poker player.

"I was just leaving." The cop rose and tipped his chin at me. "Your parents are right. Nothing to worry about, son. Of course, nine times out of ten, it's nothing to worry about."

I hoped he was right.

Dad walked him out, then returned. I'd managed to find my seat at the table, and I was sucking in deep breaths. Mom raised an eyebrow in my direction, probably wondering why I was hyperventilating. I supposed that if she was in my situation, being pursued by a killer, she would have gotten a little spooked by a cop car in the driveway, too. Of course, I didn't feel the need to explain myself.

"You okay?" Dad sat and absently tugged on one end of his bow tie.

"Yeah. Where's Annie?" I pictured her, tied up and gagged in the back of a plain white van, driven by Sweeney. He'd kidnapped her and was holding her hostage, waiting to swap her for me, and...

"She's sleeping at Julie's," Mom said.

My heart stopped trying to crawl through my throat. "What happened?"

"Mrs. Pilkington thought she saw a burglar."

"A burglar?"

"She said she saw a beam of light through one of our upstairs windows, like someone was creeping around with a flashlight. Then a few minutes later, she swore someone came out our back door, crossed the yard, and climbed over the fence."

"And?"

"She called Vienna's finest. I don't think she really saw anything. I think..." My father made a fist and tipped out the thumb, then pretended he was drinking. My parents always said Mrs. Pilkington liked her wine, early and often. "That police officer had just gotten here when we came home. He checked out the house and the yard. Couldn't find any trace of a burglar. Mom and I looked around the house, took inventory. Nothing's missing. Nothing's even a hair out of place. So, false alarm."

Mom rose and snaked her arm around my neck as I remained seated. "Having the police show up is a bit unnerving, even if it turned out to be nothing. Kind of makes you feel safe, though, doesn't it, knowing our law enforcement professionals are on the job? They don't get paid enough, do they?" She let go of me. "I'm exhausted. See you tomorrow. Sleep well, dear."

"Goodnight, son," Dad said, and my parents went upstairs.

I was exhausted, too, so I followed them up.

When I stepped into my room, I knew—just knew—this had been no false alarm.

Chapter Twenty-Three

Good actors are observant. We examine people, all kinds of people, as they move through life. Their mannerisms. Their tics. Their speech patterns. Taking everything in, like a sponge. The lady on the bus wringing her hands. The condescending tilt of the head from the cashier at McDonald's. The staccato delivery of the man at the grocery deli ordering his roast beef. *The low-salt kind, and can you make the slice veryverythinplease?* Actors soak it all up, never knowing when they may need to unpack a specific trait and incorporate it into their current role.

Patch was good at it, especially nailing people's voices. In fact, sometimes he'd disappear from a conversation because he was observing *too* hard. Trinnie also was good at it. Her specialty was understanding a person's emotions and motivations.

I had to say, I was pretty good at it myself—I prided myself on observing my physical surroundings.

And right now, those surroundings had changed.

Nothing tangible. I couldn't point to a particular object in my room and say it had been moved. It was more a *sense* that someone had been in my room. A feeling.

The quality of the air had changed. Not quite a scent, there was something different about the room.

There *had* been a burglar.

And he'd been in my room. Searching for something.

I didn't really possess anything of monetary value. I carried my phone with me and had maybe fifteen dollars tucked away in a desk drawer. Maybe a gift card or two lying around.

That's not what the burglar was after.

I rushed to my closet and pulled out the storage bin containing the research. Dropped to my knees and flung off the cover. Hands shaking, I plunged my hand through all the crap layered on top and didn't relax until I'd uncovered my research.

Still there.

Right where I'd left it. Rubber bands still cinching the files closed.

I exhaled a big sigh of relief and sat back on my haunches.

But I couldn't shake the feeling that someone had been in my room.

I got up and crossed over to the desk, yanked open the bottom drawer, the one holding the file folders. I kept scripts and headshots there, but I'd added the manila folder with the two conflicting M.E. reports so I would have quick access without having to dig through my costume bin.

My fingers flipped past the scripts. Past the headshots. When they got to where the M.E. reports should have been, there was nothing to flip. The folder was missing. Gone. *Gone.*

Stolen?

I slammed the drawer closed, racking my brain. Had I taken the folder out? I frantically searched the room. Not there.

Had I given it to Patch? Trinnie? Varney? I thought hard, but I didn't recall giving it to anyone. My stomach lurched. Now what was I going to give to Kennedy? How could he investigate the discrepancy without the reports?

Sure, he'd seen them. But he hadn't given them more than a five-second glance before dismissing the whole notion. What if there was additional information on the report that he needed to conduct his review?

I flopped on my bed. I couldn't tell Mom or Dad my suspicion, not without mentioning Varney. If they found out I'd been working with a supposed murderer, and if they knew someone really *had* broken in—the *actual* killer—they'd blow a gasket. Shit, they'd blow *all* their gaskets.

Why hadn't he taken the files in the closet? Did he not find them? Would the M.E. reports satisfy him? Was there something else he was after?

I really didn't have any other information that might incriminate him, at least nothing concrete beyond my feeling that Varney was telling the truth about his innocence. I considered our safety. Clearly, he'd waited until no one was home, so he wasn't after blood—not my family's anyway.

So many questions, so few answers.

What flaming mess had I stepped into? How was I going to get out of it? What if I had been home?

One thing I knew for sure. My head was killing me.

I peeled down to my boxers and climbed into bed. Turned off the light, pulled my blanket up, and arranged my pillow just so. As I did, my hand brushed up against a piece of paper underneath the pillow. I pulled it out and turned on the light.

In bold letters, in black ink, the note read: *I know you have more so-called evidence. The choice is yours: Either stop investigating or I'm coming to get it.*

My phone's vibrating woke me up. I grabbed it: two minutes past nine in the morning. Still foggy-headed from a night of very restless sleep, I tried to turn off the alarm, and it took me a moment to realize it wasn't the alarm buzzing. Someone was calling me from a number I didn't recognize.

"Hello?"

"Dalton? This is Bronson Kennedy."

"Oh. Hey." I shook my head, trying to clear the cobwebs. After reading the note from Sweeney, it had taken me a long time to fall asleep. And once I did, I had some crazy dreams.

"I hope I'm not calling too early, but I have some time today to devote to your concern."

"Yeah, uh, great."

"You said you were going to send me all the information you've been collecting. In addition to the M.E. reports."

"Right, right. I, uh, well..."

"What's the matter?"

I thought about coming up with an excuse to put him off for a while, but a guy with as much experience as Kennedy probably would see right through my lame attempt. I decided to go out on a limb and lead with the truth. "I don't know where the reports are."

"What do you mean? You showed them to me the other day."

I performed some mental gymnastics, trying to decide whether to tell Kennedy about the theft of the reports and the threatening note I'd received. But if I told him, and he insisted on investigating—dusting for prints, or whatever else—my parents would find out. And that sounded like the beginning of a nasty whirlpool down a very deep, very dark drain. Sucking my career right down into the abyss. "I seem to have misplaced them. As soon as they reappear, I'll send them to you."

"Christ." A pause. "What about the rest of your *evidence*?" Kennedy's skepticism flowed through the phone with force.

"I guess there really isn't anything solid." I'd compiled two fat folders of information, and they very well could contain something important, but I was afraid if I turned it all over to Kennedy, he'd blow it off like he'd blown off the reports.

It had taken me a while to arrive at this conclusion, but I believed catching the real killer was probably far down on Kennedy's wish list, considering it would mean he'd screwed up big time when his team arrested Varney. In doing so, they had refused to even *consider* other suspects, if Varney's account was correct, and if that ever went public, heads would roll. No, I was pretty sure Kennedy would be very happy letting things remain the way they were. Buried deep.

"Look, Dalton, I don't appreciate having my time wasted. This isn't some kind of joke, you know. We're talking about a cold-blooded killer here."

Yeah, we were. Just not the one you think. "I honestly don't know what happened to those reports. But you have to admit, the two different reports look fishy."

"It *looks* like someone made an honest mistake. When you've been around as long as I have, you'll understand. Incompetence runs rampant, and the best thing you can do sometimes is simply shrug your shoulders and move on."

Spoken like a true quitter. "Sorry to have wasted your time, Detective Kennedy."

"So we're putting this to bed for good, right?"

"I guess so." No fucking way. I wasn't a quitter. But I guessed we could kiss any possible assistance from Kennedy goodbye.

"Okay, then. I'll let you go. I'm sure you have lines to memorize. See you at the shoot."

He hung up, and I knew how my father had felt when he once complained for two days nonstop, to anyone who would listen, about trying to get the IRS to correct a mistake they'd made. Like you've beaten your head against a brick wall for an hour.

I needed to keep my eyes on the prize. Trinnie was absolutely right. The only way the public would believe Varney didn't kill Ogden was to find out who really did. How hard could it be to catch Sweeney, while finding some incriminating evidence? And if Sweeney thought he could scare me off so easily, he was sorely mistaken.

In fact, Sweeney's intrusion had the opposite effect, because if there had ever been any doubt Varney was innocent, it had been totally, completely, unequivocally erased. Sweeney's note meant only one thing: He was guilty of murdering Ogden.

An actor's imagination is one of the strongest weapons in his quiver. Stepping into a role—someone else's mind and body—requires the ability to become that person. To imagine what he or she was feeling, thinking, experiencing. To guess what motivated that person to do what they did. Or to say what they said.

I tried to exercise my imagination whenever I could. When I was little, I used to tell myself fantastic stories, full of heroes and villains, excitement and adventure. I'd name all the characters and concoct involved back stories. Kept me occupied for hours.

Now, if I saw someone interesting waiting for the bus or at the mall or walking their dog, I'd try to imagine what that person was feeling. How they'd react in certain situations. I'd sometimes create elaborate scenarios—entire scenes—full of action and dialogue and emotions. Remove the leash and allow my mind to run wild.

It was a trait I had trouble turning off. I also knew I worked best when my back was against the wall, when I was on deadline, when things looked bleakest, and when all hope was lost. Unfortunately, my imagination hadn't gotten that memo.

I had pretty much arrived at Hopelessville Station.

Chapter Twenty-Four

"When's Varney getting here?" I asked.

Patch, Trinnie, and I sat around a poker table in Patch's basement. I'd called everyone together so we could hash out a plan, but hadn't given them any details. Things seemed to be accelerating and we needed to act now, before anyone got hurt—or worse.

"Should be any second," Patch said.

As if on cue, there was a rapping on the basement window, followed by Varney's face popping into view. Patch jumped up, crossed the room, and opened the window, extending his hand to help Varney climb through. He grunted and cursed, but managed to get through mostly unscathed. He brushed himself off. "You know, it would have been easier if your house had a walk-out down here. Or maybe I could have just come through the front door." Varney scowled as he took a seat at the table.

"I don't think my mom would be so happy with us helping you," Patch said, taking his own seat. "Don't worry, she never comes down here. Just don't talk too loud."

"Can we get started?" Irritation tinged my words.

The others clammed up and nodded, while I cleared my throat, making sure I had everyone's full attention before continuing. "There's been a development. A rather significant one. Last night, someone broke into my house—into my bedroom—and stole the two M.E. reports."

Trinnie gasped and Patch's eyes went wide. Varney looked royally pissed.

"And he left me a note." I pulled it from my pocket and read it aloud. "'I know you have more so-called evidence. The choice is yours: Either stop investigating or I'm coming to get it.'"

"Holy shit," Patch said.

"What did the police say?" Trinnie asked.

I opened my mouth, but no excuse came out.

"You didn't call the police did you?" Her nostrils flared.

I shook my head.

"Or tell your parents, either." Her eyes narrowed.

I shook my head again.

"Dammit, Dalton..." Trinnie sounded a lot like my mother, and now she even looked like my mother, right before she chewed me out. At least she hadn't called me David.

I held up my hand in a feeble attempt to ward off an angry rant. Before she could get ramped up, though, Patch saved me. "Are you sure it's him? Sweeney?" he asked.

I explained the entire episode, in all its scary detail, avoiding eye contact with Trinnie. "It had to be Sweeney. Who else would want those reports?"

"I think it's time we call in the authorities," Trinnie said, still boiling. "I mean, this creep broke into your house!"

"A reasonable plan." I hesitated.

"Why do I think there's a *but* coming?" Trinnie asked.

"Look. Obviously, Sweeney knows where I live. Which means he could have hurt me anytime he wanted. But he didn't. Because he wants something. Namely, all of my evidence. So as long as he thinks I've still got something on him, I'm safe."

"Dalton..." Trinnie began.

"If we tell the cops or Ms. Z or Ranjay, or hell, anybody, then my parents will find out. And my acting career will be put on hold—or squashed altogether. We need to figure this out on our own." I swallowed. "Please, guys. I'm begging you here."

Varney had been quiet all this time, but he finally broke his silence. "I'm sorry your house got broken into. But it's proof Sweeney killed Ogden and I'm innocent. Why else would he want those reports, if not to eliminate evidence against himself?"

"Exactly my point," I added, glancing quickly at Trinnie to see if she'd calmed down. Hard to tell. "So this is actually good news."

"Good news?" Trinnie asked.

"Yep. We've got something Sweeney wants. Something concrete. Or at least something he thinks exists. Evidence that will put him away for murder. That's our bait to lure him in. All I have to do is meet with him so I can give him the evidence he wants. He shows up and we nab him."

"We nab him? How do you propose we do that? Exactly?"

"I don't have all the details worked out yet. But I'm sure between the four of us, we can figure something out."

"Sounds too dangerous." Trinnie said.

Varney cleared his throat. "Listen. Dalton is right. Sweeney wants the evidence he thinks we have against him. So we could use that as bait. But Trinnie is also right. Too dangerous." He paused dramatically, and I wondered if he had somehow picked up a few acting pointers just by hanging around us. "But it's not too dangerous for me. *I'll* meet with Sweeney. Then *I'll* nab him."

"How are you going to do that, by yourself?" Patch asked.

"Oh, don't worry about how. Being in prison taught me a few things. And you guys aren't off the hook—I'm sure I'll need your help, from a safe distance." Varney leaned back, jaw set in determination.

"I don't think that's going to work. I'm the one with the evidence, and he knows that. If only you show up, then he'll just think you're after revenge," I said. "Plus there's something else we need to consider. If we simply invite him to a meeting, he's going to know it's a trap."

"So what do you suggest?" Patch asked.

"We'll have to make him think the meeting is on his terms."

"And how do you propose we do that?" Trinnie asked.

"We lure him to someplace we're comfortable with, someplace where we can be in control. We need a homecourt advantage."

"Where might that be?" Patch asked.

"The school auditorium. Right there onstage," I said. "We know that place inside out."

"We can't do it during the day when the campers are there," Patch said. "And they lock the school down at night."

"Ordinarily, you'd be right, but tomorrow, the timing is perfect," I said. "Ms. Z is taking the camp on a field trip down to the Shakespeare Theatre, so we can have the place to ourselves. And the outer doors will be unlocked so the main office staff can get in."

"Okay, then. We know where we're meeting Sweeney." I turned to Varney. "Any idea how we'll, uh, neutralize him?"

"Leave that part to me. I don't suppose we can lock the auditorium after he enters, can we?"

I thought about that. During performances, all the side doors were locked to funnel the audience through the front doors to make it easier for the ticket-takers. Locked from the *inside.* Per the fire codes, you couldn't lock people *inside* the auditorium. We'd have to secure chains around the doors from the inside if we wanted to prevent someone from getting out. "We can handle that, right Patch?"

"No problem," he said.

"Once Sweeney shows up, we need to call the cops. It's too dangerous not to," Trinnie said. "Besides, after we catch him there, red-handed, they've got to believe us, right? I mean, we'll have solved their case for them. We'll be delivering a murderer to them on a silver platter."

I'd never wanted to involve the cops, knowing they'd get my parents involved, which would kill my acting career. But after we caught Sweeney, it wouldn't matter who knew about his attempt to get to me. The threat to me would have been eliminated, and my parents would no longer have any reason to prevent me from acting. I mean, the odds of *another* murderer stalking me had to be astronomical. "Okay. We'll call Kennedy as soon as Sweeney shows up and gives us the slightest bit of evidence he killed Ogden. And then we'll call 9-1-1."

Trinnie and Patch nodded, but Varney sat there, stone-faced.

"What's wrong?" I asked him.

"Nothing."

"Look, I know you feel Sweeney is responsible for you spending five years in prison. And I can't imagine how angry that must make you. But you can't do anything to harm him. That might put you back in prison, and I know you don't want that."

Varney didn't respond.

Trinnie jumped in. "Homer, what you went through was terrible. Unfair. Tragic. But it's over. Don't do anything that might wreck the rest of your life. Or ours," she said. "If something bad happens to Sweeney after we lure him there, in the eyes of the law, we might be considered accomplices."

Trinnie had a point. And right then, she sounded an awful lot like my mother.

"Don't worry, I won't do anything that might blow back onto you." Varney waved his hand. "Next topic."

His assurance didn't sit very well with me. But I decided to keep moving. I'd try again later, one-on-one, to dissuade him from doing anything stupid to Sweeney. "Okay, we need to get Sweeney to admit his guilt, that he killed Ogden. And it would be great if we got it on video."

"We can use our phones," Trinnie said. "That should work, right?"

"I'm on board with the video," Patch said. "But let's not take any chances. The lighting might be an issue, and we can't get too close to Sweeney. Why don't we get someone who knows what they're doing to take the video?"

"A professional? We can't just call Videos 'R' Us to come film this thing," Trinnie said.

"I know someone who can do it and who will be completely discreet," Patch said.

"Who?" I asked, but her name came to me right before Patch said it.

"Rizzo. She's into that stuff. Goes into work with her mom sometimes to work with their equipment. She'd help us out."

Trinnie smiled at Patch, but didn't say anything. I tried not to smile, and spoke. "I don't know about that. The fewer people involved, the better."

"I'll help her set up ahead of time. We'll stay up on the catwalk, out of the way. Sweeney will never even know she's there."

"I don't know..."

"She knows what she's doing. Come on, I'll take full responsibility. Make sure she's okay," Patch said.

Trinnie's smile grew.

It would be nice to have a professional taking video. I had a feeling Trinnie, Patch, and I would be busy helping Varney occupy Sweeney until Kennedy arrived. "It's okay with me."

Trinnie and Varney voiced their approval.

"Okay then. Patch, why don't you bring her up to speed and make sure she's got everything she needs?" I added quickly, "For taking video, I mean."

"Got it," Patch said, blushing just a little.

All this talk about evidence once again reminded me of my mother, the lawyer, putting together a case to put some crook behind bars. "Look, guys, I think it can work. But we all need to buy into it, or we shouldn't do it."

Varney nodded once and crossed his arms. "You know I'm in."

Patch and Trinnie exchanged glances, and for a moment, it looked as if they were trying to communicate telepathically. Then they both turned to me.

"Okay, I'm in," Trinnie said.

"Me, too," Patch said. "I'm in. Although I think we're all a little crazy, I'm in."

I appraised our little group, locking eyes with everybody in turn. "Last chance to exit, stage right. If anybody wants to drop out, now's the time. No hard feelings."

I waited a moment to give someone a chance to get up and walk out, but I knew nobody was going anywhere.

Something unspoken passed between us, then the moment dissolved.

"Now, are there any questions? Anything we haven't covered?"

"Just one," Patch said. "How are we going to lure Sweeney to the school auditorium at the appropriate time tomorrow?"

That assignment belonged to Varney and me.

Chapter Twenty-Five

I wanted to spend the rest of the afternoon and evening with Trinnie and Patch, getting ready, mentally, for the big day tomorrow. But I couldn't. I was tied up all evening completing the shoot. I knew I'd have a tough time concentrating, knowing what was in store, but I tried not to think of the million things that could go wrong, and instead really, really focused on the here and now. Being teenage Varney. Acting like a murderer. Even if he *wasn't* really a murderer. I guessed that was why they called all this stuff acting.

Somehow, Ranjay had secured us space at a local private school—a different from the one where the protestors had showed up. We had three critical scenes to shoot, and then we'd be finished—the actors, anyway. The production team would be logging serious hours between now and the Sunday airtime.

When I arrived, Alf was already busy schmoozing with Ranjay and Emily. He wore black slacks and a pink and purple silk shirt with matching scarf, although it was close to eighty-five degrees outside. On his feet he sported his customary baby-blue Chucks. As he talked, he played with his gold-tipped cane with the carved wooden handle. I stepped up to them and caught Ranjay in mid-laugh.

"Hey there, Dalton," Ranjay said. "Alfred was just telling a great show-biz story."

"Hello, there, young Mr. Black." Alf gathered me up in a hug.

Somehow the tail end of his scarf ended up in my mouth, so I spit it out before answering. "Hey, Alf. Thanks for coming."

"My favorite actor finishing up a tour de force? Wouldn't miss it for the world."

"I hate to spoil your reunion, but Dalton, they're ready for you in makeup," Emily said, trying to flex her assistant-director muscle. "Maybe you can catch up after the shoot."

"Works for me," Alf said. "I'll simply blend into the background. You won't even notice me."

Had he looked in a mirror lately? "Okay, Alf. We can talk after I'm finished."

"You bet. Break a leg, son!"

We had three scenes left to film, and the first two went great—just a couple of retakes. Before the final scene, Ranjay called for the actors to huddle up. "Okay, guys, one more to go. Let's make this one the best yet. Varney, don't hold anything back. You really hate Ogden. Remember, this happens about six months before you kill him."

I didn't point out that I didn't think Varney had killed Ogden. I just went with the flow. Acting.

Ranjay turned to the kid playing Ogden, a guy named Holden. "And you play this like the asswipe Ogden was, okay? I want to see a lot of intensity here, on both your parts. Remember, after this scene, you can go home and relax." He clapped his hands like a quarterback leaving the huddle. "Any questions?"

Holden and I shook our heads.

"Great! Then let's get this thing done."

Ranjay got us set up. We were in school, outside the locker rooms. Football practice had just ended, and I—Varney—was waiting for Ogden to come out. I'd sold him some weed earlier, and he hadn't paid me the full amount for the sale, so I'd extended some credit. Now I'd come to get the balance due.

"Okay?" Ranjay asked us, encouragement in his voice. "Ogden, you treat him like an inconvenience. You're so above him. And Varney, you're doubly pissed off. You want your money and you're tired of being treated like a scumbag."

I nodded, trying to channel my anger for Sweeney into my role as Varney. I felt my pulse pick up speed as I thought of Sweeney breaking into my house. I didn't think I'd have any trouble acting pissed in this scene.

"Okay, everyone," Ranjay said, backing out of the way. "Places."

Ogden disappeared behind the locker-room door. I slouched against the wall, backpack at my feet.

Across from me, the two camera operators got ready, while Emily waited for everyone to stop moving. When they did, she swooped in and slated. "Hallway outside locker room. Scene Eighteen. Take One."

She scooted away, and Ranjay called out, "Action."

The camera focused on me, and I tried to project anger and anxiety, along with some teenage indifference. A moment later, the locker-room door opened and Ogden came bursting out. I pushed myself off the wall and blocked Ogden's path.

"What do you want?" Ogden asked.

"You know damn well what I want," I said, sneering a bit for the camera, which had come in for a tight shot.

"Your money? I told you, I'm a little short right now. You'll get it, man. You'll get it." Ogden tried to step around me, but I moved over so he couldn't get by.

I jutted my chin at him. "You owe me, and you said you'd have it today. Come on, pay up. I'm not running a charity here."

"What is it with you guys, anyway?"

"Us guys? It's only me standing here."

Ogden waved his hand. "You guys. Burnouts. So untrusting. So paranoid. I told you, I'll get you your money when I get some. Surely you're not down to your last ten bucks." Ogden smiled. "Or are you trying to make some kind of point here? Stand on some kind of principle? Burnout-versus-jock kind of thing?" He stood taller, dwarfing me by about five inches.

"Just business. I sell you product. You pay me money. How

the world works." I narrowed my eyes, careful not to scowl directly into the camera on my right.

"For the last time, you'll get your money. Next week, I promise." Ogden hitched up his backpack and, once again, tried to get around me.

This time, though, I pushed him and he stumbled into the wall. Ogden whirled around, fire in his eyes, and for a moment, I actually felt scared. Holden was good, but he hadn't shown this intensity during our fifteen-minute rehearsal the other day.

"You're messing with the wrong guy." Ogden peeled off his backpack and tossed it aside. Took a fighter's stance, fists ready.

I shrugged off my pack too, then reached into my pocket and pulled out a knife. Flicked it open. It was about six inches long and nasty-looking, but it was just a prop, so it wasn't sharp. I thought about the knife in the evidence list from Varney's case file—a regular Swiss Army knife with a three-inch blade and a plastic toothpick. But that wouldn't be as dramatic as the tactical knife I held, so...artistic license. Which should have been called artistic *bullshit*.

"What are you going to do with that thing?" Ogden asked, smirking a bit. "Cut me?"

"I want my money."

"You try anything, I'll kick your ass so fast you won't even be able to yell before you're out cold. Maybe I'll cut out your kidney while I'm at it." He crouched and held his arms out. "Come on, man. Make your move."

The script called for me to say something nasty, then lunge at Ogden, leading right into a fight. After some tussling around, Ogden finally would kick my ass, disarming me in the process. This confrontation was supposed to be one of the motivating factors that led Varney to kill Ogden. But I was sure it was all a lie, and so many conflicting thoughts and feelings bounced around in my head that I couldn't remember my next line. So I improvised.

"I, uh, I want my money, asshole." I waved the knife, but

didn't attack. I fought to remember which hand I should use, my right or my left. As Varney or as Sweeney? Go with the truth, or portray Varney as Varney?

Either way, I didn't know my line, so I just danced, jabbing the knife in the air. I switched it from hand to hand, just to cover all my bases.

Ogden eyed me and I knew he was wondering what the heck was going on.

I dug deep into my memory, searching for my line, came up empty. Vamped. "My money. Let's have it, douchebag."

The faint flicker of indecision in Ogden's expression had turned to outright confusion, but he ad-libbed right back at me. "Come on, loser. If you've got any balls, make your move."

I still couldn't remember my line, so I just lunged, catching Ogden off guard. I was supposed to miss him with the knife, but since I'd messed up my line, he didn't get the right cue to dodge aside, and the knife stabbed him squarely in the chest. If it had been a real knife, Ogden—Holden—would certainly have been dead.

Although the actor's rule was to always keep going until the director yelled, "Cut," both Holden and I straightened up, knowing we'd have to shoot another take for sure. We simply waited for the inevitable. We didn't have to wait long.

"Cut!" Ranjay rushed over, clipboard in hand. He ignored Holden and pulled the screwup—me—aside.

Before he could open his mouth, I took responsibility. "My fault," I said. "I blew the line."

"Yeah, you did. But don't sweat it. Everything was good up until then." He directed his next question at me. "Need a minute?"

What I needed was to act professional. After my wayward attempt to ad-lib the promo spot, I couldn't afford any more major mess-ups. "No. No, let's go."

"Okay, then." Ranjay consulted his clipboard as he backed out of the shot. "Let's take it right as Varney pulls his knife.

Places, everyone!"

I shoved the knife back into my pocket and took my stance.

Emily slated again. "Take two."

"Action," Ranjay said, pointing at me.

I took a deep breath and pulled the knife from my pocket, but all I could think of was how ridiculous it would have been if, in real life, Varney had challenged Ogden with a lame Swiss Army knife. What else had the producers and writers taken wild liberties with? What had happened to the truth? Didn't that count for anything?

I thought about the scene where I'd created the pipe bomb. Although the components for making it were found in Varney's parents' basement, there had been no indication Varney had actually even *considered* making a bomb. In fact, those materials probably could be found in most people's basements and garages. Obviously, the writers thought pipe bombs would get better ratings. In our version, the only casualty was the truth.

My stomach soured. My head spun. I had trouble focusing.

I held up my hand. "Sorry, sorry. I...I guess I do need a minute."

Holden flashed me a *Dude!* look, then turned away to check his phone. Off to the side, I noticed Alf whispering something to Ranjay. Then it was Alf, not Ranjay, who came over to talk to me.

"You okay, son?"

I wasn't exactly sure how to answer that, so I shrugged. I may have wiped a tear away from the corner of one eye.

Alf placed a hand on my shoulder. "Sometimes portraying violent actions can be unsettling. Especially when they involve others about your age."

"I don't know what the problem is. It kinda just hit me."

Alf handed me an unopened bottle of water. "Here. This might help."

I took the bottle, unscrewed the top, and took a few gulps. Backhanded a few drops of water from my chin and gave the bottle back to Alf. I couldn't say I felt any better. Varney was getting railroaded and participating in this fiction didn't feel right. I felt as if I were conspiring against him myself, and in one very real sense, I was. "I'm not sure I can continue."

One of Alf's bushy white eyebrows jiggled. "You've never had this problem before, have you? You've always come through splendidly."

I've never been asked to portray something as real that I believed to be so wrong. "Nope. Never had this problem before."

"This is the last part of the last scene, Dalton. Wrap this up and you can take as much time as you need to regroup. And regroup you should. Playing a teenage murderer is no easy feat. My best advice: empty your mind of any negative thoughts and push through. I think you'll be glad you did when this is all over."

I knew Alf was right. I'd already finished ninety-five percent of the shoot, and Ranjay and the rest of TCN was going to air this show, whether or not I finished this final scene. If I flaked out now, my career would take a hit. I'd be the guy who couldn't quite finish. The guy who folded when the going got tough.

I thought about tomorrow's showdown with Sweeney. What if I quit then?

One thought kept me from giving up entirely: I *could* redeem myself, while at the same time killing this truth-challenged episode. Simply catch Sweeney and force Ranjay to reshoot "High School Hitman II," using the truth. Selfishly, I knew that if I didn't finish this scene now, Ranjay might just find a way to film the next episode—the one exonerating Varney—without me.

I sucked in a deep breath and steeled myself to soldier on. For the good of Varney, for the good of my career, and for a concept as simple as the truth. "Okay, Alf. I'm ready now. Let's do it."

"Atta boy!" A look of relief washed over Alf's face, and he flashed me a mouth full of brilliantly white, capped teeth, before he spun on his heels and returned to where Ranjay stood observing our little agent-actor chat. A few whispers later, and Ranjay wore his own smile.

"Okay, then. Places everyone."

Emily called out, "Take three," and we ran through the rest of the scene. Holden and I nailed every remaining line, and when we finished, every single person—cast, crew, Ranjay, Kennedy, Emily, and Alf all sported big grins.

We'd done it. "High School Hitman II" was a wrap.

Chapter Twenty-Six

All in all—despite my little screwup—it felt like the best performance I'd given yet. We'd nailed it all so perfectly that, after we wrapped, you could feel everyone practically vibrating. I felt like I often did after a great opening night—adrenaline pumping through my veins. I figured I'd have a tough time falling asleep tonight, especially with tomorrow's showdown looming.

Before people began drifting away, Ranjay assembled the cast and crew in the front lobby, right outside the school's main office. I'd avoided Kennedy the entire night, instead spending all my free time during breaks listening to Alf regale anyone he could corner with his tales of stage and screen. I wasn't sure what his middle name was, but it should have been Namedropper.

"Gather around, people!" Ranjay clapped his hands, and eventually, all the actors and techies quieted down. I stood in the front of the group, next to Alf. "First, I'd like to thank everyone for their hard work. Understandably, with the rushed schedule and the timeliness of the subject matter, this was a difficult shoot, but we came through with flying colors. I'm especially proud of how we rebounded after the protesters interrupted us. Every single one of you deserves special congratulations on a job well done." He clapped, and then a few more people clapped, until finally everyone was clapping and hollering and high-fiving each other, as if we'd won the Super Bowl.

Then Emily started screeching at us to settle down. It took a couple of minutes until the celebrating stopped, and when it did, she forced a smile. "I'd like to say a few words, too. Ranjay is right—you all did a terrific job bringing this case to life. For that you should be congratulated. I'd like to wish everyone good luck in their future endeavors. It was nice working with all of you."

This time, no one cheered. Must have been her tone. Finally, Ranjay clapped to fill the awkward silence, and everyone joined in with polite golf applause.

Kennedy stepped forward. Cleared his throat. "Now, I feel I must say a few things, for your own benefit. It's come to my attention that Homer Lee Varney himself has been sniffing around. For what reason, I have no idea." Kennedy turned his head and seemed to stare in my direction.

Several people gasped.

"If he does approach you, do not engage with him. The courts, in their wisdom, saw fit to let this guy loose, but that doesn't mean you have to give him the time of day. My best advice is to politely decline, and do your best to ignore him. However, if he even makes the *tiniest* threatening gesture, you should call the police. I still have plenty of friends on the force, so if you tell the dispatcher you know Bronson Kennedy, you'll get a very quick response."

One minute, everyone was celebrating. Two minutes later, everyone was quaking with fear. I resisted the urge to stand up and tell everyone Homer Lee Varney wasn't the problem, that it was the real killer they should be concerned with, but that didn't seem like a good solution. A boogeyman with a temper and a sharp knife was a boogeyman with a temper and a sharp knife, no matter what his name was.

No one said anything for the longest time, so Ranjay stepped back up. "Okay, then. Great job everyone. Tell your friends to watch it on Sunday."

The crowd dispersed, and Alf pulled me aside. "That's somewhat concerning, a killer stalking you and your fellow actors. I certainly hope he hasn't approached you."

"Approached me? Why would you think that?" My voice cracked.

Alf tapped the handle of his cane against his chin. "I see. Perhaps we should go somewhere more private to discuss matters."

"What matters?"

"My boy, I was a professional actor for forty years. A keen observer. An astute judge of people. And those skills serve me well now. I know which directors and producers like to gab, and I know which ones prefer to get right down to business. I know what a casting director is thinking, more times than not, just by how they speak to me. I read people like a book, and right now, your face is a horror novel. A terrifying one."

I didn't know how to respond, but I sure didn't want to talk about it there. If Kennedy found out, I'd be in big trouble—and it would completely jeopardize our plan to catch Sweeney.

"Sure, Alf. I don't really know what you're talking about, but we can discuss it at dinner." Had I been that transparent? Some actor.

"Splendid. Let me just use the little boy's room, and I'll be ready to go." Alf strode away.

I watched as the crew stowed their equipment, and nearby Ranjay, Kennedy, and Emily huddled together in a corner. The Brain Trust.

My phone buzzed with a text from Varney.

> Varney: Are you finished?
> Me: Yes.
> Varney: I need to talk to you. In person. Now.

Not a good sign. I texted back: Just wrapping up here, but I've got dinner with Alf. How about in an hour?

> Varney: Actually...now works for me.

Me: What happened?

"Nothing happened," Varney said, standing at my shoulder.

I practically jumped out of my shoes. "What the hell are you doing here?" I grabbed him by the sleeve of his hoodie and tried to drag him down the hall, out the front door. He didn't budge. "You can't be here! If someone sees you..." I was trying to whisper, but I felt my voice rise, right along with my terror.

How had Varney known where the shoot was? What was so urgent? A dozen questions sprang to mind, but there was no time for that now. I had to make sure nobody spotted Varney, or we would be in deep shit.

I managed to turn Varney around so his back was to Kennedy and the others. Luckily, Varney's hood threw most of his face into shadows.

But it didn't obscure his creepy grin.

"What's going on?" I asked, keeping my eyes focused on Kennedy and Ranjay, who were not ten yards away, saying goodbye to Emily. Pretty soon, they'd notice me standing here and come over to say goodbye to me. "Can't we discuss whatever it is someplace else?"

"I couldn't take it any longer, Dalton. I'm sorry if I'm messing things up. But my story deserves to be told, and who better to tell it to than the cop who was in charge of the investigation and the director exploiting my tragedy?"

"You can't talk to them! What about our plan to catch Sweeney? You could totally wreck that." My heart threatened to break through my chest walls.

"I'll explain to them about all the fake evidence. There's just too much of it to ignore. When I was in prison, no one would even listen to me, let alone believe what I was saying, because they thought I was just desperate to get out. But now that I *am* out, maybe they'll take me seriously."

"I don't think that's a good idea."

"If you were in my shoes, and your reputation, and the rest

of your life depended on it, you'd do the same thing."

I wasn't sure about that, and although I sort of followed Varney's logic, I didn't see how having some kind of confrontation in this school hallway would cause anyone to take him more seriously. "Let's talk about this. With Patch and Trinnie. Someplace else." I grabbed Varney's sleeve again and tried to gently coax him toward the door.

This time, instead of planting his feet, Varney started moving. In the wrong direction.

"Hey." I tried pulling harder, but the harder I pulled, the faster Varney went toward Ranjay and Kennedy.

With a jerk, Varney freed himself from my grasp and covered the distance to where Kennedy and Ranjay stood, leaving me behind. I figured my best bet now was not to let it be known that I knew Varney.

I inched closer so I could hear every word.

Kennedy and Ranjay looked up from their conversation as Varney approached.

"Yes?" Ranjay asked.

Slowly, very slowly, Varney peeled back his hood.

Kennedy recognized him first. "Well, if it isn't Homer Lee Varney in the flesh. You're too late, the shoot is finished. Nothing you can do to disrupt it now." Kennedy puffed his chest out and edged in front of Ranjay. "Unless there's some other reason why you're here."

"You're Varney?" Ranjay said. "What...what do you want?"

Ranjay seemed more amazed than frightened, but Kennedy stepped in between Ranjay and Varney, as if he expected Varney to take a swing at the director or something.

"I want to tell my story. Because it's a whole lot different than the one you're telling here."

Ranjay pursed his lips like I'd seen him do before when he was contemplating an actor's suggestion. Was he really considering listening to Varney?

He didn't get the chance because Kennedy got up into Varney's grill. "We don't want your bullshit here. Time to leave." Kennedy continued advancing, and Varney had no choice but to walk backward or get bulled over.

Varney tried to talk to Ranjay around Kennedy's bulk. "I know you'd be interested in what I have to say. I'm not guilty!"

Ranjay pulled out his phone and started taking video, ever the filmmaker. He slowly circled, trying to get a better angle.

"Yeah, yeah," Kennedy said. "That's what every single criminal says. Now get the fuck out of here."

Varney's eyes were wild. He tried to dig his heels in, but didn't get much traction on the slick hallway floor. Kennedy kept up his bulldozer routine, slowly forcing Varney from the school.

"Okay, son, ready to hit the—" I was vaguely aware of Alf sidling up to me. "What is going on here?"

I turned toward Alf. "It's Varney. He's—"

"Hey," Varney called out, and I whipped my head around in time to see Varney stumbling backward. He tried to regain his balance, but failed, ending up sprawled on the floor, Kennedy looming, one fist balled by his side.

A moment passed, and it seemed like everyone was frozen. Ranjay, me, Alf, even Kennedy, all stock still, staring at Varney splayed out on the ground. A second later, though, Varney bounced up and lunged at Kennedy, who sidestepped him neatly. Varney whirled around and aimed a wild swing at Kennedy's face, but the ex-cop turned at the last moment so the punch caught him on the shoulder. Instead of crying out in pain, Kennedy laughed, and it sounded completely out of place, considering the severity of the situation.

Ranjay captured the whole incident on his phone. Would he air it as a promo for Sunday night's episode? People did a lot of crazy things in the pursuit of ratings.

"I warned you," Kennedy said. "You should have left when I gave you the chance. *Before* you tried to get physical with me."

Varney just stood there, a feral animal, confused, humiliated.

I wanted to rush in, tell them what I knew, what I was sure

of, but I didn't want to risk screwing up tomorrow's chance at nabbing Sweeney. All my assurances and theories were fine, but there was truly only one thing that would persuade Kennedy that Varney was innocent—catching the real killer. I kept my feet nailed to the ground and watched things unfold with a sickening feeling growing in my gut.

"All I wanted was to talk to you. You've got it all wrong." Varney's voice had taken on a whining quality, and he shuffled backward a few steps, glancing at me over Kennedy's shoulder, then staring at Ranjay for a few beats. Right now, he didn't seem like the hardened ex-con who had first corralled me in the ZMart warehouse. Now, he looked like a little boy who'd just lost his puppy and nobody was around to give him a hug.

"Scram. And if I ever see you again," Kennedy snarled. "I won't be nearly as nice."

With a final glance in my direction, Varney turned around and pushed through the school's front doors, out into the evening.

"Well, that was interesting," Alf said. "Very interesting."

Chapter Twenty-Seven

Somehow, Alf and I ended up at IHOP, and we sat one booth over from where Patch, Varney, and I had sifted through all the information I'd collected. The night we'd found the two conflicting M.E. reports.

"Chocolate chip pancakes," Alf told the server. "And a double side of bacon, please."

"I'd like a toasted bagel," I said. "Dry."

The server left to put in our orders.

"Not hungry?" Alf leaned against the wall and hoisted one leg up on the seat.

"Not really." My stomach felt wonky as I thought about what had just happened. Obviously, Varney hadn't come to the shoot to see me. He'd wanted to challenge Kennedy directly. Face the man who had played a major role in stealing five years of his life. More importantly, at least right now, to me, was what Varney's confrontation with Kennedy might mean for tomorrow. Hopefully, nothing, but something in the back of my mind thought otherwise. I tried to put all my worry aside and pay attention to Alf's stories. Tried to be in the here and now instead of in the "what just happened" and the "what would happen."

"When I was on vacation once with Viola Davis, she told me—"

"You went on vacation with Viola Davis?"

"That's right. Sweetheart of a gal. A little intense, perhaps, but, well, who am I to call the kettle odd?" He chuckled. "Anyway, Vi-Dee said you had to follow your heart and do what you think was best, no matter where it led. That way you could sleep well at night. What everybody else thought didn't matter." Alf tapped his heart with his fist. "Go with what's in here, Dalton. Always. If that means taking a risk now and then, go for it."

I guessed that explained some of Viola Davis's bold choices of roles. I wasn't exactly sure what Alf was trying to tell me, but then again, I rarely was.

"So if I'm about to do something risky, I should go ahead, because I believe in the cause?"

"Exactly." He grinned, and a gold tooth sparkled in the back of his mouth. "Except you need to tell your manager everything, my boy. How can I protect you if I don't know what the problem is?"

The server returned to the table just then with our orders, giving me a little more time to debate Alf's request. If I told him the truth, would he drag me straight home and tell my parents what I'd been up to, working with a convicted murderer on a crazy quest to clear his name? Or would he conspire right along with me to seek the truth? I stared at him, trying to read the answer on his face.

All I saw was his joy as a plate of chocolate chip pancakes—and a double side of bacon—landed before him. Whose idea was it to come to IHOP, anyway?

The server set my bagel in front of me. "Just let me know if you'd like something else." She tipped her head at Alf's plate. "Chef can whip up some of those, if you'd like."

"Thanks, but I'm good." I didn't know IHOP had chefs, but I got her meaning. "Hey, before you dig in, can I post a picture?"

"Of my food?" Alf asked.

"Got to keep up the branding effort."

"Go ahead, my boy." He pushed his plate toward the middle of the table and leaned back as I took a picture of his heaping plate of food. Then I posted it on Instagram and Twitter along with the caption: *Can't ever go wrong with chocolate chip pancakes and bacon.*

"Thanks, Alf."

"My pleasure. Can't stand in the way of your branding." He pulled his plate back in front of him. "Now why don't you tell me what's going on? That was some display at the school, all right. But somehow I get the feeling I don't know the whole story. If I had to guess, I'd say you already have met with this scoundrel Varney." He paused, waiting for my response.

"Uh, would you excuse me? I need to go to the rest room?" Without waiting for an answer, I bolted. In the bathroom, I darted into the first stall, closed the door, and texted Varney. *Are you okay?*

I sat down to wait for a response. After five minutes, I gave up and headed back to the table. If I was lucky, Alf would have forgotten all about his previous line of questioning.

"Everything okay, son?" Alf asked. He pointed at his plate, where it looked like he'd finished about half his pancakes and all his bacon. "Hope you don't mind, but I didn't want it to get cold."

I waved my hand. "No. Good. Sorry." I picked up my bagel and took a bite. Cold. And a little too chewy. I put it down, not a bit hungry. "So. Tell me about your, uh, family."

"My family? They're fine. But I believe we were talking about what's going on with you. Your behavior—and the few hiccups you had during the shoot—are uncharacteristic." He smiled, spread his hands out. "I'm a full-service manager, you know. If there's something I can do to help, I will."

"I know," I said. "And I appreciate that."

"So, what's going on with you and Varney?"

I'd lied to my parents. I'd lied to Ms. Z. What were a few more? "Me and Varney? Nothing. Just a guy I portrayed, that's all. Why would I want to meet with him, anyway?"

"I was hoping you would tell me." Alf stared at me.

I stared at Alf.

"Nothing's going on." I tried to keep my voice steady and my hands steadier as I took another bite of my dry bagel. Maybe Alf would be less likely to keep grilling me if my mouth was full. I chewed very, very slowly.

He waited me out. Then when I swallowed, he said, "Whatever you tell me, I promise I'll do my best to keep it between us."

In Alf's mind, thinking I was meeting with Varney was one level of bad. If he knew a stone-cold killer was after me, he'd totally flip out and go racing to my parents—most rational adults would. Hell, even *I* would if my kid had told me anything close to that reality. But I didn't think I was in serious danger. Sweeney wasn't going to hurt me until he knew—for an absolute fact—I'd coughed up all the incriminating evidence. So I had to make *absolutely* sure he never felt my life was expendable.

I just knew we could pull this off, and I didn't want to do anything that would compromise our chances for success. And I was afraid of what Alf would do if he found out the truth. He was persistent, and if he thought I was in danger, he'd stay on my case until he knew otherwise. I had to come up with an alternate interpretation.

"Okay, okay. I wasn't completely truthful. I did meet with Varney. Once." I paused, shook my head as if I were sorry for not telling Alf sooner. "I wanted to see what made his mind tick. What he was thinking during the weeks leading up to the murder. So I could portray him accurately. I was just doing my research, and I figured if I told someone my plan—my parents, the director, or you—then I wouldn't be allowed to do it. So, yes, I did meet with Varney. For research."

Alf pushed his plate away. Stared at me. Raised one eyebrow, then the other. Tilted his head a bit. I had the feeling he was trying to determine whether I was telling the truth by examining my face from different angles. Throughout it all, I made a mental list of all the characters in Harry Potter, an exercise I'd found useful in performances when I needed to keep my expression neutral.

Finally, after what felt like a week, he nodded. “Okay, Dalton. I understand what an artist sometimes goes through in the name of research. I’ll make you a promise. I won’t tell anyone about this, if you don’t meet with him anymore.”

I nodded. “There’s no need. The shoot is over.”

He nodded back. “Yes, it is. But I’d still feel better if I heard you say you’ll agree to my little deal.”

“I promise,” I said, doubling down on my lies. “I promise.”

I felt like a piece of shit, lying to Alf, and part of me was concerned about how easily the lie rolled off my tongue.

On the way out of the restaurant, I checked my phone.

Still no response to my text from Varney.

When I got home, Annie was in the family room watching something on her tablet.

“What’s up, Sis?”

She didn’t tear her gaze away from the screen as she answered. “Nothing. What’s up with you? Terrorize any small children today?”

“Nope. Sorry to disappoint you.”

“You always disappoint me.” She finally looked my way with a taunting smile, but it quickly morphed into an expression of concern. “What’s wrong?”

“What do you mean?”

“You look like shit warmed over. And I don’t mean that as a compliment.”

I tried to lighten my tone, but knowing what I faced tomorrow, it was hard. “Nothing’s wrong. Everything’s peachy.”

“Are you in trouble?”

“No.” *Yes.*

“Is someone you know in trouble?”

“No.” *Yes.*

"Maybe you should get Mom or Dad involved."

"No." *No, no, no.* I forced a small, don't-worry-about-me smile. "Everything's fine. Really."

She set her tablet aside and grabbed my hand. Pulled me down onto the couch next to her. "Dalton, I'm your big sister. I've known you for a few years now. I know when you're behaving like a typical tool, and I know when there's something going on. And there's definitely something going on. Spill."

Part of me wanted to tell Annie what I was mixed up in—it would feel great to unburden myself. But I didn't want her worrying about me, and there was really nothing she could do to help anyway. I also knew if I told her the truth—the complete, unfiltered truth—she'd run to Mom and Dad so fast her head would spin. They'd get the cops involved and we'd have no shot of luring Sweeney into our trap. Worst of all, poor Varney's life would be ruined forever. Time for a stiff upper lip, as Alf would say. "I appreciate your concern, but there is absolutely and uncategorically nothing weird going on."

And now I could add my big sister to the list of people I had lied to.

Annie eyed me for the longest time, but I didn't crack. "You, little brother, are full of shit. But I wish you well with whatever scheme you've got cooking. If there's anything I can do, let me know." She patted my cheek. "Now, get lost, fuzzface, I've got stuff to do."

Love you, too, Sis.

Chapter Twenty-Eight

The next morning, I was up at eight, just in time to hear each parent, three minutes apart, close the front door on their way to work. I hadn't slept very well, waking up several times and having trouble getting back to sleep, way too much on my mind.

I rolled out of bed, jumped in and out of the shower, threw on some clothes, grabbed a package of Pop Tarts—okay, two packages—and was out the door in record time. Trinnie, Patch, Varney, and I were getting together to make sure we were all on the same page. As I'd learned doing community theater—and before that, in PeeWee Soccer—things went much better when everyone on the team was heading in the same direction.

I just prayed Varney would be calm and reasonable today, able to keep his eyes on the prize. I hadn't texted Trinnie or Patch last night with a recap of events, mostly because I hadn't wanted them to get worried.

I was worried enough for the three of us.

I arrived at Joe's Java, and Trinnie and Patch were already there, sipping from their latte-mocha-chimichangas or whatever fancy concoction they drank. I felt as though I baffled the barista by ordering a regular coffee, then joined my friends at the table. "Where's Varney?"

Patch shrugged. "Haven't seen him. Or any other convicted murderers for that matter."

"That we know about," Trinnie added.

"Right." I took a sip of coffee, hoping it would calm my nerves. I tapped on the table with my fingernails until Trinnie reached out and grabbed my hand.

"Relax, Dalton," she said. "This will all go fine."

"Sure." Not so sure. But, as my father always said, worrying wouldn't help a bit. I tried to shake off my feelings of dread. "Okay, let's go over the plan again."

"Shouldn't we wait for Varney?" Patch asked.

"Let's do it now. We can go over it again when he gets here." *If* he gets here. I had a bad feeling about this. As if last night's stunt had been Varney's lone attempt to clear his name, and because he got rebuffed, he was finished, ready to crawl into a hole somewhere and give up. I didn't understand that; if I had the chance to take down the guy responsible for the crime I'd been convicted of, I'd certainly stick around.

We went over the plan and everyone seemed on board. The plan was simple. Basically, we would lure Sweeney to school without him smelling a trap, offer to exchange all our evidence for his promise not to harm us, and get him to admit guilt while recording everything that happened. Yeah, the plan was simple—it was the execution that would make the difference.

"Is Rizzo ready?" I asked.

"She's testing the camera she wants to use as we speak. When we're done here, I'm going to pick her up and then we'll go get set up."

"You'd better stick close to her, make sure she gets what she needs." Trinnie tried unsuccessfully not to smile.

Patch faked a smile back. "I will." Then he turned my way. "Tell me again how you and Varney plan to lure Sweeney to school."

"I never told you the first time." I had a strategy, but it was something I needed to do with Varney's help. I knew if I told Patch and Trinnie the entire plan, they'd try to talk me out of it, and they'd worry the entire time. I couldn't do that to my friends. "Relax, I've got it under control."

"When people say that, I get worried," Patch said.

"Listen. I know I keep pointing this out, but there's no way Sweeney would try to hurt me until he gets the evidence he thinks we have against him." I glanced at my phone: nine thirty-five a.m. "Where's Varney? Think he got lost?"

Trinnie shrugged. "I hope not."

I hoped not, too. I checked the time again, and it was one minute later than the last time I'd looked. "He better get here. Otherwise, we're screwed." More specifically, *I* was screwed.

"Uh-oh." Patch stared at his phone.

"What?"

"No, no, no, no, no!"

"What, what, what, what, what?" I felt the Pop Tarts spin around in my stomach.

Patch looked up at me, deflated. "I just got a hit on a Google Alert I'd set on Varney. I don't think he's going to be able to make it today. Or any other day."

"What are you talking about?"

"According to the Fairfax County Twitter feed, Varney was arrested late last night."

"Arrested? Why?" Trinnie asked.

I had a feeling I knew why. Evidently, Kennedy had sicced his cop friends on Varney, and they had Ranjay's cell phone video as evidence.

"It doesn't say," Patch said.

I set my coffee down. "There was an incident. Last night. Right after the shoot." I went on to explain what had happened. "Kennedy must have called the police on Varney."

"Oh, shit," Patch said. "He won't be getting out anytime soon."

The three of us sat in silence for a moment, each of us running through the ramifications. Finally, Patch spoke. "I guess that's it then. Time for Plan B. Whatever that is."

I shook my head. "Look, just because Varney got arrested doesn't mean Sweeney is going to stop trying to get to me. He still thinks I have the evidence that will convict him of murder. We need to prove this guy's guilty if I ever want to sleep well again. And for the record, I do."

"I don't know, Dalton. Varney was supposed to help you lure Sweeney in. He would have been there, by your side, in case Sweeney got physical. Without him..." Trinnie held out her hands, palms up. Empty.

"I agree," Patch said. "Without Varney, it's too dangerous."

"Come on, guys. The show must go on. What happens when a performer gets sick? Next person up. All we need to do is find someone to step into Varney's shoes."

"That's all?" Trinnie asked. "This isn't a Broadway production. We don't have any understudies. We gave it a good try. But we should know when to call it quits."

I didn't want to play the part of a martyr. And I wasn't trying to be some kind of kick-ass superhero. But I wasn't about to quit when the going got a little tough. Varney's absence was just a speedbump. "Guys, you don't have to help me out here. But just so you know, I'm going through with this—with or without you. I just couldn't live with myself, knowing there's an innocent guy out there whose life is ruined, and I helped to ruin it. The absolute very least I can do is bust my butt trying to make things right."

Patch sighed. "You're not doing it alone. We're right there with you."

When Trinnie didn't chime in, Patch poked her in the arm. "Yeah, we're right there with you. I hope you know what you're doing," she said.

"No more than usual," I said. "Now, what are we going to do about Varney's role in this?"

Trinnie clucked her tongue. "I know someone we can get. A good actor. About the same size and build as Varney. And someone I think we can persuade to help us out."

"Who?" Patch asked.

Trinnie stared at me for a beat.

"Oh." I said. "No. No, not—"

"Cam Carter," Trinnie said.

I hated the idea. But he was the ideal choice.

"Well, he is about the right size. And he is an...*adequate* actor."

I glanced at Patch, and he gave me a look, his eyes wide and knowing.

"Okay, okay. It's no secret Cam and I don't much like each other. But—"

Trinnie interrupted. "Actually, that's not true. Cam likes you fine. You're the one who's got something against him."

"Oh, snap," Patch said, under his breath.

I felt my neck getting warm. Was Trinnie calling me an asshole in a roundabout way? "I don't think that's totally accurate."

"Oh, it is. I've talked to him about it. He's a good guy, and you just don't like him because you think he's better than you. You told me yourself he was a better actor. And better-looking. And better at a lot of other things, too. Did I mention he's also a better kisser?"

Trinnie reached over, avoiding my cup of coffee on the table, and held my arm. "I love you, man. But you're letting your ego get in the way here. I'm calling you out on it because that's what friends do. Besides, he *isn't* better than you. Just different. Not everything is a competition." Her dark eyes bored into me. Made me feel like a pile of dog shit.

"I need a refill. Be back in a week or so." Patch rose and drifted off in the direction of the counter, taking his cup with him.

"You talked to Cam about me?" I pictured Cam on the couch crushed up against Trinnie, and my insides churned. I tamped down my feelings.

"Don't get a big head. I don't make a habit of talking about you to other people. It just happened to come up. But this thing you have against Cam is ridiculous. There are plenty of good gigs to go around. Jealousy isn't an attractive trait." She paused, locked eyes with me. "Over anything."

"What are you talking about? Exactly?" My heart was pounding.

"Dalton, I've known you a long time, and...well, you never..." She exhaled. "Just forget it. Cam's a good guy, and that's what we're talking about here."

I sat there, dumbstruck. Had Trinnie been waiting for me to make some kind of move? Had she been feeling the same way about me that I'd been feeling about her? Had I blown my one and only chance because I was too oblivious? Too focused on my own stupid shit?

"We have a job to do now," Trinnie said. "I suggest we concentrate on that. Table this other discussion for later."

I nodded and tried to push all the Trinnie stuff out of my head. I wasn't sure I was totally successful, but she was correct, we didn't need any distractions in our quest to nail Sweeney. "As usual, you're right about Cam. He'd be great. Let's hope he's not busy."

"He's not." Trinnie smiled. "But you probably don't want to know how I know."

I didn't. "Okay. Good."

"Want me to text him? See if I can get him on board?"

"No. You need to help Patch and Rizzo. I'll drop by his house and talk to him alone. Better done in person, in case he has any objections. I can be very persuasive when I want to be. Besides, if he says yes, I need to start going over the plan with him."

Trinnie hadn't let go of my arm since she'd blasted me for being a jerk, and now she gave it a good squeeze. "You're a good guy, Dalton. You always do the right thing. Even if you need a little persuading yourself, now and then."

Naturally, Cam lived in a nice section of town. And naturally, his family's house was bigger than mine, the cars in the garage nicer, and the landscaping more lush. Even the birds chirping in the trees around his yard sounded more musical than ours.

He answered when I knocked and almost looked like he was expecting me. If I didn't know Trinnie was busy, I'd have thought she gave him a heads-up. On the other hand, I had the feeling Cam never looked surprised about anything.

"What brings you around, Dalton?" he asked. Then, remembering his manners, he said, "Want to come in?"

I stepped into a two-story foyer framed by twin staircases leading up. A ginormous crystal chandelier, containing about sixty bulbs, hung over our heads, and two oil-painted portraits stared down at us from their positions in an adjoining hallway. A marble bust, its eyeballs blank, also stared at us from an ornate pedestal. Trust me, it was creepy being stared at by a blank-eyed statue.

"Quite a place." I'm sure my amazement was evident.

"I guess. My mom's into decorating and all kinds of other house stuff. Want something to drink?" Without waiting for an answer, he turned and started off, presumably toward the kitchen. I followed.

Cam's kitchen was twice as big as ours, with a restaurant-sized refrigerator and two stoves. I imagined the *other house stuff* Cam's mom enjoyed included cooking.

He opened the fridge and retrieved two cans of Sprite, handed me one and pointed to a couple of stools at an island almost as big as Rhode Island. "Have a seat."

We sat, popped open our sodas, and as I took my first sip, I felt Cam's eyes on me, no doubt wondering what I wanted this early on a Wednesday morning. It wasn't like Cam and I usually hung out, one on one. "I need your help."

Cam set his soda down, and a small smile appeared. "Oh? Some acting pointers?" He delivered his little zinger with humor, not snarkiness. I probably would have gone with snarky. Maybe Trinnie was right about the guy.

"I'm sure I could use some of those, but that's not why I'm here. It's a long story."

He put his elbows on the counter. "Go ahead. I like a good story."

I filled him in as quickly as I could, glossing over a few of the less-flattering details, like me being abducted in the abandoned ZMart. He listened and nodded, but let me finish without interrupting.

"So, that's about it. We need someone who can step right in and help us out." My voice caught a little, but I managed to add, "And you're the perfect choice."

Cam nodded, gave me a sly, crooked smile, and I could see why he was a popular kid. "Seems kinda dangerous. People could get hurt if it doesn't go right."

"Maybe. But if we don't catch this guy, I could get hurt. And Varney's life would really suck. What's happened to him isn't fair, and I couldn't live with myself if I didn't at least try to set things right. Besides, if we can't pull this off, we can always call 9-1-1, right?"

"What kind of person would I be if I turned a blind eye to this? And what kind of friend would I be if I didn't offer my help?" He smiled. "I'm totally in."

So he considered me a friend? And he was helping out? Maybe I *should* give him another chance.

"Great." I held out my fist, and he bumped it. "Let's get going."

Chapter Twenty-Nine

While Cam got ready, I waited in my car. Our first challenge in getting our plan to work relied on me—making sure I delivered Sweeney to the school auditorium. I'd been wrestling with that problem since I'd hatched the idea of meeting him face-to-face. The answer: breadcrumbs. Electronic breadcrumbs.

A little deduction had given me the idea. How had Sweeney known I worked at camp when he'd gone to talk to Ms. Z? There were hundreds of camps in the D.C./Northern Virginia area, but he'd managed to hit upon mine. How had he been able to pick up my trail at the mall's food court? Or tailed me home after the shoot that night? Only one way I could figure.

He'd been following my movements as I'd been posting them on social media.

Up until a few years ago, I'd treated social media like any other kid. I'd follow friends and schoolmates, as well as some well-known celebrities, mostly actors in my case. But when I signed with Alf, he'd encouraged me to broaden my scope. Said I should start building a brand. So, gradually, I'd been expanding my circles to include all the cast and crew of all the shows I worked on—in school, during the summer, in community theater. I connected with people I took acting workshops with. I connected with all of Alf's other clients. And their producer friends. And director friends. And pretty much everyone in the business I *could* connect with. As Alf told me, you never knew who might be casting a part.

Also at Alf's insistence—and much to the dismay of my mother—I'd created a website. Nothing terribly fancy, it had the type of stuff that went on an acting resume. A listing of the shows and commercials and stuff I'd been in. My headshots. A few pithy statements about my acting passion. And ways to contact and follow me on social media.

I knew many of the people who followed me.

But not all.

I didn't have the time to check out everyone who wanted to connect, but in my mind, that would sort of defeat the purpose of building a brand. So I blindly accepted every friend and follower request and connected with any and all who asked.

If I was right, Sweeney had been following my moves as I'd broadcasted them to my friends and followers. I felt like an idiot now, but I was going to turn my stupidity and carelessness to my advantage.

At least my mother would be proud that I'd learned from my mistake.

Once again, I fell back on my theory that I was safe as long as Sweeney thought I had something that would put him in prison. As soon as I gave up that bit of leverage, I was expendable. A goner.

I pulled out my phone and got ready to start dropping electronic breadcrumbs, using my entire arsenal: Twitter and Facebook and Instagram. While devising my strategy—the exact wording, number of tweets and posts, the progression—I needed to consider a number of factors. I couldn't make my message seem like a trap, or I'd risk scaring him off. I only wanted to attract one person—Sweeney—not dozens of curious people. I couldn't endanger family or friends—or other innocent people, for that matter. And my tweets had to be effective. They had to lead Sweeney to me so I could then lead him to school, where we'd get his confession on video.

I toyed with the idea of sending him to the school directly, but I wouldn't be able to control the timing, and I might accidentally attract others there as well. So I decided to announce my intention to go somewhere else and hope he picked me up there. Then I counted on him following me as I led him to school. Having Varney along—or at least Cam, pretending to be Varney—was an added inducement to get Sweeney to follow. I figured he'd want to see what *both* of his opponents had in store for him.

Hopefully, my plan wasn't too convoluted.

My fingers hovered above the phone's screen. Once I'd set this in motion, I wasn't sure I could walk it back if something went wrong. I had complete confidence in Trinnie, Patch, and Rizzo. And, truth be told, in Cam, too.

Confidence wasn't the issue.

The wild card was the killer.

What choice did we have though?

I tapped out a tweet:

*Heading to Vienna Library w/HLV to finish up my *innocence* project. Turning in to authorities tomorrow. Wish me luck!*

The library in Vienna. A safe public place. Middle of the day. He wouldn't try anything there, but if things went like I envisioned, he'd pick up my trail there. I hoped mentioning that I planned to go to the police tomorrow would motivate him to take action—to confront me—sooner rather than later.

Forty seconds after I sent my tweet, I got a call from my mother, who was at work. "David? I see you're going to the library. Are you planning to be home for dinner?"

Of course my mother followed me on Twitter. How else to keep her nose in my business? "I don't think so. We've got a drama thing after that, and I really don't know how long it will last."

"Again? We hardly ever see you anymore. I can't remember the last time the four of us ate dinner together."

"Maybe tomorrow night." If I was still alive, dinner might

be nice.

Mom sighed. "Okay, dear. Oh, one more thing. Next week, I'll be trying an interesting case. Maybe you could come to court with me. Then you can see what a lawyer does firsthand. At the very least, I'll get to spend time with my boy."

"Sure, Mom. Maybe."

"Gotta run. Be safe." Mom clicked off.

Another requirement of my scheme: make sure I didn't post anything to make Mom suspicious or worried.

Speaking of suspicious, I'd been keeping my eyes open and I hadn't seen anyone suspicious on my tail. I hadn't posted anything about going to Starbucks and then to Cam's, but that didn't mean Sweeney wasn't shadowing me. He knew where I lived, and he could have picked up my trail when I left the house. I glanced up and down Cam's street. Nothing but a few parked cars.

I texted Trinnie and told her Cam was in.

> Trinnie: Told ya. He's not a bad guy.
> Me: Okay
> Trinnie: Who knows? Maybe you two will actually become friends.
> Me: Don't push your luck. Cya.

Cam came out, dressed in jeans and a large gray hoodie. He hopped in the shotgun seat.

"Ready?" I asked.

"Ready," he said.

"Then let's go. First stop, my house."

We swung by my house so I could pick up some stuff. I left Cam in the car while I ran downstairs to the storage closet in the basement. I grabbed an empty banker's box—basically a square cardboard box with a lid—and toted it up to my room. I filled it up with papers, old headshots, and a few scripts, along with the evidence I'd collected on the case. I'd made a copy of the important pieces, just in case something went sideways. The more stuff in the box, the more evidence it looked like we had, which, I figured, could only help lure Sweeney in.

I changed into an all-black outfit—jeans and T-shirt, with black sneakers. This was the standard tech-crew outfit, worn so they wouldn't be noticeable on the dark stage as they moved the scenery around between scenes.

Then I hustled out to the car, plopped the box on the back seat, and drove us to Vienna Library. We took a few side streets to make sure we weren't being followed, and I pulled over to the curb a few blocks away from the library.

I turned in my seat so I faced Cam. "Showtime. Remember, you are supposed to be Varney. Put your hood on and keep it on—all the time—pulled as far over your face as you can."

"Like this?" He put the hood on, tugged it down over his brow.

From the side, I could barely see his nose. "Turn this way a bit."

He did, and the top of the hood hung down pretty far, leaving much of his face in shadows. "Very good. Hang on."

I opened the center console and pulled out my knock-off Ray-Bans. "Here. Try these on."

Cam slid them over his ears. Readjusted his hood. Faced me again.

"Damn. You could be Varney, all right." If you were predisposed to thinking Cam was Varney—like I was betting Sweeney was—you'd have to be pretty close to realize it *wasn't* Varney. That's what I was counting on. "Remember. Don't speak. Don't leave my side. And try to act like a guy who was wrongly imprisoned for five years and is about to get a chance to face his accuser." I put the car in gear and drove the two blocks to the library.

The lot was about half full, so I found a spot between two mini-vans and backed into the space—ready for a quick getaway.

I hauled the box inside, and Cam and I found an empty table in the main area near a bank of public-use computers. I made sure my seat faced the entrance. There was only one way in and out of the library, and I had it covered. Of course, I didn't know what Sweeney looked like, at least not beyond a vague body shape.

Cam and I settled in, figuring we had a couple of hours to kill. I needed to pretend I had some last-minute details to put together before I went to the cops—that was for Sweeney's benefit. I mean, I'd tweeted that I needed to go to the library to finish things up—if it only took a few minutes, he might get suspicious.

More importantly, a couple of hours should also give Trinnie, Patch, and Rizzo the time they needed to get things ready at school.

I unpacked a few things from my box, sliding a bunch of manila folders over to Cam's side of the table. I pulled out a legal pad—thanks, Mom!—and a pen. Supplied the same to Cam.

"Now, look busy. We're supposed to be combing through all this, looking for clues that will incriminate Sweeney and get Varney—you—off the hook. So, pretend to read the files and make notes or whatever. And as weird as it might look hiding in your little hood cave, don't take it off."

"What about the shades?"

"Keep them on, too. Even if it will be hard to read."

"Roger that." Cam uncapped his pen and opened the first folder. "I can pretend to work with the best of them."

"That's the spirit."

To pass the time—and to make sure I hadn't missed anything—I began outlining what I knew about the evidence the prosecution had used to put him away.

There were a lot of things to cover, and I wrote slowly. Two hours was a lot of time to kill, pretending to be busy.

After I'd compiled a list of all the evidence Varney claimed was bogus, I paused to consider things.

Because the police had found Varney's bloody T-shirt and cap in the trunk of his car, they'd pegged him as the killer early on. Which meant they hadn't really considered any other possible suspects. He'd maintained during the initial investigation that he'd been framed, that someone had planted the bloody things in his trunk. He hadn't wavered from that position when he'd discussed his theory with us.

Based on what we'd researched, Varney had a point, a damn good one. If his car had been unlocked, *anyone* could have thrown the bloody shirt and cap into the trunk. And even if it had been locked, how hard was it to jimmy open the trunk. His car could easily have been picked at random. Also, the knife they found there had been wiped clean of prints. But why would Varney have kept it—or any of it for that matter—instead of throwing it away the first chance he got.

And according to the M.E.'s report—at least one of them—the killer had been left-handed.

None of it made any sense, and my recap hadn't done anything except reinforce my feelings that Varney had been railroaded.

This whole time, I'd been keeping an eye on the door, performing a quick inspection of everyone who entered. *Does this person look like a murderer?* I ruled out anyone over the age of thirty, and I eliminated anybody who didn't appear to be in good physical shape. Along with a healthy dose of anger or rage, knifing a linebacker probably took a fair amount of strength.

Most of the library patrons fell into the Not-A-Murderer category, but there were a few I kept my eye on.

I scribbled a few things on my legal pad, trying to make it seem like I was solving the Riddle of the Sphinx, whatever that was, in case Sweeney was lurking around. If I were him, however—and I was banking on this—I'd be out in the parking lot waiting for me to leave. Then I'd follow me, run me off the road, take my box of evidence, and slice my throat open. If I were him.

I shuddered, hoping Sweeney didn't think like me.

Of course, that line of thinking was another reason I was grateful to have Cam by my side. It was much harder to slice open two people's throats at the same time.

I scanned the library. Everyone seemed to be doing library-appropriate things. The computer stations were full. A father was leading a child around, a stack of books in his arms. Several people were sitting in big comfy chairs, reading magazines. A short line of people waited at the self-checkout kiosk. No one was lurking about with shifty eyes, wielding a sharp knife.

I returned to my imaginary work, and scrawled on the pad and erased and flipped through the notes and scowled and tried to look as if I were fighting injustice.

I checked the clock on the wall. An hour and a half had crept by. I kicked Cam's shoe under the table and leaned forward. "You doing okay?" I whispered, not wanting any of my conversation to be overheard—nor did I want to get shushed by a zealous librarian.

"Doing fine," Cam said, leaning forward as well, causing his hood to cover even more of his face. "Man, there's a lot of stuff in here. Some of it's pretty questionable. Did Varney even have a lawyer?"

"He did, but a bad one. Plus everyone thought he was guilty, so they made the evidence fit their theory, instead of letting the evidence *form* their theory. Big difference."

"Well, however it happened, Varney sure got screwed."

I wasn't sure why, but it felt good knowing Cam thought so, too.

"So what's the deal with you and Trinnie?" he asked.

I tilted my head, trying to get a look at Cam's face, but between the hood and the shades and the harsh overhead lighting casting ominous shadows, I couldn't see crap. "What do you mean?"

"You know, are you guys going out or anything?"

I wanted to ask him why he wanted to know, but I had a pretty good feeling why. "Trinnie's the best, isn't she? Totally awesome."

Cam's hoodie nodded. "For sure."

I checked the clock on the wall again. We'd been there almost two hours. "Speaking of Trinnie, let's see what's what. I'll text her."

> Me: How's it going?
> Trinnie: Almost ready.
> Me: How much more time do you need to be totally ready?
> Trinnie: Ten minutes.
> Me: Great. Are we going to pull this off?
> Trinnie: YES!
> I was thinking of something clever to text back, when she followed up.
> Trinnie: Or NO! Hard to tell!
> *Shit.*
> Trinnie: How's it going on your end?
> Me: Fine.
> Trinnie: How's Cam doing?

I pictured him with his arm around Trinnie. I pictured him kissing Trinnie. I pictured him—I shook my head, trying to banish images of them together from my mind. Focus!

> Me: Fine.
> Trinnie: Gotta run. Break a leg!

I sent her back a smiley face. If only I felt that happy. I was about to start mentally kicking myself for blowing it with Trinnie, but...we had important stuff to do. When this was over, I could wallow in self-pity all I wanted.

"Time to move out," I said to Cam.

He shoved his files back across the table, and I packed everything into the banker's box. Then I posted a message on all my social media: *Done at the library. Heading home for the night. Tomorrow, I turn in my proof. Justice will be served!*

We waited ten minutes to give Sweeney a chance to get

ready, then I picked up the box. It was best if we didn't leave the library alone—no sense exposing us needlessly.

There'd be plenty of time for us to get attacked later.

Cam and I waited until a middle-aged couple finished up at the checkout desk and then we ducked out right after them. With Cam at my side, we stayed three steps behind them as we walked out to the parking lot together, keeping an eye out for any sign of an attacker.

When the couple veered left to go to their car, we peeled off and walked—fast—toward my car, forty feet away. We didn't run, not wanting to let Sweeney know we were on to him.

On the other hand, we didn't want to go too slowly and allow him to nab us right there in the parking lot.

I carried the box on my hip. Bait holding bait. Keeping ultra-alert, eyes scanning the parking lot without moving my head, ready to take off in a sprint if someone came charging at me. Cam was doing the same.

The forty-foot walk to my car was the longest walk of my life, and when we reached it, I let out a huge breath. But I couldn't relax yet. Cam jumped into the passenger side, and I ran around the car and hopped into the driver's seat, handing the box to Cam.

I locked the door behind us as quickly as I could.

"Ready?" I asked Cam.

He clapped his hands once. "Ready."

I jammed the keys into the ignition and started up the car, but didn't take off just yet. If my plan was going to work, Sweeney had to be around, waiting to follow us. If he wasn't...

"Do you see anybody suspicious?" I asked. "Look around, but don't be obvious."

Cam moved his head slightly, back and forth. "Nobody."

I thought of Trinnie and Patch, believing in me and my theories. I thought of Varney, back in jail. Unless we nailed Sweeney, he'd always be thought of as a murderer. Our plan had to work.

I glanced around the lot, row by row. Nobody hunched over

their steering wheel, staring at me. No cars idled, motors running. I didn't see much of anything, even in my rearview—

Wait! I did a double take, and my heart skipped. Two rows behind me, in a black compact car. A guy in a Yankees cap. Slumped down in his seat, he seemed to be hypnotized by something on his phone, but...something didn't seem right. He gave off a weird vibe. Didn't seem like a normal library patron. Was it Sweeney?

Only one way to find out for sure.

"Don't look, but I think I may have spotted him. In a car behind us. Hang on."

I shifted the car into Drive and eased out of my parking space. I drove around the side of the building, toward the Center Street exit.

I debated a glance in the mirror. Part of me hoped there wouldn't be anyone behind me. Then I could go tell Patch and Trinnie we were full of it, our entire plan had been a pie-in-the sky dream, and we'd all have a good, long—relieved—laugh.

I screwed up my courage and checked the rearview. The black car was advancing slowly. Sweeney was driving, cap and sunglasses obscuring his identity.

Shit just got real.

"It's Sweeney."

"Let's do it," Cam said.

I paused at the stop sign, then hung a left, away from Maple Avenue, the main drag. We couldn't make it too easy for Sweeney, otherwise he might smell a trap. He had to earn it.

Rush hour had started, filling the streets with a fair amount of traffic. Most of it traveled along Maple Avenue, avoiding the numerous stop signs and speed bumps and slow speed limits in the surrounding neighborhoods. Commuters would rather wait at a few traffic lights on the main road than have to endure all the puttering around and stop-and-going.

I made sure I kept to the speed limit as we passed the elementary school and the police station. I turned left again, slicing between the big baseball field and the fire station, then wound around the community center. I'd grown up here, and I knew where the traffic logjams would be, as well as where there might be speed traps. I turned right on Park Street.

Not too fast. Not too slow. Couldn't lose Sweeney.

Next to me, Cam stayed quiet, letting me concentrate on the driving.

At the next stop sign, I turned right. Once I made sure Sweeney had also turned, I gunned it until the next cross-street. Then, when I was sure he could see me, I turned left. I repeated this pattern, alternating lefts and rights, for a while. I wanted him to think we'd finally spotted him and were trying to elude him. That way, when we eventually let him catch us, he wouldn't suspect a thing.

With every few zigzags, we were slowly but surely making our way closer to school. Once in a while, a car would get between me and Sweeney, so I slowed down or turned down a sidestreet until he caught back up. I needed to give him some line, then reel him back in, playing him like the giant swordfish he was.

We'd made a big circle and were now back on Cottage Street, heading toward Maple Avenue. I'd left him behind, so I slowed down, just like I'd been doing all along. Only this time? No Sweeney in the rearview.

I slowed down even more.

"What's wrong?" Cam sat up straighter in his seat. "Why are we slowing down?"

"He's not behind us anymore." I pulled over to the curb.

"What do we do now?"

"I guess we wait."

We waited. A full minute. No dark sedan.

Had I lost him? He'd been able to keep up with us, through far hairier intersections. Had he gotten tired of the chase? Had I blown our one good chance to nail him? He'd been right behind us!

"Maybe if we drive around a bit, we'll bump into him, and we can pick up where we left off." My words sounded hopeful, but I felt our prey slipping through our fingers. Poor Varney.

"Sounds like a plan to me," Cam said, without much enthusiasm.

I pulled away from the curb. At the next intersection, I stopped at the four-way stop sign. Stared into the mirror, hoping—praying—Sweeney would reappear so I could lead him to school.

Nothing in the mirror.

I eased my foot off the brake and turned my attention forward. A car had stopped ten feet in front of me, right in the middle of the intersection, blocking my way.

Sweeney.

Chapter Thirty

"Watch out!" Cam yelled.

I stood on the brakes, and my car came to a skidding stop a mere eighteen inches from Sweeney's door.

He stared at me with a crazy grin. Greasy black hair, chiseled cheek bones, some scruff on his chin that he probably thought looked cool. He made a gun with his fingers and pointed it at my head. My hands shook with fear, fueled by an adrenaline rush. I wasn't sure which was scarier, almost hitting his car or his death stare.

We'd found him, all right.

I didn't wait to see what came next. I jammed the gearshift into Reverse and hit the gas. The car lurched backward and I spun the wheel and the back end fishtailed into a stop sign. The sickening sound of bending metal cried a warning: Get the hell out of here!

I overcorrected from hitting the signpost and lurched up onto the curb. I jammed the gearshift back into Reverse, and this time, the crunching noise came from the passenger side-view mirror being shorn from the car.

Again.

"Dude," Cam kept saying, over and over, each time with more feeling.

I slammed the car into Drive and hit the gas, giving some poor resident a vicious lawn job as I barely managed to steer back onto the street. Sweeney was turning my way, so I spun the wheel again and completed an insane three-point turn, just like in every chase scene I'd ever seen in the movies.

I floored it and roared off, barely avoiding Sweeney's car as I sped past him in the opposite direction. I dodged another car coming my way as horns blared and tires screeched.

"You okay?" I asked Cam.

"Dude!"

I took that as a *yes*. At the end of the block, after getting my car—and my pulse—back under control, I slowed to allow Sweeney to catch up.

This time, it didn't take him long. Ten seconds, and he was hot on our tail and closing fast.

I blew through the next stop sign, barely missing a slow-moving landscaping truck, then tapped the brakes again, to make sure Sweeney was still behind me. Only a few more blocks of this crazy speed-up/slow-down chase until we made it to the school.

Somewhere karma was shining down on me, because when I got to the last gnarly intersection, where Nutley Street hit Maple, the light was green and my path was clear. I turned left, and swerved into the right lane.

Sweeney was on my ass. Perfect.

I barely hit the brakes as I negotiated the right turn just past the gas station and onto the school access road. A quick glance in the mirror told me Sweeney had made the turn, too. I was sixty yards ahead of him and needed every inch. After I shot past one tiny side street, there was only one place I could possibly go: South Vienna High.

Without even slowing down, I flew over the parking-lot speed bumps, my head grazing the roof of the car with each one. Out of the corner of my eye, I could see Cam holding on for dear life. I skidded to a stop in front of the doors closest to the auditorium.

"Let's go. Hurry!"

I grabbed the banker's box from Cam and jumped out of the car. I wanted Sweeney to spot me with the goods. Cam tumbled out, too, and we sprinted for the double doors leading inside. As we did, I could hear Sweeney's tires skidding on the gravel.

When we were five feet away, a door swung open, and Trinnie waved us in frantically. The three of us bolted down the hallway, just making it around the first turn as we heard the door opening behind us.

This is where we hoped our assumptions were accurate. We figured that out on the streets, Sweeney would want to stay as close as possible so he wouldn't lose us. Here, though, in an unfamiliar setting, he'd probably be more cautious. He knew we were there, somewhere, with the evidence. And he figured—accurately—we'd be afraid of him.

What he didn't know was that it wasn't just me and Cam, who was masquerading as Varney. We had our friends as backup. That probably wouldn't occur to Sweeney, mainly because he probably didn't have friends of his own who were willing to lay down their lives to help. To further maintain the surprise, our friends had parked around the back of the school.

If our plan was going to fall through, it would be now, when we were in the hallways where a school administrator could spot us running around. One of the reasons we had needed to kill so much time at the library was to wait until all office staff had gone home. Although it was summer vacation, some of them still kept normal hours. There was always something going on at the school—athletics, band, camps, drama—so our presence in the auditorium hadn't seemed out of the ordinary. Most likely, they figured we were with the drama camp, just fine-tuning a few things before an upcoming performance.

At the moment, though, there was nobody around. Perfect.

Trinnie, Cam, and I slowed as we reached the front auditorium doors. As we did, I glanced down the long hallway behind us. No sign of him. We'd locked all the other doors to the auditorium, so this was the only way in.

I held open the door and gestured for Trinnie and Patch to pass through, but I needed to wait until Sweeney came around the corner before going in myself. We needed him to see us dart in so he would follow. I stood there, eyes glued to the corner of the hallway, gripping the door handle, ready to rush inside as soon as I got a glimpse of him.

A flash of Sweeney's arm came around the corner, and I sprang into action. I raced down the center aisle toward the front of the auditorium, chasing after Trinnie and Cam. They leaped up onto the stage, and I followed seconds later. We cut right, disappearing into the backstage area.

We paused for five seconds to catch our breath, but that was all we could spare. I turned to Trinnie. "Is the camera ready? The lighting?"

Trinnie nodded. "I think so. We tested it all out, me onstage, them recording. You could see and hear okay. Rizzo said something about fine-tuning something or other. It'll work. It has to."

"And Patch?"

"He's ready, too," Trinnie said.

"Great. Let's go."

The three of us weaved our way through all the backstage junk until we found a spot where we could see the front auditorium doors. I glanced up at the catwalk and gave a little wave. It was too dark up there to make out Rizzo, but she was up there. Somewhere. Waiting to start rolling the cameras.

I looked to the back of the auditorium, even though I knew I wouldn't be able to see Patch crouching down in the last row of seats, ready to lock Sweeney in.

Meanwhile, my stomach was doing somersaults.

I'd say most actors got nervous right before a show. What differed was the degree of nervousness. I read once that being a little anxious prior to an activity helped you focus and achieve maximum performance. Not enough anxiety, and you might fall a little flat—too much, and you risked forgetting your lines and stressing out entirely. Luckily, my nerves usually bolstered my performance. Usually. Right now, I had the feeling I was a little too amped up.

Judging from the deer-in-the-headlights expression on Trinnie's face, I'd say she was pretty revved up, too.

I couldn't see Cam's face. As we had discussed, he was to keep his hoodie on at all times so Sweeney wouldn't know he was being duped. I just hoped he hadn't seen the news about Varney being arrested.

We kept our eyes on the doors, waiting, sweating.

A minute later, one of the middle doors cracked open slightly, and Sweeney's body became silhouetted by the light from the hallway.

"And...action," I whispered to Trinnie and Cam.

Sweeney stood motionless in the doorway for the longest time. Had I underestimated his desire to see what evidence we had? Was he going to turn and run? Finally, he stepped inside and began walking down the center aisle.

When he was halfway down, Patch—dressed in black, head-to-toe—emerged from his hidey-hole, and keeping down, quietly looped a towel-wrapped chain through the door handles and secured it with a padlock. Then he crawled down a side aisle to join Rizzo up on the catwalk.

No escape for Sweeney through the auditorium doors now. To get out, he'd have to cross the stage and take us down.

If Sweeney heard Patch locking the doors behind him, he didn't act like it. He came strolling down the aisle and stopped fifteen feet from the stage.

"Come on out, Dalton," Sweeney yelled. "I know you're here. I know you've got what I want. Hand it over, and no one will get hurt."

Sweeney had watched too many gangster movies.

He took another step forward, glancing around. "If you don't, well, I know where you live. You know, that nice house where your family lives, too."

"Okay," I called out. "Let's talk about this."

Sweeney whipped his head in the direction of my voice, but didn't move forward.

He must have had questions. How many of us were here in the backstage shadows? Were the police involved somehow? And if he did decide to do something drastic, did that prove he really was the killer? Why else attack?

"Okay, let's talk. Why don't you come out here where I can see you?"

I nodded to Cam and Trinnie, and she grabbed my hand, squeezed it, and whispered, "Break a leg."

I nodded again, then slowly started walking across the stage. A spotlight blazed on, and I kept walking until I was smack in the middle of the circle of light, careful to hit my mark exactly. I needed to be sure I was in the frame Rizzo and Patch were shooting. "Climb up here and we can talk."

The house lights were on, at their lowest setting. From my vantage point, I could barely make out the sneer on Sweeney's face as he hopped up onto the stage. He approached, and when he was about ten feet away, I held up my hand. "That's far enough."

"You're giving *me* orders? That's rich."

A second later, another spot went on, lighting up Sweeney. He craned his head up toward the light, but I knew from experience he wouldn't be able to see Rizzo or Patch. Too bright.

"Look, I have what you want, right? So just be cool." My voice was high-pitched and wavered. In my head, when I'd practiced this scenario, I'd been more of a badass.

"Oh, I'm cool." He looked over my shoulder. "Where's the box of stuff? And where's the murderer, Varney?" His sneer had turned into a full-blown grin.

"First, we need to come to an agreement."

"How's this for an agreement? You give me the stuff, and I don't harm any of your loved ones."

I needed to coax out a confession for the video. "Why did you do it?"

"What?"

"Kill Ogden."

"Who says I killed Ogden?"

"If you didn't, then why do you want the evidence that clears Varney's name?"

"Why doesn't Varney join us? I'd like to see what he says about things." Sweeney laughed, and I had a feeling there was a joke I wasn't in on.

"Sure." We'd planned for this, so when I waved into the wings, Cam walked onstage, but he stopped well behind me. Another spotlight went on, illuminating him. His hood was pulled forward, and the harsh light from above kept his face entirely in shadow.

"What's the problem? He afraid of me?"

"In case you try something, one of us will be able to go for help."

Sweeney tapped the side of his head, mocking us. "Ah, good thinking. But you know what, I don't believe that's actually Homer Lee Varney. And you know what else, I don't think you have any real evidence against me. I think you, and all your drama geek friends hiding behind the curtains, are grasping at straws."

"It's just me here with Varney," I said. "Nobody else."

"Then who's turning on the spotlights?"

"They're automatic. I programmed them earlier."

"Bullshit," Sweeney said, full of bluster.

Of course, he wasn't wrong; all of our lights had to be manually controlled. Despite Ms. Z's repeated requests, a fancy lighting system wasn't in the school's budget.

I tried to gauge Sweeney. Had our ruse been blown? If I didn't come up with something fast, Sweeney would walk away, and we wouldn't have his confession on tape, and Ogden's killer would walk free, and Varney would forever be labeled a murderer. Time for some improv. "Listen closely. While researching the case for my role, I found some very damning evidence, something the crooked forensics lab screwed up."

"What evidence is that?"

"After the troubled crime lab had been shut down, they retested evidence in some of the big cases. And wouldn't you know it, the knife found in Varney's trunk? The murder weapon? They rechecked the knife and found a partial print on the blade, right by the handle, one they hadn't seen before. I bet it matches yours." Of course, I had no idea whether what I was spouting made any sense, or was even feasible, but improv was all about going out on a limb.

"Bullshit," Sweeney said, but he didn't say it with the same bluster this time.

"That's not all. They retested some DNA evidence on Ogden's T-shirt that doesn't match Ogden *or* Varney. It's the DNA of the real killer. And I bet you're a perfect match."

"You're full of it."

"Yeah, well, there's more." I was in this far, I figured I'd lay it on even thicker. "The police also have an eyewitness, one who just came forth after seeing a rerun of 'High School Hitman.' One who knows you're guilty. You are so screwed."

Sweeney flexed and unflexed his fists at his side.

I kept up my verbal assault. "I'll ask you again: If you didn't kill Ogden, then why do you want the evidence that clears Varney? I mean, why do you care at *all*?"

Sweeney pursed his lips, thinking. "To answer your question, I'm curious as to why you think I killed Ogden. Why you're planning on taking this to the police. Don't you think I have a right to know the basis for being accused of murder?"

"Until a minute ago, I don't believe we'd ever said anything about *you* being guilty. I think we've always maintained this evidence merely clears Varney." I paused a beat. "But isn't it interesting that you think evidence exists that would implicate you in a murder. In fact, if you hadn't shown up here today, we'd never have known who you were."

Sweeney's smile disappeared. "You don't know who you're

messing—"

Suddenly, the spotlights went out, and the stage was bathed in light.

"Shit!" Patch shouted from above. Evidently, he'd hit the wrong switch on the lighting panel.

Sweeney's head shot up, and he'd have to be blind not to see Patch and Rizzo standing next to a tripod. Patch was fumbling around with an electronics control panel.

"You're filming this? I should have known. Little shitheads." Sweeney turned my way again, and now he had a gun in his hand. Pointed at me. "Gimme what I came here for!"

"Run! He's got a gun," I shouted. "Kill the lights!" I dove to the side and before my body hit the stage floor, we'd been thrown into darkness. Nice recovery, Patch.

I rolled to my left, then ran, hunched over, aiming for the cover of backstage. When I reached the side curtains, I paused and glanced back. It was very dark, but the distant house lights glowing lightly in the auditorium proper provided just enough light to see shadows.

And a shadowy figure was coming after me.

I whirled and moved deeper into the backstage maze. Most backstages are jam-packed. Scenery, furniture, props—all the stuff that's needed for whatever show is being put on—are crammed into every available nook and cranny. Sometimes, two or more shows are sharing the same stage concurrently. At South Vienna, space was at a premium, so the drama department even used some of the space for long-term storage.

I dodged around an old recliner and behind a grandfather clock, not checking over my shoulder, not wanting to see Sweeney gaining on me.

I heard him curse behind me, though, as he bumped into something.

I plunged deeper into the darkness, past a bicycle, a floor lamp, a picnic bench, as I headed for the prop closet. There, I flicked my phone on for just a second so I could snag the baseball bat a previous class had used in a production of *Damn Yankees*. I gripped it tightly as I slipped behind the closet. If he found me, I'd be ready.

I tried to control my wild breathing and thought about the others. We'd mapped out a plan for this contingency in case things went straight into the flaming dumpster. We were to separate, so Sweeney wouldn't be able to get all of us with one attack, then we were supposed to call Kennedy first, followed by a call to 9-1-1.

I sure hope someone had already made those calls, because I didn't want to risk pulling my phone out right now. The glow would surely attract Sweeney.

Of course, Trinnie knew every inch of the cluttered backstage as well as I did. Hopefully, she had been able to grab Cam and lead him to a safe hiding spot. Ditto for Patch and Rizzo.

Sweeney wasn't going anywhere. All the auditorium doors had been chained—and locked—from the inside.

The only door we could leave from was a backstage door, the one closest to Ms. Z's office. The one closest to where I stood now. So if Sweeney found it, and left, I'd hear him and be on his tail in a minute.

We had Sweeney trapped. All we needed to do was keep from getting killed until the cops arrived, and we'd accomplish our mission.

"I know you're back here, Dalton." From the sound of Sweeney's voice, he was close, and getting closer. I gripped the bat tighter. "Come on out. I won't hurt you."

Flashbacks to when Varney had me cornered in the abandoned ZMart. That time had ended okay. Although Varney had captured me...

"How about this? Tell me what your so-called evidence is and I'll let you and your friends go. It's bogus anyway, you know. I didn't kill Ogden. Homer did." Sweeney's shuffling feet sounded like he was right on the other side of the closet.

More shuffling. The seconds ticked by. I was sure he could

hear the pulse pounding in my chest.

"Come out, Dalton." He was so close I could almost smell his bad breath.

Now or never.

Chapter Thirty-One

I whipped around the corner of the closet, cocking my bat as if I were about to slam one into deep center. It was solid wood, the real thing, and it would do some damage if it connected. Sweeney saw me and turned, just in time to see the business end about to connect with his head. He ducked at the last moment and the bat smacked into the metal closet, reverberating like a gong. A large ceramic garden gnome fell off the top of the closet and brained him. He collapsed in a heap.

I stood over his inert body with the bat. Bash his head in? Crack those chiseled cheekbones?

Sweeney stared at me, eyes glazed, stunned. Then he looked down and seemed to notice the gun still in his hand. An evil grin appeared.

I swung at the gun and missed. But the barrel smashed his forearm, and the gun went flying, skittering underneath an old sleeper sofa. Sweeney cursed at me as he scrambled to his feet. "I'm gonna kill you."

Not if I could help it. I swung the bat again and conked Sweeney in the side of the head. He went silent and crumpled to the ground.

I didn't wait around to see if I'd killed him. I'd come back with reinforcements. I dashed away, skidding around a tight right turn. I blasted through the backstage side door into the hallway and practically plowed over a big guy in a rumpled suit.

Bronson Kennedy, in the flesh. Thank God, the cavalry had arrived.

"Whoa, where's the fire?" he asked. Gently, he took the baseball bat from me and set it on the ground.

I gasped for breath. "In there. He's in there."

"Take a deep breath and tell me what happened, okay?" Kennedy grasped my upper arm and steered me over to the wall, so I could lean against it while I caught my breath.

"He followed me here. The guy who killed Ogden. And then he attacked, trying to silence me, so I couldn't bring the evidence to the authorities. I creamed him with the bat."

"Is Nate Jenkins dead?"

I stared at him and shrugged, not quite sure what to say. Sweeney's real name was Nate Jenkins?

"Where's that evidence now?" Kennedy's grip on my arm tightened.

"It's safe. He didn't get it."

Wait a minute.

How did Kennedy know Sweeney's name was Nate Jenkins?

"Give it to me, and I'll see it gets to the right place."

Had Patch called Kennedy? And 9-1-1? I figured someone had. But Kennedy had arrived way too quickly. "How did you know I was here, anyway?"

Kennedy blinked a couple of times. Rapidly. "I saw your post on social media. I'm connected to everyone from the show."

Things weren't adding up. I'd posted my location from the library, not wanting to risk anyone coming to school to say hi and mess things up. I hadn't posted anything *anywhere* about me being here. And I'd never mentioned the name Jenkins—mostly because I didn't know that *was* Sweeney's name. Someone else had clued Kennedy in to my whereabouts.

An icy finger scratched my spine. Could Jenkins himself have alerted Kennedy? Were they in on this thing together?

It all fell into place with a sickening thud. Kennedy was a dirty cop. And worse, he held me tight.

I tried to squirm out of his grip, but he grabbed my other arm, too.

"Dalton, you should have listened to me and left all of this alone. Now we have ourselves a situation." Kennedy's suit jacket smelled of cigarettes.

"You were involved in killing Ogden, weren't you? And the original report was correct—the killer was left-handed."

"I was careless and let a copy of that report slip by. No one would ever have noticed. But you had to be such a dedicated actor, researching your role. Let's see you act your way out of this mess."

"Let me go."

"Where's your box of evidence?" He squeezed my arms.

"You won't get away with it."

"I still have friends on the force. You wouldn't believe what I can get away with. Or what I can do to you. What I *will* do to you, if you don't cooperate. You see, going to jail isn't the worst thing that can happen to someone."

A flash of clarity struck me. "You had Varney arrested, didn't you? Had him thrown back into jail on some bullshit charge."

"He attacked me. You saw it. Remember, I still have friends in powerful places." He started to drag me down the hallway. I tried to dig my heels in, but he was too strong and the floor too slippery. Plus, he'd had a lot of experience hauling bad guys around during his long, corrupt career. "Come on. Stop fighting. You want me to cuff you?"

"Fuck you."

"Just keep moving." Kennedy kept dragging me down the hall, and I kept resisting. We tussled for another minute or two, until he outmuscled me and shoved me along.

"You know, we called 9-1-1, right after Jenkins, or whoever it is, pulled his gun on us."

Kennedy laughed. "Oh, I know. I heard it come through on the scanner. I knew the responders so I told them I was on the scene, and it was all a prank. Told them I'd take care of it. It took a bit of convincing for them to bend the rules like that, but eventually they got the message. Life's a bitch sometime." He spun me around and pressed me into the wall, spread-em fashion. "I'm going to search you. If you move a muscle, I'm gonna beat the shit out of you. Got it?"

I did what I was told and braced to get frisked.

Chapter Thirty-Two

Then I heard a *thonk*, followed by a *thump-thump*, and I no longer felt Kennedy's hands on me. I whirled around.

Cam stood on one side of Kennedy, holding a wooden sword, and Patch, armed with my baseball bat, stood on the other. Rizzo stood a ways back, filming the whole thing with her phone.

Kennedy clutched his shoulder. "I'm a former police officer, boys. Don't get yourselves in trouble here. Put down those clubs and we'll talk."

"He's lying," I said. "He's going to torture me until I give him the evidence. He's in on it with the real killer. He may have been a cop, but he's dirty. He helped kill Ogden, and he got Varney thrown back in jail."

"Is that right?" Patch asked Kennedy.

Kennedy didn't answer, just sneered.

"I'll take that as a yes," Patch said in a calm voice. Then he barked, "Go!"

Cam faked a swing of the sword, and Kennedy raised his hands to ward off the blow, but Cam countered with a three-sixty spin and whacked him in the ribs coming around from the other side.

Kennedy groaned and stuck his hand into his jacket, but before he could pull out a weapon, Patch went down on one knee and extended the other leg, whipping Kennedy's legs out from under him. Kennedy started to fall, then half-regained his balance but—aided by a hearty shove from Cam—stumbled and smashed head-first into the cinder-block wall.

He slid down the wall, onto the floor, like a cartoon character hitting a freight train.

"Exactly like I choreographed," Patch said.

"You choreographed his head crashing into a wall?"

"Well, *almost* exactly like I choreographed it," Patch said. "I hope we didn't kill him."

A lot of that sentiment going around.

We watched for a moment, until we were sure his chest was moving up and down. "He's still alive." Patch's voice echoed the relief we felt.

"Maybe we should tie him up?" Cam's voice was also a little shaky. Now I knew what it felt like, clobbering a guy, the nauseating sound of a hard object meeting flesh. Not a good feeling, no matter what crimes the guy had committed.

"I think he's got handcuffs on him. Those'll work."

We rolled Kennedy over and found them in a pocket, then cuffed his hands behind him. We also discovered a gun in a hip holster. Cam carefully removed it and held it at his side.

"We heard the side door open, figured it was either you or Sweeney," Patch said. "Either way, we thought we'd investigate." He glanced around. "Where's Sweeney? Did he escape?"

"First of all, Sweeney's real name is Jenkins. And I have no idea where he is. Last I saw him, he was in similar shape to Kennedy here. Sprawled on the floor, semi-comatose."

"He's probably long gone by now. Escaped in the chaos. A fugitive at large," Cam said. "If he has half a brain, anyway."

"Let's hope," Rizzo said.

"Wait a second. Where's Trinnie?"

Everyone looked around. "She was right behind us," Rizzo said.

Oh shit.

Patch pulled out his cell, but I grabbed his hand before he

could text her. If she was hiding, even the slightest buzz of the vibration might give her away. "We can't risk exposing her. The cops should be here any minute, but we need to find Trinnie before Jenkins does, if he's still around. Make sense?"

Head nods all around. "Look everywhere for her. Turn this place upside-down. But we need to be careful, and whatever you do, if you spot Jenkins, don't approach him. I knocked his gun away, but he may have retrieved it, or he may have another weapon." I made eye contact with everybody. "Remember, let him escape if you have to. We need to find Trinnie."

More nodding heads.

"Okay, Patch and Rizzo, you stay together. Search the lobby area, and see if maybe she's hiding in one of the restrooms."

They raced off down the hallway.

I turned to Cam. "You stay here and make sure Kennedy doesn't take off." I nodded at the gun in his hand. "You okay with that?"

"Sure. I'll manage." He hefted it a couple of times.

I started down the hallway, back toward the auditorium.

"Hey, where are you going?" Cam said. "It's too dangerous to go by yourself."

I took off, ignoring Cam's plea to return.

If I was lucky, really lucky, Jenkins would still be lying unconscious right where I'd dropped him, and I could ease everyone's anxiety. I slowly opened the backstage side door.

I crept along backstage, using the scenery flats as cover. If Jenkins was conscious, his eyes would already have adapted to the darkness, so he'd probably be able to see me before I saw him.

I paused when I reached the prop closet where we'd fought. Tried to hear his breathing, but the pounding pulse in my head was too loud. During our fight, I'd knocked Jenkins's gun from his hand, and it had disappeared under some heavy furniture. Had he recovered it? Of course, if he'd awakened and found his gun, it was unlikely he'd still be sitting there. But you never knew.

I took a deep breath, then jumped out from behind the closet.

No Jenkins.

Relief unclenched my jaw muscles. A split second later, fear reclenched them. Had Jenkins found Trinnie?

I tried to chase the emotions from my mind and think logically. Where was that asshole?

I was pretty good figuring out characters' motivations; I think it's what made me a good actor. And if I were Jenkins, I wouldn't leave until I was sure I had all the evidence against me. Which he thought was in the banker's box.

We'd stowed it in plain sight, next to a few other boxes on a shelving unit backstage. If we needed it during our negotiation with Jenkins, we'd fetch it and bring it onstage. We hadn't gotten to that point when things went haywire.

Had Jenkins figured out where we'd left it?

I inched my way along, quietly, but quickly, toward the shelving unit, keeping alert for any sign of Trinnie. I crouched behind a rolling makeup case and peeked around the corner.

The box was right where we'd left it, on the shelf next to a plastic bin of assorted hats.

Then a thought struck me, and my heart stopped.

The video. Jenkins had realized he was being filmed, right before all hell broke loose. If I were him, I wouldn't leave without that incriminating evidence.

I tiptoed through the wings until I could get a sightline up toward the catwalk and all the metal scaffolding where the crew hung lights and other special-effects equipment. The catwalk was basically just a metal plank with metal railings, suspended thirty feet up in the air. Because of the danger, Ms. Z required that all the crew members be specially trained to work up there, and she made everyone pass a safety test.

Patch and Rizzo had set up their equipment right in the middle, so they could get a good view of center stage.

As far as I could tell, the camera was still up there. I guessed that in the rush—and with me yelling for everyone to run for their lives, they hadn't wanted to be slowed down hauling the equipment with them. And rightly so.

The only problem? I needed to get it down. The concrete evidence we had on Jenkins was incomplete and sketchy, but when combined with the video pseudo-confession, it would be enough to put Jenkins away for a long time.

The catwalk was accessible by a metal spiral staircase backstage. I raced across the stage, hoping not to be spotted, and bounded up the stairs, trying not to make too much noise on the metal treads. I hadn't spent a whole lot of time up on the catwalks—my interests were more onstage, but I had completed the training course.

No running. Hold onto the railings. Go slow. Basic safety precautions. None of which I had time for now. The video camera was in the middle of the span. My goal was simple: Finish what we hadn't had time for. Grab the tape or memory stick or whatever was in there, and scram.

I walked across the span to the tripod and bent over the camera, but before I could open it up and dig out the memory card, I heard the distinctive sound of footsteps on metal stairs. I jolted upright. Jenkins stood at the end of the catwalk.

And he wasn't alone.

Chapter Thirty-Three

My insides turned to jelly. Jenkins had his arm around Trinnie's neck. I couldn't be sure, but from the position and angle of his other hand, it looked like he held a knife.

Given his history, I shouldn't have been surprised.

"Hello there, Dalton." Jenkins pushed Trinnie forward, brandishing his knife in his left hand.

I took a step backward. "Let her go. The cops are right outside."

"Then we'd better make this quick." He closed the gap between us to ten feet, near enough so I could see the fear in Trinnie's eyes.

I poked my hand under my shirt and stuck a finger out. "I have Kennedy's gun. Don't move or I'll shoot."

"Yeah? Then let's see it."

I stared at him.

"I didn't think so. Good thing, too. You'd probably blow your fingers off."

"Long way down, isn't it?" Jenkins said. "Now, give me the camera and I won't hurt your friend here." He thrust her toward the edge of the catwalk, then yanked her back as she screamed. "It's a long way down."

"Let her go, and you can have it," I said, grabbing the camera and the attached tripod.

"Let me have the camera, and I'll let her go."

I stared at him. If I stalled long enough, the cops would be here.

"I'm counting to three," Jenkins said. "Then I'm going to start carving up her face."

A dozen courses of action flitted through my mind. None good. I chose the best one.

"One," Jenkins said.

I licked my lips.

"Two."

"Okay. Okay. I'll give you the box, then you let go of Trinnie. Just like you said." I figured he couldn't hold both her and the equipment, and only one held his ticket to freedom—the video recording. "Here you go." I lunged at Jenkins and thrust the camera right at him.

Instinct took over and he grabbed the camera and let Trinnie go. I grabbed her hand and pushed her behind me, so I was facing Jenkins. No way was I letting him escape.

Jenkins held the camera itself, but the tripod extended toward me. I reached out and grabbed it. Gave it a yank. Jenkins held the camera tight. A tug-of-war stalemate. But Jenkins was stronger. He tucked the knife in his belt, and with both hands, he pulled harder. Trinnie saw what was going on, and she grabbed me around my waist and pulled, too. A tug-of-war thirty feet in the air on a narrow catwalk.

We pulled, and Jenkins pulled even harder to maintain equilibrium.

All of a sudden, I let go, and Jenkins tumbled backward, falling on the catwalk. I darted forward and with my foot, I shoved the camera over the side.

But it didn't go crashing to the ground.

Somehow, the tripod legs got wedged in the metal latticework and the camera balanced precariously there, in midair, thirty feet up.

"Goddamn it!" Jenkins drew his knife and charged at me.

I reached up, swiveled a spotlight in his direction, and flicked it on. It was as if someone had turned on the sun five feet away from his face. Jenkins's hands flew up to cover his eyes, and he dropped his knife. It bounced once on the catwalk, then caromed over the side. Three long seconds later it hit the ground. It *was* a long way down.

Trinnie and I were single file on the narrow catwalk, me in front. I whispered to her over my shoulder, not taking my eyes off Jenkins. "Be ready."

"Okay."

Jenkins stepped forward and batted the spotlight away. It teetered a bit, then focused on the giant cardboard rainbow in a back corner of the stage. He roared forward, but instead of going for the camera, like I figured, he came for me.

Shit! I whirled around, and Trinnie had no choice but to turn, too. We clattered down the metal catwalk as carefully as we could to get away from Jenkins. Ms. Z had told us all about the guy who fell off and broke his neck from being careless. True or not, it had gotten everyone's attention.

Jenkins banged behind us. Evidently, he hadn't heard Ms. Z's story, because he ran as if he were on solid ground, not on a rickety metal grate three stories high. I practically felt his body heat as he grew nearer.

I pictured him tackling me from behind, then heaving me overboard. Then doing the same to Trinnie. He'd overtake us, I knew it. Time to try another approach.

I spun around, and held my hands up as if to surrender. "Okay, okay. Hold on."

Jenkins grabbed me by my shirt. "You little shit."

Behind me, Trinnie had stopped running, and I knew she was coming back to help. "Stay right there, Trinnie. No sense both of us getting hurt. I got this." I craned my head over my shoulder, and our eyes connected for a second. I tried my hardest to beam my thought waves to her. *Stop. I've got a plan. Trust me.*

She must have gotten the message, because she didn't try to intervene.

Inside, I was relieved. If something happened to her because of me, I wouldn't be able to live with myself.

Jenkins jerked my head around to face him, and his half smile turned into a maniacal grin. "Yeah, I killed Ogden. And I enjoyed it. Just like I'm going to enjoy killing you. And your friend."

I'd heard his confession, but I feared it would go down with me and Trinnie, as soon as Jenkins hurled us off the catwalk to our deaths below. Talk about taking a curtain call.

"Who else knows about your theory?" Jenkins smelled like crap, and his breath smelled worse.

"So you can kill them, too? No way." I wasn't really afraid of heights, but with the knowledge that one wrong step meant a long fall down to a hard surface, I started to hyperventilate. I didn't have much time.

I bit the inside of my cheek—a focusing technique Alf once taught me—and mustered all my strength. I figured I had one shot at this and it had to count.

Jenkins moved his hands to my throat. "Tell me what I want to know, goddamnit, or you're going over the edge. Now."

I sucked in a deep breath. Then I kicked Jenkins in the nuts as hard as I could.

"Fuck!" His hold on my neck loosened. I brought my arms up and turned my hip into him, using leverage to force his hands off me. Then I took a lesson from Patch and leg-whipped Jenkins. He went down hard, his back landing square on the protruding metal lip of the catwalk floor. He screamed in pain, then rolled over.

The wrong way.

His legs and torso slid over the edge of the catwalk, and his hands scrabbled for a hold. Somehow, he managed to grab the lip with one hand. He dangled over the stage, legs pumping, screaming. "Help me! Help!"

Just then, I heard voices and shouts from the stage below. "Fairfax County Police. Hang on. We're coming up for you."

I ignored them and, on hands and knees, crawled over to Jenkins. If I pried his fingers off, he'd go crashing to the ground. Probably to his death. The world would be rid of a stone-cold killer. All I had to do was unhook each finger, one-by-one. Or better yet, I could stomp on his whole hand a few times. That would do the trick.

I gazed down at him, and our eyes met. His were full of fear. What did mine reflect? Hate? Fury? Vengeance?

"Help me, you little shit."

It would be so easy. After what he had done to Ogden. And Ogden's family. And Varney.

And after what he tried to do to me and my friends? It would be simple and completely justified.

Jenkins couldn't manage to grab the lip with his other hand, and he was struggling, big time. "I'm slipping."

But would Ogden's family get justice? Would the cops and the courts go after Jenkins for murder? Or would they sweep everything under the rug, not wanting to admit the mistakes they made with Varney? Who would win if that happened? Certainly not Varney.

"I can't hold on much longer."

My mother always taught me to Do the Right Thing.

I reached down and grabbed one of Jenkins's wrists with both my hands, braced my feet against the railing, and held on with all my might. Trinnie rushed over and lent a hand, and together we prevented Jenkins from falling to his death.

If I had anything to do with it, Nate Jenkins wasn't getting off easy by dying.

No villain was going to steal the show with an over-the-top death scene.

Not in a Dalton Black production.

Chapter Thirty-Four

Mom was majorly pissed and Dad was pretty hot, too, when they found out I'd been helping Varney without telling them. But I apologized—sincerely, and often—and I played up the angles of fighting for injustice and going to extremes to help a falsely accused innocent man. Eventually, they softened. To help seal the deal, I offered to go into work with Mom. She was happy on two counts: She got the chance to show me how lawyers spent their days, and she was able to show me off to her partners and officemates—the boy who had actually fought injustice and won! The son who had captured a killer!

Truth be told, this whole fighting for justice thing had gotten under my skin—in a good way. Maybe I could study law, as my Plan B. No matter what, it was a better Plan B than being bait for a killer.

The last three weeks had been crazy busy.

TCN rushed into production a new and improved—updated with the latest facts—version of "High School Hitman II." We shot every day, pretty much developing the script in real time. And since I helped Ranjay write the episode—much of it recapped my actual experience unearthing the real killer—I got a writing credit. Another line item for my IMDB entry.

Usually, after a school show, there'd be a cast party, but right after we'd finished filming "High School Hitman II," many of those involved—the professionals, anyway—had quickly moved on to their next assignment. With all that had happened, though, Patch, Trinnie, and I decided we deserved a party, regardless—sort of a combination cast party/viewing party/general blowout. It hadn't taken much to persuade Mom and Dad to let us have the party at our house.

So we invited whatever cast members were still around, everyone in the school drama department, and dozens of our closest friends. Ms. Z came with her wife, Whitney, and Alf, who was still in town, arrived in a white three-piece suit and baby-blue tie, which matched perfectly his blue Chucks and blue-and-white scarf. Unfortunately, Ranjay and Emily couldn't make it, but they sent their regards. Along with a cake with the word *Congratulations* written in fancy script icing.

Now, about thirty of us were crowded into the family room to watch the new episode. We'd all seen it when it had originally aired the week before—and several times since—but there was something about watching yourself on TV that never got old.

The crowd hooted and hollered whenever I appeared on-screen as teen Varney in the flashback scenes, and they cheered when Trinnie and Patch made their cable TV debut, which they totally rocked.

Things got uberweird, too, in a meta-kind-of-way. Because the audience had already seen me portray Varney as a teenager in the first episode, I couldn't play myself—the real teen-actor-turned-investigator—in the current-day scenes of the sequel. They had to bring in another actor who resembled me.

They hired Cam!

Of course, we all carried on whenever Cam appeared as me. I had to admit, he did a bang-up job portraying the dashing and courageous Dalton Black.

We watched the episode twice, with just as much enthusiasm the second time, then people drifted off to enjoy the party.

The techies, dressed in black from head-to-toe, migrated to the basement for a session of full-contact karaoke, and a large gang of school friends congregated out on the back deck. My closest buds—those who had faced down Jenkins with me—gathered in the kitchen. I'd gotten stuck in the family room, recounting the harrowing ordeal to the adults: Ms. Z, Whitney, Alf, and my parents, who had heard my version almost daily since it happened. They couldn't seem to get enough.

"I understand how the killer followed you, but how did the detective end up at school? Was he following you, too?" Ms. Z asked.

"Not really. Jenkins picked up my trail at the library, like I planned. He kept Kennedy apprised of my location the whole time. In fact, they'd been in constant communication ever since Jenkins had seen 'High School Hitman' and realized I'd pegged the real killer as being left-handed. When he saw I had evidence that would point the finger at him, he contacted Kennedy, and they figured they had a problem. Namely, me!"

"How was that detective involved in the first place?" Alf asked.

"He and Nate Jenkins had a drug-dealing operation going. Kennedy would skim drugs from the busts they made and funnel them to Jenkins to sell on the street. It turned out Jenkins and Ogden were dating the same girl, and Ogden found out about the drugs. Threatened to blow the whistle on Jenkins to get him out of the picture so he could have this girl all to himself. Jenkins, with a great deal of urging from Kennedy, retaliated by killing Ogden, and then Kennedy railroaded Varney, framing him with phony evidence and altered reports. Varney didn't stand a chance."

"But why was Jenkins so worried? I wouldn't think a report stating the killer was left-handed would be enough for him to panic," Alf said.

"He and Kennedy both were afraid that me poking my nose into things would lead to everything unraveling. The fudged fingerprint reports on the knife. The scrap of paper with Ogden's address they planted in Varney's belongings. The fact that Kennedy smeared Ogden's blood on Varney's T-shirt and baseball cap to implicate him. Once somebody started digging into it, Jenkins would have been arrested. And Kennedy was afraid if that happened, Jenkins would rat him out to save his own skin."

"I can't believe Kennedy was able to get away with it," Whitney said, putting her arm around Ms. Z.

"A crooked investigator in the crime lab was also indicted. Kennedy paid him off to help doctor the evidence. In fact, this guy rolled over on Kennedy, in exchange for a lighter sentence."

Ms. Z shook her head. "And Varney's life would be forever ruined if you hadn't helped him. You done good, Dalton."

"Yes indeed, my boy, you done splendid," Alf said, clearing his throat, a sure tip-off that he was about to launch into some charming show-biz story, one I'd probably heard a dozen times. My cue to exit, stage left. I rose while Alf prattled on in his vague British accent. "In fact, that was something I learned from my good friend, Johnathan Depp—J-Depp, as he likes to be called. He said that when the going gets tough, the tough get tougher, and the toughest get going toughly and..."

I slipped from the room and headed toward the kitchen. Before I got there, the doorbell rang, and I detoured to the front door. Opened it. Varney.

"Glad you made it. I was afraid you'd miss the celebration. Enter, enter."

He shook his head. "Can you come outside for a minute?"

"Uh, okay." I stepped out, closing the door behind me, and joined him on the porch. "You sure you don't want to come in? There's food."

He flashed a tense smile. "Thanks, but I can't stay long. Crowds make me a little nervous, and..." A shrug. "I just wanted to stop by and say thanks. For everything you did."

"It wasn't so much—"

He held up his hand. "Dalton, without your help, I'd forever be thought of as a murderer. My life would have sucked, enormously. Hell, I'd still be back in jail, if Kennedy had his way.

But you believed in me and my innocence, and I can't tell you how much that meant—*means*—to me. Not many people would have stuck their necks out to help someone in my situation. I owe you everything, and I'm not exaggerating a bit."

I didn't know what to say to that, and I might have wiped a tear or two from my eyes.

He reached into his pocket and pulled out a chain with a small silver medal on it. Held it out to me. "This is for you. It's a Saint Genesius medal. He's the patron saint of actors."

I took the medal. Turned it over in my hands. Examined the small oval. Engraved next to the image of the saint were little comedy and tragedy masks. More tears welled up, and I back-handed them away.

"It's not much, but I hope you like it. Maybe it will give you luck at your auditions."

"Thanks. I...I don't know what to say." I slipped the chain over my neck.

"Tell Trinnie and Patch that I thank them, too, will you? And Cam."

"Sure thing."

"I'm moving to Tucson. I have relatives there, and it will be good to get a fresh start." He stuck out his fist, and I bumped it. "So long, Dalton. I'll never forget what you did for me, and if I can ever repay the favor, just let me know." Varney nodded once, then stepped off the porch and crossed the lawn to his car without a backward glance.

I finally made it to the kitchen. Patch and Rizzo were next to each other, leaning against the counter, giggling. Rizzo wore white shorts and a blue blouse, and she sported a new hairstyle. I almost didn't recognize her, since she wasn't dressed entirely in black. Something definitely was up, because Patch *wasn't* clutching a plate overflowing with food.

"Nice party," Rizzo said.

"What's so funny?" I asked.

They looked at each other, and I felt a weird surge of electricity in the air.

"All the giggling?"

"Nothing," they said in unison and then giggled some more.

"Sure. Whatever." I left them alone, knowing when I wasn't part of an inside joke.

Trinnie and Cam were on the other side of the kitchen at the table near the large bay window. I joined them. "Getting enough to eat?"

"Yeah, it's great. Thanks for inviting me." Not only was Cam a good actor, he was polite, too. Damn him.

"Thanks for your help in this. We couldn't have done it without you."

Cam smiled. "What are friends for? Anyone else want something to drink? Soda?"

Trinnie and I declined, and Cam got up and went to the back deck to quench his thirst.

I nudged Trinnie and nodded at Patch and Rizzo, who were now taking turns whispering in each other's ears. "Crazy, huh?"

"*Clarisse* and *Miguel*, you mean?"

"Yeah, them."

"They are kinda cozy. Weird to see Patch like that. But cute, right?" She smiled. "I understand she even persuaded him to sign up for a couple of auditions."

"I knew I liked Rizzo," I said. "I'm glad that Patch is happy."

Trinnie leaned over and whispered in *my* ear. "You're a great friend, Dalton David Berglund Black. It's nice that Patch found someone he likes. And who likes him back."

"Yeah, it is."

Trinnie leaned back. "We're not far along or anything, but I found someone I like, too."

And it wasn't me. "I'm happy for you."

She took my hand. "Really?"

"Yes. I want you to be happy."

"Thank you." She squeezed my hand and rose. "You know, I think I *am* thirsty. I'm going to find Cam. Later."

I watched Trinnie leave the room, and I hadn't been just spouting crap, I truly did feel happy for her. She deserved every ounce of happiness she could find.

Ever since we'd brought down Jenkins, I'd been thinking about some things, and it finally became clear to me that I didn't always need to be center stage, that I wasn't always the star of every show. In fact, Trinnie, Patch, Cam—everyone, really—was the star of their *own* production, and in their shows, if I was cast at all, I was merely a supporting actor. And one of the first things they teach young actors is never to upstage the star. For some inexplicable reason, I'd been blind to this before—I guessed I wasn't as observant as I thought. Of course, this revelation gave me a *lot* to work on.

As I was ruminating, Alf bustled into the room. "There you are, Dalton. I need to speak to you. Got some splendiferous news!"

"What's up?"

"Just got off the phone with one of my movie contacts in Hollywood. After 'High School Hitman,' he expressed some interest in you, so I sent him a reel."

"How come you never told me?"

He tapped my shoulder with his gold cane handle. "Pish-posh, so many of those inquiries don't go anywhere. I didn't want to get your hopes up. Anyway, after he saw you in the sequel, he realized you were perfect for a part he's casting. He wants you to audition. Out in L.A. The City of Angels. La-La Land."

My heart fluttered.

"So, my boy, what do you think?" Alf asked.

Hollywood, here I come!

ACKNOWLEDGMENTS

My name may appear on the cover, but it takes a whole lotta people to get a book into a reader's hands. Without their help, this manuscript would still be languishing on my computer's hard drive.

My sincerest thanks go to:

Eric Campbell, Lance Wright, and the rest of the dedicated team at Down & Out Books. Their passion for putting top-notch crime fiction books into the hands of readers is unsurpassed, and I'm proud to be part of their family.

Thanks to Cynthia Bushmann, my excellent editor.

The amazing cover artist, Zach McCain.

The many readers and critique partners I've worked with through the years: Dan Phythyon and Ayesha Court. Dorothy Patton. Mark Skehan. Doug Bell. John Stevenson, Jill Balboni, Kim Stevenson, and Samantha Stevenson. Andy Heyman, Todd Hall. Tara Laskowski. Barb Goffman. John Betancourt, Carla Coupe, Karen Diegmueller, Bonner Menking, Adam Meyer, Megan Plyler. Ed Aymar.

The Rumpi: Donna Andrews, Ellen Crosby, John Gilstrap, and Art Taylor. Great writers, great friends.

My awesome beta readers: Shari Randall, Fred Rexroad, Becca Schwartz, Heather Powell, Emily Bierman, and L. Ryan Storms. Truly invaluable!

My supportive friends in Mystery Writers of America, International Thriller Writers, Sisters in Crime, and The Writer's Center. My cyberpals on Facebook, Twitter, and throughout the blogosphere.

The P.J. Parrish sisters (Kris Montee and Kelly Nichols), Reed Farrel Coleman, Elaine Raco Chase, Noreen Wald, the late Ann McLaughlin, Jeff Deaver, Jim Grady, Hank Phillippi Ryan. Excellent teachers, mentors, and blurbers!

Booksellers, librarians, and, of course, my faithful readers.

Eric Smith, for, literally, his email giving me the idea for this book. The cover could easily have read, "by Alan Orloff and Eric Smith." Giant hugs also to TeamSmithRocks.

My terrific agent, Michelle Richter, and the entire group at Fuse Literary.

My extended family, for always having my back.

My parents, for everything.

My children, Mark and Stuart, and my wife, Janet. Their unwavering encouragement and everlasting love make it all worthwhile. Double thanks to Stuart for introducing me to the whole world of drama (and for making my research for this book so much easier—he lived it!).

Thanks everyone!

I Play One On TV is **ALAN ORLOFF**'s tenth novel. His thriller, *Pray for the Innocent*, won an ITW Thriller Award, and his PI novel, *I Know Where You Sleep* was a Shamus Award finalist. His debut mystery, *Diamonds for the Dead*, was an Agatha Award finalist; his story "Dying in Dokesville" won a Derringer Award; and "Rule Number One" was selected for *The Best American Mystery Stories 2018* anthology. He is currently the Florida Chapter President of Mystery Writers of America.

Alan likes cake and he likes arugula, but not together. Never together. For more info, visit him at AlanOrloff.com.

On the following pages are a few
more great titles from the
Down & Out Books publishing family.

For a complete list of books and to
sign up for our newsletter,
go to DownAndOutBooks.com.

Radicals
Nik Korpon

Down & Out Books
May 2021
978-1-64396-185-9

When a mysterious cyber-terrorist organization begins erasing Americans' medical debt, enigmatic FBI cybercrimes agent Jay Brodsky must focus on an attack threatening to destabilize the US economy.

But when the trail leads to his own family, Jay will be forced to confront everything he never knew about his parents and his long-missing sister and decide where his true loyalties lie.

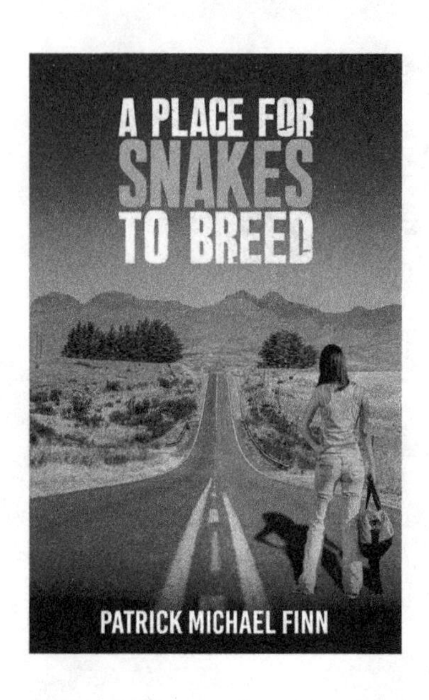

A Place for Snakes to Breed
Patrick Michael Finn

Down & Out Books
June 2021
978-1-64396-207-8

The desert spares no souls.

Set in the scorched and unforgiving deserts of the American Southwest, *A Place for Snakes to Breed* follows Weldon Holt's desperate search for his daughter Tammy, who is lost in the vicious landscape of interstate truck stop prostitution and its nightworlds "where the fruit of human trade is harvested by razor blades and cheap pistols."

Dead-End Jobs
A Hitman Anthology
Andy Rausch, Editor

All Due Respect, an imprint of
Down & Out Books
June 2021
978-1-64396-212-2

A collection of eighteen short stories about contract killers by some of the hottest crime writers in the business.

“An incredible collection of powerful and haunting stories that exist in that shadowy realm between tragedy, nihilism and noir.” —S.A. Cosby, author of *Blacktop Wasteland*

Houses Burning and Other Ruins
William R. Soldan

Shotgun Honey, an imprint of
Down & Out Books
May 2021
978-1-64396-115-6

Desperation. Violence. Broken homes and broken hearts. Fathers, junkies, and thieves.

In this gritty new collection, one bad choice begets another, and redemption is a twisted mirage. The troubled characters that inhabit the streets and alleys of these stories continually find themselves at the mercy of a cold, indifferent world as they hurtle downward and grapple for hard-won second chances in a life that seldom grants them.

CPSIA information can be obtained
at www.ICGtesting.com
Printed in the USA
LVHW101921190922
728751LV00003B/283

9 781643 962139